AN ISLE OF MIRRORS

A SHADE OF VAMPIRE 88

BELLA FORREST

NEW GENERATION LIST

Thayen - Adoptive son of Derek and Sofia
Richard – Son of Jovi and Anjani *(Wolf-Incubus Hybrid)*
Astra – Daughter of Phoenix and Viola *(Daughter-Sentry Hybrid)*
Isabelle – Daughter of Serena and Draven *(Sentry-Druid Hybrid)*
Jericho – Son of Caia and Blaze *(Fae-Fire Dragon Hybrid)*
Voss – Son of Aida and Field *(Wolf-Hawk Hybrid)*
Dafne – Daughter of Lethe and Elodie *(Ice Dragon-Human Hybrid)*

THAYEN

Something was happening in our beloved Shade, and Astra was somehow smack in the middle of it. There were more questions than answers, and the few answers we did get were either puzzling or downright horrifying.

The real Isabelle was missing. Serena and Draven were worried to the point of developing an ulcer, while the pristine copy of their daughter had once again been secured inside the hospital's west wing. We'd been sitting outside her room for the better part of an hour, watching her as she stared back at us with a triumphant smirk. As though she'd somehow won.

Kailani had locked this entire section down to keep both hallways clear for easy access to the clone's room, if needed. The security staff numbers had been doubled in the meantime, and we saw them patrolling the entire wing every other hour, clad in their black leather uniforms and sporting GASP earpieces. It all made me feel like we were under siege. The Shade hadn't seen this kind of security activity for decades, which was proof that whatever was happening here was literally hitting close to home.

My stomach ached as I looked around at those present in the hallway. Rose and Caleb seemed on edge, which was understandable. They'd taken over from Derek and Sofia, and they'd made a promise to keep everybody safe. Lumi was constantly thinking about what had happened and how it could be resolved, keeping her share of wise words to a minimum. She remained baffled at this point, since none of the comprehensive tests they'd put Isabelle's clone through had revealed even the slightest clue that she might be fake. On the contrary, the doppelganger had even fooled the Reapers with her faux soul.

"We'll do another sweep of the nearby woods soon," Kailani said after a long period of heavy silence, and Hunter nodded his agreement.

"If Richard's clone plans to make a comeback, we'll be ready for him," he replied, straightening himself as he got up and took Kailani's hand. "It's going to be okay."

"That's relatively easy for you to say," Richard muttered, leaning back in his seat, arms crossed and a muscle ticking nervously in his sharp jaw. "*You* didn't come face-to-face with literal copies of yourselves..."

"But you survived. That's what matters," Astra told him.

Phoenix and Viola flanked her, the three of them sitting across the hallway from me. On my side, Draven and Serena were quiet, staring through the large glass panel between the clone's room and us. "Mom and Dad are organizing an emergency meeting in the Great Dome," I said. "They're reorganizing the sweep teams to cover the entire island again, but in different groups. Corrine, Ibrahim, and Arwen are bringing their magical A game to the table. Hopefully, they'll be able to provide some detection methods for these portals. There's still a lot we don't know."

"What about Mona?" Phoenix asked, looking at Kailani. "I know she and Kiev were vacationing on Strava when this nightmare started, and we shut the portal down. Wouldn't she be able to assist?"

"Mom said she'll speak to them, but it's better to keep the portal completely shut for the time being, especially with these shimmering gashes popping up all over the place. Besides, Astra is the only one who was able to sense them," Kailani added. "What could Grandma Corrine or Mona or anyone else possibly do at this point? Even Viola, a full Daughter, wasn't able to help."

Viola sighed deeply. "Well, I have yet to finetune my powers into detecting portals before they open, but I'm sure I can figure something out. Besides, I can still try to help verify souls, as a Daughter."

"Maybe Corrine and the witches just don't want to give up," I suggested. "They'll keep trying until they find something that sticks. I suppose this whole thing is pushing everybody to newer levels of performance in that respect. If we can't get Mona involved, too, at least for the time being, it's okay. I know our people's safety is paramount, and leaving the island's portal open might give dangerous opportunities to any clone that might enter the scene, going forward."

Draven sighed. "If this is really foreign magic—like nothing we've seen before—I'm not sure how we'll be able to detect it. Astra has an uncanny natural ability, and even that is weak. I think we need to focus more on physical defenses. If they cloned Richard, chances are they'll have cloned more of our people, too. We have to be on the lookout."

"That's part of the agenda for the meeting," I replied. "Supplying our agents with weapons and spells they can use to defend themselves and to capture incoming clones. Gah, I can't believe this is really happening..."

Kailani offered a shrug, her dark brown curls dancing over her shoulders. "Hey, let them come, if they wish. I've got the room warded up like crazy. Only Draven, Serena, me, Astra, Soul, Kelara and Thayen are allowed in. And thanks to Soul and Kelara, we've got additional death magic wards to ensure that only the originals can set foot inside. That was no easy feat."

"Unfortunately, we are all you've got in terms of Reaper assistance," Soul said, joining the conversation as he and Kelara returned from outside. He didn't look happy. Only the two of them remained, though the entire First Ten crew had been here less than an hour ago. "Our other siblings may be free, but they are still undertaking the occasional task for our maker. They were just summoned back by Death. An urgent matter, she called it, without any regard for what's going on here. Then again, she did warn us not to get friendly with the living..."

"A force of habit, I presume," Kelara added. "Soul and I barely convinced her to let us stick around. She wouldn't tell us what was so urgent, either. Anyway, we've reached out to other Reapers but have yet to receive answers. Time wasn't too happy about being called back. He said I should keep a telepathic line open and reach out if there's an emergency, and he'll try to sneak away, repercussions for disobedience be damned. I tried to get Death to send us more people, but she's not interested in your problems. Not for the time being, anyway. She did ask that I keep her posted."

"Typical." I scoffed, leaving my seat and settling by the glass panel. I took a moment to watch Isabelle's clone. Had Soul not confirmed that she was a fake, I would likely have been ready to accept that our beloved Isabelle had really gone off the deep end. It was a terrible feeling to have, and the guilt only amplified as I wondered where she was. They'd taken one of our own.

The clone seemed calm, hands cuffed to the tabletop with charmed links and a plethora of death and Word spells, just to be sure. I had a vague sensation that this would somehow end up being bigger than all of us, but I couldn't put my finger on how, exactly, or what the incoming shift entailed. But there was a huge change coming, and I doubted we were ready for it.

"The reorganized patrols will have a redefined scope," I continued, setting the topic of Death aside as I moved my focus to Rose and Caleb.

"They'll be combing for portals and any other anomalies. Basically, if there's anything out of place, even if it's a crooked blade of grass where there shouldn't be any, they'll look into it. Unfortunately, this is the best we can do right now," Rose added.

"I wish I could do more," Astra said.

"You'll be ready when we have another clone to test," Soul replied. "It's only a matter of time. Richard's doppelganger failed his mission, and I expect others will follow in his footsteps."

Something else bothered me. "Isabelle is missing, so I can assume it's how whoever made the doppelgangers got her DNA and copied her. But Richard is here. How'd he get a clone?"

"That's a good question." Concern darkened Kailani's gaze. "The culprits must have infiltrated The Shade somehow. Either they're invisible or shape-shifting, pretending to be one of us... I don't know, but it's making it even harder to trust our current reality, if you think about it. I mean, if we can't see our enemy, if we don't know who they are or what they can do and how... damn..."

That was a frightening thought indeed. Looking around, the others' expressions told me we were all on the same page as to what this meant. Maybe Isabelle and Richard were not the only ones who'd been doubled by whatever nefarious methods were used, and there was a chance we may deal with more of their kind, soon enough. Soul was right. If Richard's copy had failed in his mission, others modeled after us might follow.

Stan and Ollie, Soul and Kelara's faithful service ghouls, moved slowly as they took up their guarding positions by the clone's door. They were dark and quiet, even gloomier than usual. It made me curious. "What's wrong with them?" I asked. "They seem out of sorts."

"They're troubled by the clone issue," Kelara said. "They've never seen anything like this, either, and I'm guessing they were hoping for more run-of-the-mill work after Visio. Think about it. Even after twenty years of relative quietness, Visio still haunts us all, the ghouls included. I would've liked another twenty years of the same relative quietness, too, to be honest, but... here we are. Dealing with something weird and frightening. Stan and Ollie are much more receptive emotionally speaking than most Reapers might assume."

Serena got up and came toward me so she could get a closer look at Isabelle's clone. "I've been thinking," she murmured. "Richard's clone only attacked Astra to distract from helping her..." She nodded toward the girl, who was eyeing us with a mixture of contempt and concern. What I wouldn't have given to be able to hear her thoughts. "We've got her secured, though, so our best chance at running into more clones will likely be here, in or around the hospital."

Kailani agreed. "Which is why Thayen and Astra have agreed to stick around for the time being, along with Richard. They've made a good team so far, and since Astra seems to be the main target, keeping her close to the clone will probably kill two birds with one stone."

"And they're using the shimmering portals to go in and out of the island, but we don't know where they lead," Serena added, glancing at Astra. "But you were able to feel more from the one Richard's doppelganger escaped through, right?"

"Something significant, yes," Astra replied. "The pressure was different in its vicinity. The air was thicker and heavier, like something huge was clamping down on me. There was a spark of electricity, too, but I would need to be around one of these portals for longer to fully examine its effects on my being."

"You'd need an open portal, ideally," Serena concluded, and Astra offered a faint nod.

"Which is why I'm also sticking around for now," Kailani said. "If any of our agents come across an open portal, I can immediately zap Astra there." She held back a weak chuckle. "She hasn't figured out how to do that on her own yet."

"Give her time," Viola replied, giving Astra a warm smile. "There are things a Daughter knows how to do at once, and there are things she must learn. On top of that, Astra is strongest in Eritopia. Out here in The Shade, her connection to our power is weakened. I think it's amazing she was able to give us so much already, all things considered."

"I wholeheartedly agree," Kailani said.

I cursed under my breath, feeling helpless. "I can't even use my glamoring to manipulate a clone. For all the fuss I've made about having this power, it's proving pretty useless under these circumstances."

"Wait, hold on. Don't knock it down yet," Soul interjected. "The clones don't have real souls, like I've already said, but the knockoffs they do have were good enough to fool a Reaper at first. Chances are the fakes function like the real souls, so I think it's too early to say it wouldn't work. Keep trying. The fake soul might respond to your glamoring, if you find the right buttons to push. It's not a certainty, though it is absolutely worth a shot! You're getting better at it with every attempt, anyway, but you have yet to discover the full extent of its power and reach. You need more time, more practice."

"Time isn't exactly on our side," I said, still frustrated.

"Well, what else can you do?" Soul shot back, raising an eyebrow. "Mope in a corner?"

I shook my head. "I don't mope!"

"Then you keep practicing. You spend every minute that you have pushing yourself." Soul pointed at Isabelle's clone. "You've got someone perfect for target practice right there. I'm sure Serena and Draven won't mind, despite her similarity to their daughter."

Serena gently squeezed my shoulder. "Not at all. Please, Thayen. If you can help, if you can improve your ability... go ahead. Glamor this girl until you get somewhere."

Draven nodded his agreement.

"Soul's right. Practice makes perfect," Astra replied. "You don't know what your limits are. This is a good time to figure them out."

"Seeley and Nethissis promised to train me," I said.

"Death had them reassigned," Soul grumbled. "But it's fine. You've got

Kelara and me, plus a whole family by your side, kid. You'll get to where you need to be."

Deep down, I was nervous—not about the glamoring, really, but about the prospect of failure. I didn't want to go into the clone's interrogation room and walk back out empty handed. What if I simply wasn't able to bend a fake soul? But there was something in Astra's intensely dark eyes that made me relax, if only for a second. She'd taken after Phoenix with the dark eye color, though they did turn pink when she used her Daughter abilities. I felt reassured by her faith in my power. Her confidence in my ability meant a lot.

"Okay. I'll give it as many shots as I can," I said, bracing myself for what would come next. Placing my palm on the door, I waited for the spells to recognize me. I gave the hallway one last glance and found myself feeling safe and trusted. Rose and Caleb watched quietly as the door opened with a delicate click, and I went in.

I took a moment to breathe. The air inside the doppelganger's room was slightly adjusted—infused with a mixture of aerosol medication and therapeutic oil vapors to help keep her calm. It was one of Kailani's many tricks to keep prisoners subdued. It seemed to be working, since the girl barely acknowledged me until I reached her table, the door automatically closing behind me.

She raised her gaze, steely gray eyes drilling holes into my head. I didn't see any hate in them, only a chilling determination to kill and get away with it. That had been her only goal from the very beginning, from what I could see. And now her target was right outside while she was trapped in here, secured with the heaviest spells our witches could devise.

"Okay, Thayen. Now... remember what I told you," Soul said, his voice echoing through a telepathic connection. "Focus on her soul. Well, on that exquisite forgery that's passing as a soul. It can mimic emotions, and she was responsive to someone's orders when it came to killing Astra. There's a good chance you might be able to reach her with your glamoring."

"I just need to dig deep enough." I nodded slowly as I looked at Isabelle's clone.

A cold grin spread over her face. "What? You want to try poking through my head again? Your previous failure wasn't enough, so you're here to embarrass yourself further?"

"Something tells me that by the time I'm done with you, that smile will be long gone," I shot back, narrowing my eyes as I tried to latch on to whatever tendril of energy I could pick up. This was a matter of opening myself up more. It required focus.

I felt the power inside me. The shard was alive, making my heart hurt a little whenever I tapped into it. I followed that sensation and allowed it to expand and take over my body, then my spirit. A flame brewed in my throat as the shard became an incandescent presence within, its influence spreading out like wildfire.

"You can't twist me around," the clone said. "I'm not designed for this stuff."

I needed to get the inferno under control, focusing the heat onto my target and increasing its strength until she could no longer resist it. Something between us connected, and my heart tightened a little as I made contact. This felt different than the first time. Either I was finally doing something right, or the shard had learned to follow my lead a little better. Sometimes I thought of it as a sentient entity of its own.

The clone's grin vanished, and her nostrils flared.

"There we go," I whispered, pushing myself and digging deeper into what I'd found. She was definitely there in spirit, though it wasn't a real spirit. She was animated by something, and I'd managed to tap into it. Describing it in terms that made sense would've been a titanic feat, so I chose to concentrate on what I could understand—the electrifying layer that surrounded her core, through which my glamoring had just pierced. Isabelle's clone was fighting back, rejecting me, but I wasn't done yet.

Slowly raising a hand, I reached out toward her. As if that force inside her might respond. As if it might come out to touch me so I could grab it and squeeze it into submission. My fingertips pricked, and I closed my fist, breathing heavily as the doppelganger gasped.

Her eyes widened as she realized what was happening.

"Thayen, wait," I heard Soul say.

But I couldn't wait. I'd found the very center of the clone, and I was about to take control. Every atom in my body tingled, my head as light as a feather. I wanted this more than anything, and I would do anything in my power to get her under my command.

"Thayen!" Soul shouted.

Something tickled my lip. Instinctively, my tongue flicked out and caught the taste of blood. This was supposed to mean something, but my mind had slowed down, and I couldn't process it. For only a second, I looked to the right, where they'd all gathered just behind the glass pane, each of them worriedly focused on me. No, not worried. Terrified.

"What is it?" I asked, my voice barely audible.

"Your nose is bleeding," Astra replied, pointing at me.

"Yeah... I can taste it."

"I think you need to stop for now," Soul said. "I don't think that's supposed to happen, kid!"

I shook my head and chose to keep pushing instead. "Nah, I've got this."

She was squirming in her seat, and I could feel her agitation in my chest. Astra was banging on the glass, but I ignored her. I was too close to achieving something here, and I couldn't bring myself to lose this opportunity. Not with what was at stake.

"I've got you," I said to the clone.

"Thayen, stop! I think bending a fake soul is having a negative side effect!" Astra reached me in a matter of seconds, and I felt her hand gripping my wrist, but I was sliding down a strange spiral of weird sensations. I had lost control, and I wasn't even sure when it happened. A second earlier, I'd managed a perfect hold on the clone's faux spirit, and now... I was flailing and coming apart at the seams, unable to pull myself back into the present.

"What's happening?" I heard myself ask. An infinity of white covered my eyes. I couldn't see anything anymore.

"You're passing out, Thayen," someone said. Maybe Astra. Or maybe Soul. I wasn't sure anymore. It was as if my body had suddenly divorced my soul, leaving me behind at the crossroads between consciousness and eternal sleep.

My sense of space vanished, and I felt like I was floating for a split second before I hit the ground. The light was quickly replaced by darkness, a deep sleep sneaking up on me and pulling me deeper into the abyss.

My consciousness slipped through my fingers.

ASTRA

(DAUGHTER OF PHOENIX AND VIOLA)

Thayen was on the ground. I kneeled beside him, listening to his slowing heartbeat. A sense of urgency came over me, and I placed my palms on his chest. I wasn't sure what I was doing, merely following my instincts.

The clone's breathing was ragged. Thayen's control over her had come to a sudden halt. He'd really pushed himself this time. Soul was checking her vitals, though she seemed to improve with every second that passed.

"How is he?" Soul asked, giving me a worried look.

"I'm not sure," I replied, allowing the energy within me to reach through Thayen and jolt him back into consciousness. The surge was sudden and powerful enough to make him gasp sharply as his eyes popped open. "There we go."

"What the..." Thayen managed, blinking rapidly as he tried to assess his surroundings. A glimmer of familiarity was evident in his gaze as he quickly scanned the hospital room. He remembered where he was and what he'd been doing. That was a good sign. "How long have I been out?"

"Half a minute, tops," I said. "Are you okay?"

He nodded faintly. "I think so." I helped him into a sitting position, checking his pulse in the process. "How did I black out? I mean, I blacked out, right?"

"There's some confusion persisting," Soul noted. "Not unexpected, considering how your lights went out. You overexerted yourself, Thayen. You pushed too hard, and your body couldn't take it. Plus, Astra might be on to something. Bending a fake spirit might take more practice and strength than what you currently have to work with."

"It makes sense," I said. "A fake soul would function much like a normal one, therefore making it susceptible to glamoring. The "moral codes" are learned, along with the concept of right and wrong, and therein lies the true difference between us and them, I suppose. At least we know I can, in fact, glamor a fake soul... but its toll is worrying."

"I thought my vampire nature was good enough to hold my power," Thayen replied as we both got up. He frowned as he stared at Isabelle's clone for a moment. "How is she?"

"She's fine. A little woozy, perhaps," Soul said. "Listen, your vampire biology sustains the shard and the glamoring power, but if you overuse it— if you force yourself beyond your physical limits—stuff like this is bound to happen. You will never reach the peak of your ability this way. Take it easy."

Thayen scoffed. "We don't have time for me to take it easy."

"Deep breaths, come on," I told him. "You just need to take a moment and find a better approach, that's all. You caught her for a short while, so we know there's a possibility you can control her forged spirit, despite yesterday's attempt. You're capable of more than you can imagine, Thayen. But we can't risk you hurting yourself in the process."

I pulled out the chair across from the doppelganger, and he sat down, carefully measuring his breaths. He'd already accomplished something incredible in proving that the clones weren't as immune to his glamoring as we'd thought—Isabelle's clone had been impressively good at resisting him the first time around, but on his second try he'd managed to find cracks in her defenses. We'd all seen her break into a cold sweat.

"There is hope," I whispered in his ear. "If you keep poking, she'll eventually cave in. You just can't damage yourself, because if you're our only way of finding out what she and the other clones are up to, then we absolutely need you awake and healthy."

Thayen smiled. "Roger that."

"Feeling better?" Soul asked, then gestured to the clone. "She's stable."

"Screw you," the doppelganger shot back. She gave Thayen a nasty look. "You'd better stay away from me, freak."

I chuckled softly. "I think you hit a soft spot."

"Oh, I most certainly did," Thayen said. He wiped the beads of sweat from his forehead with the back of his sleeve and repositioned himself in front of the table. Facing Isabelle's clone, he placed his hands on the table. "Time for round three."

"Just don't overdo it," Soul replied. "We'll try as many times as needed until she breaks."

"I am totally on board with that," Thayen said and took another steadying breath.

Isabelle's clone didn't look too comfortable in her seat. He scared her. She probably hadn't thought he'd have such an effect on her. This was as new to her as it was to us, which meant that her superiors—whoever they were— didn't have a full grasp of what Thayen's glamoring entailed. That shortcoming could work in our favor going forward, provided we got even a snippet of useful intel from this creature.

I understood Thayen's time-related frustration. Isabelle was still missing, and we weren't likely to find her anywhere in The Shade. The faster we broke the clone down into some kind of submission and cooperation, the better our odds of saving my cousin. Isabelle's double was restless, but Soul pinned her down, his hand clamped on her shoulder. "Sit still," he said. "Let loose, Thayen."

"No," the clone mumbled, her fear obvious. "Stay out of my head." A smirk fluttered across Thayen's lips.

"I think her defenses are weak," I said.

That was all Thayen needed to try again. I could almost feel the electricity surging and charging the air around us. The hairs on the back of my neck tickled, and I felt the need to inhale deeply, as my head felt suddenly lighter than usual. I was closer to Thayen as he used his ability this time, and I seemed to be reacting to it. It was an interesting sensation, as if my fingers were mere inches away from lightning itself. If I touched it, I would be thrown back against the wall—or at least that was what it felt like.

I stayed completely still while Thayen opened himself up and pierced through the clone's resistance. She grunted, dry swallowing as he dug deeper. She started shaking, but he didn't let go. Soul had been right. Thayen was getting better with each use of his power, and it showed in the speed with which he was dismantling the clone's defenses.

"Tell me, who sent you?" he asked, his voice as cold as a winter storm. It sent shivers down my spine, spreading over my skin like frost across the glass in the middle of a sudden blizzard. "Speak. I want the truth."

"No..." she blurted, shaking. She was under tremendous pressure, her shoulders lowered and her fingers twitching. It was as if Thayen had dumped a truck on her back, and she was struggling to keep it from crushing her.

"Who sent you? Who are you? Where did you come from?" Thayen demanded. Sweat covered his face, but he seemed to have a better grip than during the previous attempt. "Tell the truth!"

"No!" she cried out. The pain must've been horrendous to make her react like this.

I had little sympathy for her, however. She'd tried to kill me, and she had very likely taken my cousin from us. No, whatever Thayen was doing to her, she deserved it. "The more you resist, the worse it'll get," I said. "Is it worth it?"

"If the rivers run red with your blood? Yes," she hissed, but Thayen slapped the tabletop hard enough to startle her.

"Who sent you?"

"I... I can't!" the clone replied, her beautiful features crooked from the pain and the anger. She felt helpless, and I didn't need my weak aura-reading to tell me that. It was written all over her face.

"Tell me!" Thayen pushed and pushed until she finally snapped.

"You... you can do anything, but you can't stop it," she whispered, blood dripping from her nose.

Soul leaned in closer to Thayen with a troubled look. "Your nose is bleeding."

"Hers is, too," he replied, keeping his focus on the clone. "Come on, tell me."

"You... you can't stop what's coming," Isabelle's clone said. "I'm not the only one. We... we are many.

Unstoppable." Her eyes rolled into her head, and she slumped over the table.

Thayen gasped, and I instantly gripped his wrist, checking his pulse again. "You know the drill," I told him. "Deep breaths. In, out, in, out. Slowly."

He followed my lead, and I gave him a tissue to clean his nose. There was less blood than before but still enough to warrant some concern. Thayen had limits, and we didn't really know what breaking them would mean.

"She's unconscious but alive," Soul declared, briefly touching the clone's back with his scythe, the blade glimmering white as it analyzed the creature.

"Did you hear what she said?" Thayen replied.

"We all did," Rose said from the other side of the glass panel. The others remained gathered around her, concerned looks on their faces. I couldn't really blame them. Isabelle's clone had held on tight against Thayen's attacks, but she'd still let something slip.

"My clone isn't the only one besides hers, then," Richard replied, arms crossed. "For sure, there are more out there."

"We are many," Thayen repeated. "We are many and unstoppable... That sounds creepy as hell."

"Where is she coming from? What lies beyond those shimmering portals? How did her makers get our DNA, to begin with?" Thayen asked, becoming increasingly agitated. "And if there are so many more of her kind, where are they? Are they already here?"

Or were they on their way to The Shade as we spoke? What purpose did they serve? Why did they want me dead? Unfortunately, Isabelle's clone had not given us much to go on except for more questions and no answers. I dreaded getting used to something like this. I loved a good mystery now and then, but this was not what any of us wanted or needed, and I worried I wouldn't be the only one they wanted dead.

Thayen wasn't finished with the clone, however. Once she woke up, I knew he'd push her again. With each stab at her faux spirit so far, he'd gotten her to react. She'd told us something important, but we needed more. So much more...

TRISTAN

Anunit wanted us to pass her three trials before we sealed our deal. Her methods and motivations worried me, but I was also curious. I could see why Death wanted this Reaper apprehended, and I wondered what she would do once we delivered Anunit to her. Unending had spoken to me telepathically shortly after agreeing to the Reaper's initial terms. She'd assured me that Death would likely remove her power and perhaps reassign Anunit to some remote hellhole as punishment for her deeds.

We still had a long way to go before we got to that point, however, so I chose to focus on the present. If we pulled through—and if Anunit kept her promise, bound by death magic—Unending and I would have a family of our own to look forward to. While we'd already discussed the possibility of adoption, my wife was battling a powerful desire she'd inherited from the original soul she'd been based on. The more she remembered, the more human she seemed to me. Unending's yearning for a child of her own was something I'd learned to respect and understand. And since we still had this chance with Anunit, no matter how strange, we owed it to ourselves to try it before turning her over to Death.

"We cannot stay here much longer," Anunit said as she took a moment to enjoy the view from Red River Mountain. The crimson stream poked through the rocky top and snaked its way along the jagged ridge before it went deep into the dark emerald woods. By the time it emerged at the bottom, swollen and much wider, the water was crystal clear. "Not that I don't like this place, but we have work to do."

"I presume we're getting started with the trials?" Unending asked.

"Well, you want to get down to business, don't you?"

"Of course," she replied.

"What does the first trial entail?" I interjected, eyeing Anunit carefully. I'd known enough people from all walks of life to be able to spot deceit fairly easily. Concerned she might not be telling us the whole truth, I kept a wary eye on her at all times.

Anunit reached out with both hands. "We need physical contact for the journey, as you well know. Come on." "Where are we going?" I asked.

Unending gave me a warm smile, and her voice resounded in my head with nothing but love and appreciation. "I'm glad you've got my back in this."

"The Feoinn Jungle," Anunit said. "It's where your first trial begins."

"What's there?" I asked.

"Will you just take my hand? I don't like being in one place for too long, especially since I'm about to break the Reaper laws again for you two."

We did as she asked. As soon as our hands touched, the world warped around us as though the colors and shapes had been resting atop a still surface of water, and Anunit had put a brush through, swirling and mixing it all together. I felt dizzy for a moment, until everything fell back into place, and we were somewhere else entirely. We were in a different part of Rothko, judging by the alignment of stars in the sky, a corner of this world that seemed forgotten by the Aruni. It looked empty and uninhabited, a wild jungle stretching for thousands of miles, its trees the height of buildings and its waters restless enough to pound the stone that skirted the coastline.

A variety of shades of green unfolded before our eyes—wavy trees as tall as Californian redwoods; sprawling shrubs with huge waxed leaves and brightly colored flowers sticking out in different directions; a moss-like carpet covering the entire jungle floor, with patches of pink and red blossoms here and there; and bright white rocks dotting the ground like nature's own attempt at landscape gardening.

"This is incredible," I murmured, trying to take it all in.

Birds sang from the lush crowns, and Rothkian primates swung down from above before jumping from branch to branch to get as far away from us as possible. They couldn't see us, but they could certainly sense us. I had a feeling I'd see many more the deeper we went in, but for now I needed to know what we were doing here.

"This is the Feoinn Jungle?" I asked, and Anunit nodded once. "What's the purpose of our visit?"

"Deep in these woods, about a hundred miles northeast, there is an isolated village," she said, gazing into the distance. "It's home to creatures that supposedly shouldn't even exist anymore."

"What sort of creatures?" Unending asked with a slight frown.

"The Spirit Bender's kind," Anunit said, looking at her intently.

I heard my own gasp, yet it sounded like it had come from somebody else. "Wait, what?"

"Soul fae?" Unending asked, her galaxy eyes growing wider.

Anunit nodded again. "If that's what you call them, sure. Soul fae."

"That doesn't make sense. Spirit was the last of the species," Unending said. "Death told me—"

"Death has been lying." Anunit cut her off. "A bunch of them survived long after the Spirit Bender's matrix died. Our maker had them contained and sealed off in this jungle with no contact with the outside world whatsoever. She intervened in the affairs of the universe, which is woefully unethical, of course..."

I shook my head slowly, following Anunit's gaze into the dark and wooded distance, imagining what that village would look like. The image in my mind's eye reminded me of the Amazonian jungle and its isolated tribes, and I couldn't shake it. What would it be like to live somewhere for eons and not even know there were other civilizations beyond my little patch of wildlands?

"They were nearly extinct, don't get me wrong," Anunit continued. "You know Rothko's Hermessi are vicious and unforgiving. But Death put a protective shield around their new home in the jungle, impenetrable by the elements' wrath, with a self-contained environment designed to keep them alive and healthy. It irked the Hermessi, of course, but they couldn't do anything about it. With time, they just looked away, focusing on the other species that came afterward. And so, the soul fae survived, albeit in small numbers. I think Death tweaked their fertility rate to keep them under control. She needs the soul fae, but she can't let them get out of control."

"How so? Why would she even intervene in the course of nature? It's the one thing she's been so adamantly against," Unending said, giving me an irritated look. "After her Visio speech, this really bothers me."

"It's hypocritical of her, I agree," I replied.

"Like I said, she needs the soul fae," Anunit repeated with a cool grin.

"What for?" I asked.

"Spirit's ability is characteristic of the species. They can bend souls to their will. Any kind of souls. Reapers included. I'm thinking Death is keeping the soul fae as some sort of emergency backup plan, in case... I don't know, she can't control our kind anymore. When Spirit convinced Brendel to steal Thieron, I figured she'd unleash the soul fae, but she didn't because she still had our support. I guess things weren't dire enough to warrant the soul fae's revelation, at least in her mind. Death has gone to great lengths to protect them, to make sure no one found out about them."

Unending cursed under her breath. "Not even us..."

"Yes, well, our maker isn't perfect. Thing is, Thieron isn't the only item stolen from her. Spirit snatched a few things himself. Things she'd hidden in other worlds before she had them all moved into the Vault," Anunit added. She had my full attention, but Unending was horrified.

"Huh?" she managed.

"He snatched some of her artifacts before they were gathered and stored inside the Vault. You know about the Vault, right?"

Unending looked at her, then at me. "I don't know about the Vault," I replied, though I wasn't sure why. This whole conversation was turning into a messy blur.

"It's a collection of the artifacts Death created over the centuries, long before Spirit rebelled. Objects imbued with death magic and a purpose. Some small and insignificant to most, while others could shift the balance of power in any empire. They used to be stored in various realms, for safety," Unending explained while Anunit nodded in agreement. "About nineteen years ago, after Spirit's demise, Death built the Vault. She ordered the Reapers to search every location she gave them and to retrieve the objects she'd hidden there, to put them in the Vault. It's supposed to be a secure location. Remote and known to a select handful. We're only supposed to access it with her permission, and only if she deems it necessary."

"That might've come in handy during the Visio war," I said. Of course, I understood the timeline, but damn, it would've been nice to have had such artifacts handy in our fight against the Darklings and the Spirit Bender.

"Had it existed twenty years ago, sure," Unending said. "Most of the objects there were stored elsewhere until Death had the Reapers comb every known dimension for them. Some have been retrieved. Others are still missing, no longer where she thought they'd be. Those, apparently, were stolen by Spirit. I don't know why Death didn't create the Vault from the very beginning, but I reckon she didn't expect Spirit to turn against her. Once Spirit became such a capable enemy, Death probably didn't want to risk moving and exposing them. Maybe they were safer where she'd left them, until his demise. At least, that's an explanation that makes sense to me—Death had already lost some objects to Spirit, so she couldn't take a chance and lose the others, too. Once he was gone, she built the Vault and centralized everything there." Unending looked at Anunit. "What did he take? And what was he planning to do with the artifacts?"

"Well, I don't know about all of them, just the one he brought here. Spirit stole it long before the Hermessi's rebellion, before he even emerged as an adversary of Death, if I remember correctly. Spirit told me he'd left it inside the soul fae village because it was the safest place he could think of. I believe he once had the intention of using it to do a trade with Death for something else, though that never panned out. This object... He called it a Mixer," Anunit replied. "It merges scythes together. You know he dropped a few Reapers in his time. Most of them on Visio, in fact. But he destroyed a few in other places, and he gathered their scythes in a safe place. I believe he intended to fuse them into his own weapon with the help of this Mixer, at some point. Though I'm not sure why, because he was scarily powerful already. He put Death under the Thousand Seals, after all."

The more she spoke, the better I understood Unending's troubled expression. "Why didn't he fuse them, then?

Surely, it would've given him more power during the Hermessi wars... right?" I asked.

"There's a Reaper who guards the soul fae village," Anunit said. "Spirit could never get past her, though not for lack of trying. Of all of Death's agents, she's the one he failed to defeat. He left the Mixer in that place on purpose, making a deal with the Reaper to keep it safe. You should understand that Spirit was extremely upset when he discovered the village and found out that Death had been lying about their demise. I think it was part of why he was so determined to make her suffer."

"Wait, so Spirit made a deal with this Reaper? The same Reaper Death put in charge of protecting the soul fae village?" I replied, struggling to wrap my head around this hidden piece of history.

Anunit was rather amused by our befuddlement. In hindsight, Death's subterfuges shouldn't have come as a surprise, but alas, she was the gift that kept on giving—and not in a good way.

"And most importantly, what Reaper was it that Spirit couldn't best?" Unending added, raising an eyebrow.

"We call her Joy, though she never gave us her real name," Anunit said. "She probably knows we could use it for a death magic spell. She's a fox that way."

"Joy," Unending repeated, lowering her gaze.

"Does it sound familiar?" I asked her.

"No. But given everything else Death has kept from me, I'm not surprised. I do wonder what power she has that helped her remain undefeated."

Anunit sighed, looking disappointed. "I've had my run-ins with her, as well. She is fierce. Dangerous.

Destructive. I'd rather not mess with her again."

Suddenly it all clicked into place, like pieces of a puzzle coming together for a full and absolutely disturbing picture. "Hold on. You want us to retrieve the Mixer," I said. "You want us to go into that village, somehow—and I say somehow because I assume it's warded against any form of intrusion—and you want us to deal with this Joy person, then get you the Mixer. Am I getting that right?"

"You're a smart man," Anunit said.

"Before we even get to that point, let me rephrase an earlier question," Unending interjected. "What deal did Spirit and Joy make for him to put the Mixer in her village? And why did it go south?"

Anunit chuckled lightly. "He wooed her. He promised her the moon and the stars, and she believed him. For centuries, he stopped by once in a while, just to... you know, get all lovey and dovey with Joy, to keep her happy. At some point, I think he got busy with something else, or some*one* else, I don't know. Point is, Joy was easy to scorn in that sense. By the time Spirit came back and tried to get the Mixer, she'd turned on him. I reckon Death must've warned her about him, but I don't know the particulars. I do know she was too ashamed to tell Death about the Mixer being there, in the first place. She would've had to explain how she'd held on to it for so long, while Spirit had been plotting against Death. I figure Joy thought she'd just keep the Mixer here, hidden from Death and Spirit and anyone else, and Death would be none the wiser. Joy's ego is gargantuan..."

"And this is our first trial," Unending concluded, still frowning. She clearly wasn't sure about all this.

Anunit shrugged. "If you want your shot at life and a kid, yeah."

"So, you plan to use the Mixer to meld the scythes you've collected into yours," Unending said.

"Ahem. They'd be more useful if they were combined with my own." She revealed her own weapon—a beautiful work of metal art with an almost circular blade and a silvery handle. It glistened under the moonlight, shimmers dancing across the steel as she turned it over.

Unending didn't hide her concern at this demand. "You want to assume the power of those Reapers as your own? No wonder Death wants you captured..."

"I only desire it so that I can better protect myself against her," Anunit retorted. She seemed offended. "My whole existence revolved around my service as a Reaper until I gave hope to some of my disillusioned brethren by sending them back into the world of the living. Suddenly, I became an enemy. Frankly, I like my so-called life just the way it is, and I don't do this kind of favor for just any Reaper. I'm not a threat to Death, but she treats me like one, so I need the Mixer because I have to protect myself from her. That's my only reason."

"What will stop you from using it against innocent people?" I asked, equally untrusting.

"Why would I use it against innocent people? Tristan, I've been staying under the radar for some time now. On the run. Always looking over my shoulder," Anunit said. "I just want to be able to stop and breathe for longer than a few days in one place. That's all."

Unending jabbed a finger at her. "If we do this and you hurt people with the Mixer, I will do worse things to you than Death ever would. It won't make you stronger than I am. Hell, a thousand scythes won't make you stronger," she warned. "Anunit, I need your word that you won't disappoint me."

The Reaper exhaled sharply. "I know better than to piss off a First Tenner. I was hiding from Spirit for a while. I know what that's like, and I don't need you tailing me on top of Death, thanks." She offered me a dry smile. "Anyway, this is the deal. Take it or leave it. If you choose the latter, I hope I never see you two again, and good luck with your adoption efforts. But if you choose the former, I'll be happy to consider you my friends and escort you both as close to the soul fae village as possible. Either way, make up your minds. I don't have all day."

I would've liked some time to properly discuss this with Unending. She was thinking the same thing. "There are a few aspects of the whole situation that don't quite add up," she said through our telepathic connection. I also had a ton of questions, though I wasn't sure if either Unending or Anunit would be able to answer them. "I don't like being rushed into something so major..."

"It seems like we don't have much of a choice," I replied. "Anunit won't give us the time we need to investigate this properly. We'll have to prepare for the worst and hope for the best."

"Something tells me we can't turn back now, anyway. We need to see what Anunit is planning for her future.

"We have to capture and bring her back to Death, anyway. Whether she helps us with what we want or not."

"Yeah... so, saying yes to this first trial is still our best way forward," I concluded, using my mind to communicate with her.

Unending took my hands in hers and leaned closer, whispering in my ear. "It's going to be okay, my love."

She had an air of confidence, of security, like she knew more than she was saying. It made me curious, but we'd been together for long enough for me to trust her with everything I had.

One step at a time, I told myself.

One step at a time, and Unending and I might not only get our chance at a family, we'd also get answers to my many questions about the soul fae village and Joy, the bitter and undefeated Reaper.

TRISTAN

*A*nunit walked with us through the jungle for a while, getting us as close as she could to the warded area of the soul fae's village. From the outside, the jungle had seemed like any other wild place in the world, filled with rapidly growing greenery, curious animals, and the kind of humidity that made my shirt stick to my skin. But this place was different.

The most notable peculiarity was the existence of luminescent green veins that stretched through every single leaf, no matter how small. The light pulsated as if the jungle itself had a steady heartbeat. It was alive. The branches moved slightly, like ribs expanding with each breath. The deeper we went, the brighter the emerald glow.

"This is so weird," I said as we followed a narrow path between the enormous trees.

"It's a living organism, comprised of many smaller ones," Anunit replied, leading the way. "Don't let the eyes scare you. It's just how this place evolved."

"What eyes?" I asked.

My answer came fairly quickly, as I spotted movement to my left. Turning my head slowly, I saw a pair peeling open on the trunk of a tree. I nearly screamed, covering my mouth as the eyes widened, settling on me. The bark lids crackled as they blinked. The irises were full and black, and they seemed to be peering right into my soul.

Unending gently gripped my elbow and pulled me away so we could continue our journey. "They're just watchers," she said. "I've seen them before in other worlds that are likely extinct by now. Truth be told, I've always believed them to be the result of lingering or stray magic of some kind."

"Do... do they communicate with one another? The trees, I mean," I managed.

"I'm certain they do," Anunit replied. "But they don't speak to anyone or anything else. I think what happens in these woods stays in these woods."

At least the animals kept their distance. They had plenty of dark places to hide as we passed them by. The closer we got to the center of the jungle, the heavier my feet felt. This wasn't exhaustion I was dealing with. We'd only been walking for a couple of hours, cautiously moving through this place to better understand it. Anunit had advised us to learn a little bit about the terrain in case things went south with Joy and we could no longer teleport away to safety. Her guidance made sense, and I could certainly see why we needed to know our way around this jungle.

The mossy floor was riddled with hidden ditches and holes. One wrong step, one careless move, and we could easily break an ankle or worse while fleeing for our lives. "This is as far as I can take you," Anunit said as she stopped and turned around to face us. "I cannot risk exposing myself to Joy. Considering how badly Death wants me, I'm certain the Reaper might find a way to trap me without even leaving her precious warded area."

Unending let out a weary breath. "It feels different here. Like the air is skimmed."

"My legs are made of lead," I added.

"It's probably the death magic charms that Joy sprinkled all over the jungle, especially in the village's vicinity," Anunit explained. "The closer you get, the harder it'll be to move, to fight. Regular Reapers like me feel the charms more than a First Tenner like you will."

"I presume the living are also affected," I said. "Based on the sensations I'm dealing with."

"Absolutely. But it's okay. Joy's purpose isn't to kill but rather to slow down a potential enemy," Anunit replied. "Her orders are clear. No one is to come in contact with the soul fae. No one is to even see or hear them. To make sure said orders are followed, Joy spent a few years putting together some death magic charms and traps to keep the curious explorers away. So far, it's worked well."

Unending narrowed her eyes. "What can you tell us about your run-ins with her?"

"Only that I still regret it," she said, shaking her head slowly. "I was pretty weak by the time I reached the warded area, but I thought I could pull it off. Desperation gave me quite the push, until I realized I was absolutely no match for Joy. She's First Tenner level, Unending. You must be careful with her. She knows more than I do, and I don't know how much Death has taught her, so I have no idea what her limits may be."

"From what we've learned, Unending and Spirit were the only ones with near-complete knowledge of death magic," I said. "I mean words, sub-words, sounds. Like ninety percent or more. But if Joy's been around as long as Unending and Spirit... it would be reasonable to assume Death might've taught her almost as much, if not just as much, for the sake of keeping the soul fae safe."

"I think so," Unending replied. "I'd certainly teach Joy everything she needs to keep even the likes of us at bay. Especially after Spirit found out there were still some soul fae alive. I wonder if he ever confronted Death about it."

Anunit shrugged. "I'm so used to Death keeping secrets and telling half-truths—if not outright lies—that nothing surprises me anymore. I reckon it's part of why Spirit was so against her. It wasn't just that she refused to let him go. She preached this sanctity for our kin while she went ahead and did everything she'd asked us not to. Leading by example was never Death's forte, hence all the calamities that transpired. The terrible consequences of her decisions."

"What can you tell us about Joy, as a person?" Unending asked. "What is she like?"

"She's cold. She's a cold bitch. Joy doesn't care who you are or what you want. Her sole objective is to protect the soul fae, and she will stop at nothing to do that," Anunit said. "I told her, quite clearly, that I had absolutely no intention of touching or even interacting with them. That I only needed the Mixer. She did not care. Actually, I think my request annoyed her, since she couldn't give it back to Death without telling her how she'd gotten it, in the first place. How she'd kept it stashed here for Spirit, Death's arch enemy. In Joy's defense, she didn't know what Spirit was plotting at the time, but our maker was never really the merciful type, if you think about it. So, Joy got angry. She came at me with everything she had and nearly destroyed me. Which is why I need you. Perhaps now you understand."

Unending nodded slowly. "I do. Well, we will hopefully see you soon."

"Good luck," Anunit said.

We continued up the path without her, but I could still feel her watching us from afar. "What do you make of Anunit so far?" I asked.

"She's not to be fully trusted," Unending said, echoing my own thoughts. "I feel like there's something missing from her story, but Death wasn't able to fill in those blanks, so we'll have to figure it out ourselves. It doesn't mean Anunit isn't telling the truth, though. We have something she needs—we can try to fetch the Mixer and who knows what else the other two trials entail. She has something we need in return, so we're operating on the basis of a trade."

"So, it just means she might not be wholly forthcoming, perhaps to make sure we get her what she needs and can't get on her own," I replied.

"Probably. We'll have to meet Joy for ourselves and see what kind of Reaper she is. Maybe Joy will have a different side of the story from what Anunit has told us. It's just hard for me to believe anything a friend of Spirit's says, especially a friend he trusted with so much of his knowledge. We'll see where this leads, I suppose."

Looking around, I noticed more eyes opening on the trees. They followed us as we made our way up the path, their branches rattling in the nocturnal wind. Long black shadows stretched across the moss carpet, blending into the nearby darkness. Only then did I realize what was happening here. "Hold on," I said, stopping for a moment.

The light from the luminescent veins was concentrated around us but dimmed in the distance. The glow also followed us as we moved, as if the jungle were lighting our way through. That was why there was still darkness dominating the area, yet we had the courtesy of the green glow to keep us company.

"The forest... it's giving us a guiding light," I said, looking at Unending.

She quickly understood I was onto something. "Oh, wow. You're right.

This is interesting."

"Won't that give us away when we get closer to the village? Joy will see us coming from a mile away," I replied. "I think Joy will see us coming with or without the glow," Unending said. "You heard Anunit. There are charms all over this place. Traps, too. I don't think it's just the jungle that makes our presence known." "You think maybe she already knows we're coming."

"Yes, so we must be careful," Unending said, and we linked hands as we continued our journey north.

Unease festered inside me with every step I took. I was afraid, and I had every reason to be, but Unending's presence by my side soothed me. I'd married the most powerful Reaper in existence, and I knew she'd stop at nothing to keep me alive.

Something clicked under my heel, and I froze. Unending gave me a terrified look. "Do not move," she whispered, then dropped to her knees and cleared some of the moss around my boots, revealing a stone plate with familiar symbols carved into a pentagram pattern. "Oh... crap."

"What is it?" I asked, my voice barely a wheeze. Sweat began dripping down my face and seeping into my already moist shirt. My blood ran cold, and I wasn't sure how I'd get out of this predicament. I didn't really need Unending to tell me what the plate was, since I already knew it had been designed to hurt people. It didn't take a genius.

"It's similar to the landmines used by humans," Unending said, cautiously running her fingers over the runes. "But it's loaded with a Reaper's personal energy. It's weaponized against Reapers, and it will easily obliterate a living person. You won't stand a chance."

I gave myself a moment to let it all sink in. "Okay. What do we do?"

"I can teleport you away, but we need to make sure we don't end up on another one of these. We also need to be as far from this plate as possible, because I have no idea what the blast radius will be."

"Won't it leave a hole in the jungle itself, if it's a big one?" I asked, my tone uneven, my throat scratchy with anxiety. "Would she do something so extreme?"

"Nature recovers," Unending said. "But you'd be pulverized, and I cannot let that happen, my love."

"I understand. You should zap us somewhere off the beaten path, then," I suggested. "I assume these traps are more limited where the terrain is harder to cross."

Unending stepped back, her brow furrowed. "Give me a second." She vanished, and I was left on my own. I tried not to shiver or make even the slightest movement. Taking deep breaths, I waited while she scoured the woods for a safer place to drop me. The traps would hurt her, too, so she had to be extra careful as she briefly scanned the increasingly hostile terrain just to save my bacon.

My wife was an absolute badass, I thought to myself. She reappeared and took my hand, smiling with sparkling confidence. A split second later, we vanished, and only the faint echo of the blast reached us as we were teleported a mile farther north, smack in the middle of the untamed wilderness. The trees suddenly came to life, veins illuminating and eyes opening to find us standing and shaking like leaves. We'd escaped a terrible, violent fate.

"Are you okay?" Unending asked.

"I'm alive. I'm whole. Yes, I'm definitely okay." I chuckled, though I was still very much on edge. She didn't let go of my hand as she guided me deeper into the woods.

"This will be slightly safer, I think," she said.

We trekked through the untamed and uneven jungle, keeping away from any noticeable paths. Other people may have come around at some point or another, in smaller or larger numbers, for a variety of reasons. Some may have survived. Others perhaps had died, while the rest would have scattered upon dealing with Joy's many hidden traps. But the forest floor seemed to have remembered them all, keeping their paths from being swallowed by the sprawling ferns with succulent-like leaves.

"Have you told Death telepathically about this place? Or about Joy? I mean, about you knowing about it?" I asked as we carefully advanced through the wilderness, the glow persistently following us around.

"No. I want to see what it's like first. I want to see it for myself. To maybe understand why she kept it a secret, why she lied about the soul fae's demise."

"But you will tell her, right? I doubt Joy will keep this a secret," I said.

"Of course. I do wonder if she'll be okay with me taking the Mixer." Unending chuckled. But that raised a different question for me.

"What if she says no?"

Unending stopped, giving me a sideways glance. "I'm not sure what we'll do. We can still try to take it and deal with the consequences later. Let's see what this place is about first. Then we'll handle Death."

"But if we don't or can't get the Mixer, what then?" The prospect of halting the mission here bothered me more than I'd originally thought it would.

"Then we'll stop our quest," she said. "And we'll adopt. I'll find a way to exist with this yearning. Maybe a child of another world will keep me busy enough to stop my mind from crumbling. I don't know. I don't have all the answers, my love. Let's just take this one step at a time and see where it leads."

Finally, we reached a clearing that looked rather strange. It was empty, and the air rippled all around it. I needed no magical skills to figure out that we'd found the warded edge of the village. "It's an invisible shield," Unending murmured, analyzing it carefully.

"We found it, then."

"Which means we must pay extra attention to anything and everything from now on," she replied, slowly reaching out a hand to touch the transparent membrane. The surface shimmered ever so slightly, barely bothered by the physical contact. I had a feeling it wouldn't be easy to breach. Beyond it, the soul fae were probably going about their lives, unseen and unheard by the outer world. Joy was likely patrolling the area which, judging by the wide arch of our side of the membrane, was probably at least a few miles wide.

In there, somewhere, was the Mixer. Our first trial had begun, and I couldn't see myself turning away from it now. We'd made it this far. Unending's expression spoke of confidence and wise concern. I squeezed her hand and gave her a wink.

"We've got this. Right?"

She smiled. "Hopefully, yes."

I was fine with a hopeful yes. It was better than a no or a maybe. We just had to figure out a way in. It seemed doable in theory, but without a full understanding of the death magic that had been keeping the village safe for so long, I doubted we'd succeed. But I was with Unending, one of the brightest of her kind. That had to count for something.

THAYEN

Astra and I remained outside "Isabelle's" room for a while. We'd agreed I'd give myself a longer break before trying to glamor the clone again. I needed time to recover. Kailani had taken the others to the nearby terrace to eat. They'd all been so worried and focused on these strange events that nourishment had been the last thing on their minds.

Kelara and the ghouls had joined Lumi and the living, though she had no need for food. But our people required comfort and kindness, company and reassurance more than anything, and the Reaper had understood that. Besides, Stan and Ollie could do with a chunk of fresh meat, as well. Isabelle's clone didn't need this much attention from us, anyway, and I doubted it did Serena or Draven any good to stick around and watch her. Especially when their daughter was still missing. Isabelle's clone was a mean and unforgiving creature. She'd mess with their heads given the chance, so I was more than happy to see them leave with the others.

Soul, on the other hand, had gone to do a sweep around the hospital perimeter, just in case there might be a portal opening nearby. It was a long shot, but I knew he just didn't have the patience to stay in one place for too long.

Meanwhile, Astra and I struggled to figure out our next steps. We didn't have much to go on, which made any action risky without all the data. At least Isabelle's clone was still sleeping, her head resting on the table. My glamor push had done quite the number on her, apparently. I was already looking forward to trying again, having acquired a taste of my ability's growing strength, and I wanted to make myself truly useful. Soon enough, I thought, dealing with a certain lingering feebleness—a sign that I had absolutely overexerted myself earlier.

"You'll dig deeper when she wakes up," Astra said, as if reading my mind. "I wonder if there have been any more portal sightings since Richard's clone escaped."

I shook my head. "I doubt it. Our people are constantly combing The Shade and the redwoods, but they haven't seen anything."

"I wish I could sense the portals from afar, but alas... I cannot."

"It's not like you can wander through the forest day and night on the off chance one will pop open," I replied. "You need a break."

"And you need to rest, too," Astra said. "Stop stressing over the doppelganger."

"How do you know I'm stressing?" I shot back with a faint grin.

"I can tell," she grumbled. "Your spiritual energy is a mess, though I'm barely able to read it. The weight of the world should not be on your shoulders."

"I just want to sort this out before it gets worse. We've all agreed there's a chance more clones will show up at some point," I said. "And the more I can do with my glamoring, the better for everyone. If I can train myself to be able to make them tell us everything, then we'll have an undeniable advantage. Don't you think?"

Astra sighed. "That nosebleed was a symptom, Thayen. You cannot exhaust yourself in this pursuit. Take it easy; give your ability time to expand and grow without it whittling away at your health. There is no point in you glamoring a clone if it eventually reduces you to a bleeding mess."

"What am I supposed to do? Give myself a day or two? Kick back with a book?" I was irritated by my inability to overcome these physical limitations. What good was a Reaper's power if I couldn't use it like a Reaper could?

"Maybe start with a deep breath," Astra said, eyeing me worriedly. "Unwind for a moment. Stop assuming it's your responsibility to fix everything. Isabelle's clone will cave in eventually. Whether it happens in the next few hours or days, it doesn't matter. It will happen."

"What about Isabelle? She's still out there somewhere," I insisted.

She looked down, as if uncomfortable to hold my gaze. "If she were dead, I'm sure we'd have found her body by now."

"What if they took her body to wherever the clones came from?" I asked.

"Whoever is pulling the strings here already knows we have their clone. I think we would've come across... the real Isabelle if that were the case. They would have no reason left to hold on to it. Given how practically evil they are, as evidenced by our 'friend' here, they would probably throw her back into this world just to get back at us for taking their clone," Astra replied.

I didn't like the sound of Isabelle's body not having turned up so far, but I had to admit it was a solid line of reasoning. A mild sense of peace came with it—a faint reassurance that maybe Isabelle was very much alive and waiting for us to save her.

"Let's not mention any of this to Draven and Serena," I said. "The corpse part, I mean. They're dealing with enough as it is."

Voss came down the hallway, carrying a duffel bag on his shoulder. "Hey, you two!" he called out. "Sofia and Derek want you back at the Great Dome. They couldn't get through to your comms pieces. Apparently, your Telluris connections aren't working, either. I was on my way to start the patrol shift, passing by the Great Dome, when they called out to me. My comms aren't working, either, it seems..."

"So, they only sent you?" I asked.

Astra tried her earpiece first, then Telluris. "I'm not getting an answer." She gave me a concerned look.

"No. They told me they sent Chantal and Soph ahead, too. They're not here?" We shook our heads, and he pursed his lips as he reached us and dropped the bag on the floor. "There's something funky going on here... I obviously have no way of reaching the girls now..."

I tried my own comms lines and Telluris, but just like Astra, I wasn't able to contact anyone. It bothered me. Something was definitely about to happen. I could feel it in my bones. And I didn't want it catching us split up like this.

Astra gave me a curious look. "Do you think we're dealing with more clones?"

"I wouldn't put it past them. Dad did say we should expect more fakes, though we're not yet sure how many of us they were able to replicate, in the first place. Not to mention how," Voss replied. "It's all very confusing to me. I wish things were normal again."

"Things were never really normal here, though." I said as I got up. "But this warrants further investigation. Before we head for the Great Dome, Astra and I will rush over to the terrace and pick the others up. We'll have Stan and Ollie come over to keep you company and make sure no one tampers with the doppelganger's room. It's virtually impenetrable, anyway."

He eyed me intently. "Yeah, I'll hold down the fort here, but hurry. The fact that our comms are down is a major issue. We need to get ahead of this quickly."

"I know. Like I said, we'll grab Lumi and the gang and we'll head back to the Great Dome. You'll have some ghoul backup soon enough," I said, patting him on the back as I walked toward the exit with Astra. "The clone's in deep sleep for now."

"Just be careful, okay?" Voss replied, taking my seat.

I gave him one last look before we went through the double doors. Astra had a permanently raised eyebrow, as if something had been bothering her for a while. "What's wrong?" I asked.

"Nothing. I just think we're missing a crucial piece of the puzzle here, and until we find out what it is, we'll keep hitting these glass walls."

The hospital's ground floor was sparsely populated with a handful of nurses and doctors waiting for any walk-in patients. I didn't mind. It meant our island was healthy and rarely in need of medical assistance. Besides, we had bigger fish to fry.

Outside, everything seemed peaceful. Warmth permeated the enormous clearing where the hospital had been built—the late spring temperatures helping the citrus blossoms burst open and spread their lemony fragrance all around. The permanent night gave us a starry view of the sky, the moon slowly moving across as it bathed everything in a delicate pearlescent light. For a moment, it seemed as though nothing had really happened.

As though it had only been a wicked dream.

Soul appeared outside, giving us both a surprised look. "What are you two doing out here?" he asked, and I told him about Voss and the sudden lack of comms available.

"Then we'd best get the others," Soul said, and the three of us headed west. The terrace was only a couple hundred yards away. Beyond the giant old oak trees and the magnolia garden, the Vale humans had erected a cobblestone alley with posh little shops and gourmet bistros, each with an open-air terrace and fresh flowers in cast- iron pots decorating their tables. The whole area was secluded from the hospital's traffic, making it perfect for the occasional cup of coffee or, in my case, crystal glass filled with fresh deer blood.

It served as our miniature French alley, complete with a sweet water stream—one of the many that flowed through The Shade. We couldn't see it from here, but I could already smell the latest batch of croissants that had just left the oven. It made me miss my Trakkian days, but I had found different comforts in my life as a vampire.

"I can teleport us over there," Soul nodded ahead. Both Astra and I were inclined to agree, since time was of the essence at this point, but a familiar voice cut through.

"Stop right there!" Chantal shouted from somewhere behind us. I quickly turned around. We still had a view of the hospital clearing— just enough to see several figures bolting through the woods beyond. Instinctively, I ran toward them, and Astra and Soul followed.

I could see Chantal running, but she wasn't alone. Soph, Zane and Fiona's half-daemon daughter, and Voss were with her, just a few yards from the edge of the forest. They were chasing after someone. The sight before us didn't make sense. "Wait, isn't Voss—"

"What the..." Astra cut me off, equally stunned. We all recognized the creature they were trying to catch.

"Come on," Soul said, grabbing us both by the wrists.

"No, wait, Voss is supposed to be up in the hosp—" I didn't get a chance to finish my sentence as everything went black for a split-second. We materialized closer to the chase just as Voss, Soph, and Chantal ran past us. They were going after... Chantal.

"Holy crap," I blurted, my blood running cold.

There was a clone of Chantal darting between the redwoods and moving at an impressive speed. She threw fireballs back at her pursuers, her skin shimmering silver under the moonlight that pierced through the tree crowns. And the Voss we were seeing… was that a clone or the real one? Who was the Voss we'd left upstairs? My brain could no longer compute this entire sight.

"I said stop!" Chantal demanded, fury drawing a deep shadow between her eyebrows.

Voss shifted into his wolf form and went ahead, getting dangerously close to the clone, while Soph picked up the pace and extended her daemon claws. Chantal flung fireballs back at her doppelganger, careful not to hit Voss in the process.

"Well, this is weird," Soul mumbled, watching Chantal's clone shrink in the distance with Voss hot on her trail.

Soon they were all tiny dots against the dark green backdrop of the forest.

"We need to go back to the hospital," I said. "Voss!"

It didn't take long for the realization to fully sink in.

"Oh, no," Soul managed, finally realizing what I'd been trying to say. Not that I could really blame him. This whole situation was confusing to all of us.

He grabbed us both again, teleporting our stunned asses straight back to the hallway outside of the clone's room, where Voss's doppelganger was already hard at work on breaking the door open. He wasn't able to get through, however, despite the weird-looking bladed object he'd been using. It didn't look like anything we'd ever used or even thought to design—the blade was long and split in three, each extension molded into a different shape. One was long and slim, much like an icepick, while the other two were wider and undulated, with sharp tips. Tiny lights flickered on the handle as the Voss clone kept pressing them in a certain order and cursing under his breath.

"For heaven's sake," Astra croaked. "When will this stop?!"

This doppelganger had passed as one of us. That wasn't supposed to be a surprise, given how well-made Isabelle and Richard's copies were. They'd fooled us before. But this one had chosen a more covert approach, getting us out of here so he could do whatever he'd been sent to do. From the looks of it, breaking Isabelle's clone out of that room was still a priority, though he had clearly not gotten the memo on all the magical wards that had been put in place.

He grew still and looked back at us, lights still blinking on his strange instrument. "This wasn't supposed to happen," he muttered.

It made me angry beyond belief. Isabelle was the only one they'd taken, while the others' clones were waltzing around and messing with us. It didn't make sense. However, it did mean that their maker had infiltrated The Shade more than once, since they'd been able to gather so much DNA material for their fakes. Why had they abducted Isabelle, in particular, then?

Whatever their agenda, I allowed my rage to take over. Voss's clone was going down. We were getting to the truth today, one way or another. I'd had enough of the mystery and the nonsense, of the unwarranted and inexplicable violence, of the chaos that had infiltrated and turned my world upside down.

I let my claws out and revealed my fangs. He knew things were about to get bad. His expression told me that much as I lunged at him.

ASTRA

(DAUGHTER OF PHOENIX AND VIOLA)

What followed happened quickly.

I barely registered the movement as Thayen attacked Voss's double. The foreign tool ended up on the floor. I snuck around the two-man skirmish and grabbed it before the doppelganger could get to it. Soul stood on the side and watched the fight—he'd intervene if needed, but I had a feeling he wanted to see how Thayen would handle the clone, perhaps whether he'd try to use his glamoring ability or not.

Thayen was thrown against the wall as the clone spread his wings in a menacing fashion. Only then did I see what made him truly different from the real Voss. Each feather had been replaced with stainless steel blades. The sight made my stomach churn because I understood their purpose before Thayen could even blink.

"He needs help," I said, giving Soul a nervous glance.

He vanished, reappearing a couple of feet behind the clone. Somehow, the clone knew what he was doing, and horror gripped me by the throat and stopped me from warning the Reaper of what was about to come his way. "Watch out!" I eventually managed, but it was too late. The clone had already fluttered his deadly wings. Soul disappeared again, and I wasn't sure where he'd gone.

"Damn it!" Thayen said, pushing himself back up.

I unleashed my Daughter energy, my hands glowing pink as I pointed them in the clone's direction. Channeling all the rage I'd been gathering over the past couple of days, I released a flurry of shimmering pulses in his direction. He used his steely wings as a shield, but it gave Thayen the split second he needed to use his glamoring ability.

The clone didn't see it coming. He froze, grunting as Thayen took hold of his fake soul. It was barely a grip, but it was working. "Don't move!" the vampire commanded him.

Concentrating an energy pulse in the palms of my incandescent hands, I prepared myself for a devastating attack. Voss's clone couldn't move—this was my chance to destroy him before he did any more damage or hurt anyone else. He'd come here to set Isabelle's doppelganger free, and I would be damned if I was going to let either of them walk out of this place. Enough was enough.

"Do it now!" Thayen called out. "I can't hold on for much longer. He's resisting, and he's way better at it than Isabelle's copy!"

"That means they're learning," I muttered, then let go of the pulse.

Voss's double couldn't pull his wings forward as a shield again. Thayen's hold on him was weak but still enough to tamper with his defenses. A figure bolted between us, and something shone so bright that I had to close my eyes.

"Astra, move back!" I heard Thayen shout.

Something rammed into me with the strength of a supercharged bull. My whole body hurt as I was slammed against the wall. I cried out, coughing and wheezing as I landed on the floor. Finally able to see again, I looked up to find Chantal standing beside me, a crystal-like disk with a diameter of about two feet in her hand—as it moved, I noticed how it reflected the light. This was another foreign object, and she wasn't Chantal but her able-bodied clone.

The enemy had come out to play, and they'd brought some toys to the party.

She raised the disk and prepared to bring it down hard, its edge sharp enough to sever my head with one swift move. Voss's clone broke free of Thayen's hold and went after him with his bladed wings. I couldn't help him; I had one hell of a problem of my own to handle.

"Where the hell did Soul go?!" Thayen croaked as he deflected the doppelganger's attacks. He'd brought up a chair to keep some distance between them, though I doubted it would do much good in the long term. The clones were set on kill mode.

Chantal's copy tried to cut my head off, but I kicked the side of her knee and threw a barrier out. It hurled her backward like a rag doll until she hit the glass panel from Isabelle's clone's room with a painful thud, but she wasn't done. Throwing fireballs at me, she managed to get up and turn her copied fire fae ability to the max in a bid to pummel me into a scorched mess. My Daughter instincts flared, and I pulled an energy shield around me. It stopped the fire from reaching me, but each blow took a toll on my stamina.

I could feel myself weakening. Much like Thayen, I'd only come up with a temporary solution. We needed much more to defeat these bastards.

"Fire in the hole!" Soul shouted, appearing next to the eastern wall. He touched the blade of his scythe with two fingers, and a phosphorescent pattern emerged on the marble floor, glowing green. He'd been hard at work, I realized, crafting an attack spell.

It all came to a sudden halt, as even the clones understood that something nasty was afoot. Soul elbowed the wall, and it came crumbling down. He motioned for us to jump through the opening. "Move! Move! Move!"

I didn't hesitate, and neither did Thayen. We dashed toward the gaping hole before the clones could scramble toward us. We jumped, and a massive explosion tore through the entire floor of the hospital. Screams echoed somewhere nearby, but I knew Soul would've evacuated anyone within the vicinity of his spell—standard Reaper procedure to keep the innocents safe.

I pushed a barrier beneath me, and it hit the ground and bounced back, softening our fall. We landed and rolled to the side. Soul had already joined us, scythe still glinting in his hand as he looked up. Reddish flames had blossomed through the hole, spewing plumes of black smoke and debris as the blaze consumed everything in its path. I couldn't see Voss or Chantal's clones anywhere. My heart was beating fast, and I was dangerously close to hyperventilating.

"What in the world..." I murmured, trying to catch my breath.

"You two okay?" Soul asked.

Thayen and I nodded at the same time and shared a confused look.

"What sort of blast was that?" I replied.

"Proprietary blend of mine," Soul said. "Isabelle's clone is still safe in her warded room, however. The whole hospital could come down, and her room would remain untouched. A solitary cube atop a pile of smoldering rubble."

"You were gunning for Voss and Chantal's clones, right?" Thayen asked, albeit sarcastically. "You almost blew us up, too."

Soul nodded. "Sorry about that. I'm not sure it did anything. You two were fast, but the doppelgangers weren't half bad, either."

"This is weird. What was Chantal's copy doing here? I thought the real Voss and the others were chasing her down," I said. "I'm not making much sense of this…"

"The more you trouble yourself over it, the harder it'll be to process the facts, and one fact I can give you right now is that there may be more clones of the same individuals running around now," Soul replied with a shrug. "One step at a time, Astra. Also, nice save," he added, pointing at the object coming out of my pocket. I'd almost forgotten about the tool Voss's clone had tried to use on the door to free Isabelle's doppelganger.

Thayen pressed the distress button on his earpiece. We'd barely had a moment to breathe, let alone try and call for help again. "Can anyone hear me?" He was trying the general channel. None of the others had worked thus far, and I wasn't sure this would do any good, either. "We need backup at the hospital right now," he said. "Voss and Chantal's clones attacked us. No sign of them for now, but Isabelle's clone is secure… Come in! Any GASP member on this channel! Hello?"

"I doubt you'll be able to get through to them," Soul replied, stating the painful obvious. "My telepathic communications have been cut off, too. Whatever these clones are using, whatever kind of magic this is, it's tampering with all our networks, undead or otherwise."

"It was worth another shot. Desperate times, desperate measures, yadda, yadda… What the hell do we do, then?" Thayen asked, the scratches on the side of his face already healing. The clone's bladed wings had sliced through his GASP uniform, leaving patches of skin exposed. He'd drawn blood, but nothing the vampire couldn't handle.

I'd gotten off easy, too, with just a few bruises that would heal by nightfall. However, I knew this was just the beginning. It would get worse soon enough. Soul raised his scythe again, his brow furrowed as he went into fight mode. "They're coming."

"Who?" I asked. I got my answer as Voss and Chantal's clones emerged seemingly from nowhere. They both wore red lenses. "Oh, crap, they're using our invisibility magic!"

Soul took on Voss's clone with his dangerous wings, but the doppelganger produced a device that released a black smoke-like gas. It hit the Reaper right in the face and immediately forced him screaming to his knees. "No! Stop it! No!" Soul cried out, covering his eyes.

Chantal's clone sprayed the same substance at us. I managed to get back a couple of steps, and I also pulled my GASP-issued face mask over my mouth and nose, but it didn't help much. The particles were spreading fast, reaching my nose through the filtering fabric as I inadvertently sucked in a breath. It burned right through me, making my head hurt. Reality warped itself around me, and I caught a glimpse of Thayen grunting as he collapsed into a fetal position.

Whatever this stuff was, it took effect very quickly, and the masks were useless.

Every muscle in my body ached, convulsions taking over with such violence that I feared my bones might break. I lost any sense of light and dark, of objects and space. Pain expanded like a heatwave, making me whimper before it pushed me over the edge and into a crippling state of despair. I had no control over myself or my emotions. I'd lost it completely.

Hitting the ground hard, I felt my lungs fill with water. Where had it come from? Was this even happening? I was drowning. I seemed to be drowning. *Is this real?* Struggling to breathe. Unable to survive. Death came knocking. I could hear her giggling in my ear, inviting me to just... let go. But why would I? No, I'd fought too hard up to this moment. I'd resisted their attacks. I was a Daughter. Drowning wasn't a way to kill me. This didn't make sense. Or was I not really drowning? Was this just a malevolent illusion? If so, how could I get past this deathly point?

"If Isabelle couldn't take you down, then I will." Chantal's clone snickered as she towered over me, the reflective disk still in her hand. I wanted to throw out a barrier to push her away, but I couldn't even draw a life- saving breath anymore, let alone defend myself.

Despair took over, my ears ringing and my heart thudding. The adrenaline rush made everything worse as the anticipation of my impending demise took center stage in my consciousness. This was it. I could smell it. The rancid stench of failure.

A spine-tingling roar broke through. Chantal's clone screamed. Chills rushed past me as I inhaled deeply for the first time in what seemed like forever. The air was cold, and I managed to peel open my eyes just as a flurry of ice shards swooshed down after the doppelganger. I recognized Dafne in dragon form about fifty yards away, her jaws opened wide as she unloaded on the clones, left and right.

Voss and Chantal's copies were forced to move away from us. Some of the shards sliced through them, but they were still moving. They both aimed their weird spraying devices at her. I forced myself into a sitting position. My arms were weak. My body weakened and my breathing labored, but it occurred to me that the black mist's effect was brief and profoundly psychological, just enough to mess with our defenses so the clones could deliver the kill shot. Fortunately, Dafne had come upon us somehow.

The worst part was that the spray had affected Soul, too, and he was struggling to pull himself back together. The stars had gone out from his eyes, leaving behind nothing but darkness as he looked around and tried to understand what had just happened.

Dafne hissed and lowered her head, releasing more ice shards all around her in a bid to keep the clones at bay, but they were both determined to hit her. A fire dragon emerged from the woods—majestic but smaller than most I'd seen. I only needed a second to recognize Jericho as he made it rain fire on the doppelgangers.

Voss's clone managed to escape the flames, bolting into the redwood forest, but the blaze caught Chantal's clone in full. She screamed in agony as the fire consumed her. She dropped and rolled on the ground over and over, but nothing helped. The flesh melted off her bones, black smoke rising as she took her last breath and stilled. Looking at her charred remains, I realized what was so off about the way she'd died.

"She's a fire fae," I said quietly. "The fire isn't supposed to kill her..."

The body was barely a figure with legs and arms and a head, a black and reddish crust covering every inch of her. Dafne and Jericho approached her cautiously, while Thayen helped me up. He looked better than I felt, but I was thankful we'd both made it out of this alive.

"Long live the dragons, huh?" he said, only partially amused. "Are you okay, Astra?"

"They did something to us." I glanced at the clone's body. "Is she really dead?"

Dafne huffed and pulled her head back just in time, as the burnt doppelganger sprang up shrieking and ran off into the woods. It left us all stunned and unable to react as we tried to wrap our heads around this.

"Well, this is endless shades of wrong," Soul grumbled, finally up and in a better state than before. "What was that black mist thing? It messed with my head on so many levels... I'm still shaking!"

"Isn't anyone wondering how a fire fae clone could succumb to the one element she is supposed to be impervious to?" I asked, my voice trembling as I leaned into Thayen. "Also, how the hell did she manage to just get up and bolt away like that? I don't... I don't get it."

Dafne and Jericho approached us, staying in their dragon forms. They both sniffed the air, their reptilian eyes scanning every inch of the place. Dafne was the first to shift back into her humanoid form, and I gave her my jacket so she could cover herself.

"Thanks. Chantal, Voss, and Soph are on their way back with my stuff." she said. "I came across them in the redwood forest, not far from the Great Dome. They were chasing after Chantal's clone. As for your question regarding it and fire... I'm gonna take a wild guess and suggest that maybe whoever's making these fiends doesn't have all the information. Or maybe they have faulty genetic material? I don't know, just a theory at this point."

"Even so, this is insane." I sighed, the adrenaline gradually wearing off to reveal the physical trauma I had just overcome. My legs were shaky and weak, but Thayen stayed close as I tried to gather my thoughts into something coherent.

"I don't know much about the clones' genetic makeup," Dafne added, "but Voss and his crew lost Chantal's clone. I picked up a faint trail and followed her up here."

Jericho sat on his hind legs, threads of smoke billowing from his nostrils. "And what's your deal?" Soul asked him.

It made Dafne chuckle. "He tagged along. He and his crew were chasing after Richard's clone again. There are definitely more of these creeps around. Though I fail to understand their purpose. The comms systems and Telluris are both down—none of our messages have been getting through."

"What in the world are we going to do?" Thayen wondered. "Clearly, they won't stop coming for Astra, and they'll keep trying to release *their* Isabelle."

"True. But they're also off by a few degrees," Soul noted. "Some are accurate clones, like Isabelle's. Others are... tweaked."

"Voss's clone has blade wings and Chantal's has a vulnerability to fire," I said.

"Jericho's blaze hurt her, but it didn't kill her." Dafne nodded slowly. She glanced at the fire dragon, raising an eyebrow. "You can shift back now. It's kind of weird being the only naked one. Well, half-naked, anyway."

Thayen chuckled. "I think that's exactly why he's not turning. Someone else has his clothes, likely those in his crew."

"Aw, Jericho is bashful." I allowed myself a giggle.

Surrendering to the despair that had tested me earlier would've meant defeat. I refused to yield before these clones, and I sure as hell wasn't going to let them disrupt our way of life anymore. We'd just survived a heinous attack, but we'd also discovered a few changes in their strategy. They had tools and methods to fight us. That suggested they were better organized than we'd originally assumed.

Their failures had taught them to try different things, but they clearly lacked all the information they needed to succeed. As baffling as it all was, I found a glimmer of hope in knowing that they were essentially winging it, much like the rest of us.

ASTRA

(DAUGHTER OF PHOENIX AND VIOLA)

few minutes later, we found a medical robe for Jericho to put on. The rest of his crew were still chasing down other clones. From what Jericho and Dafne told us, there had been at least four strange sightings, and nearby teams of GASP agents were spotted going after the slippery doppelgangers. Our biggest problem was with the communications channels. The earpieces weren't getting through to anyone, and Telluris didn't seem to be working, either.

I used my Daughter magic, deeply rooted in the natural elements, to conjure up a watery mist that spread through and around the burning hospital. The flames died out quickly. Considering we still had Isabelle's clone to guard, we decided to stick together and head back to her room to make sure she was definitely okay in there. Soul and the witches might've put the mother of all wards on that box, but we still had to check. Besides, the others in the hospital who'd been present during the attack must have run out to warn everyone.

"We'll be seeing some senior officers soon," Dafne said as we moved through the long, narrow hallway leading up to the clone's room. "I saw people running away from the hospital on my way here. They'll figure out that the comms are down and start sending envoys to warn the civilians."

"Plus, we still have the island-wide announcement system," Jericho added, fastening the robe's belt around his waist to make sure it didn't flutter. "Thanks for jumping in, by the way."

Dafne gave him a sideways glance. "What's that supposed to mean?"

"I just figured you'd rather hole up in the Black Heights or something."

"Why?" the ice dragon replied, while Jericho began to fumble his words.

"Because… you're the recluse type?" In that respect, the fire dragon was on to something. But given the circumstances, along with the fact that Dafne had been present when Isabelle's clone had first tried to kill me, I wasn't at all surprised that she'd chosen to stick around instead of heading back to the Black Heights.

"You're not making much sense," Dafne chuckled. "What happens in The Shade, anywhere in The Shade, concerns us all. Dad's the one who doesn't come out much, but I've been here since the beginning with Isabelle's doppelganger. Obviously, I'll do what I can to help police the island. You know, with the killer clones prancing around like nobody's business."

Jericho exhaled, unable to take his eyes off her. "You are absolutely right. I shouldn't have doubted you."

"Meh. You fire dragons have a way of being judgy sometimes, with regards to my species, anyway."

"Ice dragons make that easy," Jericho shot back. I'd almost forgotten about this antiquated line of thinking. It wasn't an issue anymore, but the dragons still brought it up once in a while to playfully poke another.

Dafne was actually amused. "See? Judgy. Proves my point."

"I know Jericho has already said it, but thank you for stepping in when you did," I interjected, offering her a smile. The last fight had rattled me, and I doubted I'd be okay anytime soon, but I had to push through. This was nowhere near over. On the contrary, I had a feeling our nightmare was only just beginning.

"Don't mention it. I just followed the smell of trouble," Dafne replied. Her grayish blue eyes darted all over the place as she analyzed every inch of space ahead. Most of the floor had burned enough for the walls to turn black. Ashes lingered in the air, flakes of papers and medical paraphernalia, towels and uniforms that had been reduced to nothing. Looking at it now, I realized how lucky we'd been to find an intact garment for Jericho in the reception area of the hospital, which hadn't incurred as much damage.

We could see the broken windows and the door to the clone's room. From what I could tell, Soul had been right. The protection spells had kept it safe and virtually intact, causing an interesting contrast of pure white walls and the marbled floor against the charred aspect of everything else around it.

"Have you been able to reach any of the Reapers yet?" I asked Soul, and he shook his head.

"I'll go get Kelara as soon as we check on Miss Knockoff in there," he said. "Something's off here, and I don't like it. The only time comms are cut is when there's an assault coming, and I doubt the four clones running around in the woods are the first wave."

"What about the ones we fought?" Thayen asked. "Weren't they the first wave?"

"Nah. Two of them were manageable," Soul said. "I think we should assume the worst is yet to come."

When I reached the glass panel, I breathed a sigh of relief. Isabelle's clone was very much alive and tethered to the table with charmed cuffs. She seemed annoyed by our presence. "I was hoping you were all dead," she grumbled, leaning back in her chair.

I had trouble getting the burnt smell out of my nose. This place had been a haven, a place of healing and peace. The mere fact that they had attacked it felt like an act of war, and Soul's warning made me worry about where they might strike next.

"They're obviously after Isabelle's copy," Jericho said. Occasionally, he stole glances at Dafne but looked away whenever she shifted her focus to him. Under different circumstances, I would've found their dynamic cute.

Thayen looked at the device we'd rescued from Voss's clone. "And we still don't know what this thing is..." "He was trying to use it on the door," I replied. "It's got to be some type of lockpick."

"And that disk Chantal had. And the black spray... that was the worst," Soul said, visibly troubled. "It affected me directly. I've never seen anything like that before."

Dafne scoffed, shaking her head slowly. "Whatever foreign magic they've got, it seems to have an effect on everyone, alive or otherwise. They did some of their homework right, since our GASP-issued masks are useless for this stuff. It's a shame Chantal's clone ran off with the disk. I would've loved to take a look at that thing, too." She paused to give Jericho a stern frown. "You should've turned the heat up on her."

"I went full throttle!" Jericho exclaimed. "It's not my fault she's resilient. She was cloned after a fire fae. It's a miracle I even hurt her at all. That wasn't supposed to happen. I used my fire to at least distract her with an enormous amount of flames. I'm surprised it took so well."

"For what it's worth, you did a good job out there," Dafne admitted. It seemed to have an impact on Jericho, as he looked away, his cheeks blooming red for a moment.

"Thanks. You weren't too bad yourself."

Soul cleared his throat, demanding our attention. "I'll go out and get Kelara. We're spiritually bonded, so I know where to find her, even without our telepathic connection."

"Is she still at the terrace?" Thayen asked, slightly concerned. "Surely, she and the others would've heard the blast. There were witnesses running away from the hospital."

"I'll find out. Maybe they had issues of their own," Soul replied, then vanished.

While checking the hallway for any details I might have missed earlier, I replayed the entire fight in my head. It had been manageable, like the Reaper had said, until they pulled out the black spray. Whatever that was, it messed with our heads in ways I feared we'd never truly overcome. The sensations I struggled with still haunted me, the horror already settled in my chest and unwilling to ever go away.

It was as if a nightmare had followed me all the way into the waking world, long after a restless sleep. I looked at Thayen and noticed his troubled expression. "What is it?" I asked him, and he replied with a shrug. "Come on, talk to me."

"I can't shake it off," he said, his shoulders dropping. "I don't know what they put in that black spray, but... I think it's doing something to me."

"To the both of us," I replied. "And we will get through it. For now, however, we must keep moving."

Jericho and Dafne gave us both a pair of worried frowns. "What's Thayen talking about?" the ice dragon cut in, measuring me from head to toe. I told her about the black spray and the effect it had on us. She and Jericho had come in wrathful and violent, and they hadn't noticed the devices that the clones had used against us. By the time I was done describing every sensation that Thayen, Soul, and I had dealt with, I could tell they were both disturbed.

"It hasn't done anything to us, physically speaking," I added. "I would've felt it, for sure. But my psyche, and apparently Thayen's too, is… I don't know. 'Damaged' is perhaps too strong a word."

"You should have Viola or Lumi look at you both," Dafne advised.

I nodded my agreement. "As soon as we get over this next hurdle. You heard Soul. We're in the first wave." "Oh, absolutely," Richard interjected, stalking toward us from the other end of the hallway. I didn't need to put my hand through his chest to recognize him as a clone. He carried a mirror disk much like Chantal's copy, and he had a murderous look on his face. But the fact that he was alone baffled me.

I wasn't the only one who noticed, either. "What's a clone doing up here on his own?" Jericho wondered aloud, following up with a low growl.

"We can't shift in here," Dafne warned him. "It'll tear what's left of this hospital apart."

"You don't need to," Thayen said, his posture stiffening in anticipation, as only a few yards remained between us and Richard's clone. "You said it yourself, Jericho. He's alone. We can take him."

"You can certainly try." The doppelganger chuckled. He bolted toward us, and I reacted with a powerful barrier. The rippling pulse shot forward, nudging Thayen aside as it hit Richard's clone in the solar plexus and knocked him back.

In an instant, he was back up, grinning like a deviant as he brought the mirror disk up in one hand and the black spray in the other. My stomach tightened as I realized we weren't prepared to deal with another horror trip like the one before.

"Thayen, stand back," I shouted and hurled another barrier at the fiend. "Dafne, Jericho, don't let him reach you with that thing!"

Dafne was quick to react and improvise. She grabbed what was left of a chair and threw it at Richard's clone. It distracted him long enough for Jericho to swerve behind him and kick him right between the shoulder blades, expelling the air from his lungs.

Thayen dashed forward and drove his knee into the clone's back, pinning him down, while I grabbed his wrists and slapped on a pair of charmed cuffs.

"Like this… is going to stop me." Richard's double laughed between bouts of coughing and wheezing from Thayen's pressure on his back.

"Wait, hold on," I murmured, understanding the subtleties in his tone. "Thayen, get off him."

The vampire got up, and I rolled Richard's clone over. Only then did we all see the strange object serving as a belt buckle. It was shaped like a tear, featuring tiny channels in a circular pattern. Light flickered through each indent, moving from the edges in toward the center. My senses blared as I realized it was a countdown of sorts, the object beeping louder as the light filled it from within.

"We need to get away from him," I managed. I dragged Thayen as far as I could before his own instincts kicked in, and he started running beside me.

We all raced down the hallway, headed for the stairs. Richard's clone was left behind, laughing maniacally in our wake. I didn't even get a chance to look over my shoulder before a violent blast ripped that whole hospital wing apart. The thundering shockwave followed in a split second, ramming into us with the force of a high-speed train.

"Go, go, go!" Thayen shouted. We nearly tumbled down the stairs, aided by the blowback, and crossed the lobby on the ground floor. I fell to my knees, sharp pain shooting up my thighs, but Jericho pulled me up.

We burst through the doors as the entire already damaged structure came down, rubble exploding outward and hitting us all in the back and the legs. Anger coursed through my veins as I whirled around and released the widest barrier I'd ever been able to conjure. It deflected most of the flying pieces of the hospital's shattered walls, along with the swelling puffs of dirt and dust that inadvertently followed.

My muscles ached, but I was still standing.

A few minutes passed in wretched silence as we watched it all come down, Isabelle's clone's room was left in the middle, untouched and safe, while everything else had fallen apart around it. Iron beams had melted, deformed and twisted by the powerful explosion. Most of the bricks had been turned to reddish dust and pebbles. Glass had been sprinkled everywhere, capturing some of the moonlight in its tiny shards. And clouds of powder danced through the clearing before settling in a thick layer over every surface.

This was a piece of The Shade that the clones had destroyed. A part of our lives. They were going to great lengths to wreak havoc and to get Isabelle's double out of here. It had to mean something.

"Are you okay?" Thayen asked.

I nodded slowly. "Yeah, just worn out."

"No kidding! That was one hell of a barrier you threw out," Jericho replied, genuinely impressed. I couldn't stop myself from blushing.

"Well, at least our precious doppelganger is still okay," Dafne noted, staring at the box surrounded by rubble and dirt and burnt ruins from which black smoke rose in thin columns reaching for the heavens.

Branches broke somewhere nearby. We turned to see Voss, Soph, and Chantal running toward us. Out of an abundance of caution, I raised my hands and positioned myself in front of Thayen, Dafne, and Jericho. "Stop right there!" I said, loud enough for the three to hear. "Don't move another inch!"

I wasn't sure I could push out another barrier, but they didn't know that.

"What are you doing?" Thayen asked me, his voice low.

"How do we know they're the real Voss, Soph, and Chantal?" I asked, giving him a nervous glance. He nodded as it dawned on him why I was concerned.

"Whoa. What's this about? What just happened here?" Voss asked, his eyes widening as he tried to take in the entire scene. It was a lot to process.

Soph frowned in my direction. "What's up, cuz?"

"As you can see, we've had some clone trouble," I said, my voice trembling. "And we know of four other copies you've been dealing with out in the field. Considering how adept they've been at infiltrating our ranks, I'm thinking we need to implement a vetting process going forward. You know, to make sure you guys are the real thing."

"We can start by having Voss spread his wings," Thayen suggested.

"That might not be enough. What if there are multiple clones with different enhancements?" Dafne replied.

Voss, Chantal, and Soph exchanged curious glances. They were an odd team. Voss was the tallest, having taken after his father, Field. He did as Thayen asked, however, showing us his wings. They looked normal.

Chantal seemed tiny in comparison, her silvery eyes sparkling with concern, and there were a few leaves caught in her pale blonde hair. They'd been doing their share of running through the redwood forest.

Soph stood out—she was a full head taller than Chantal yet at least that much shorter than Voss, with daemon horns and Zane's vibrant red eyes. I knew Fiona had asked her to come over from Neraka, but I hadn't had a chance to catch up with her since this whole mess had begun. The only common elements these three shared were the GASP uniforms of black leather, utility belts, and weapons sheathed on their backs.

"It's not enough," I told Voss. "Forgive me, we need to do more to protect ourselves."

"She makes a fair point," Soph conceded, looking at Voss, then back at me. "I'm told you were able to distinguish the lack of a real soul within Isabelle's clone. Think you can try that with us, too?"

Thayen leaned in close to me. "While Soul is gone, you're our only functioning clone detector."

"Right. Okay," I replied with a nod, then moved forward. "Soph, you come first. Slowly, please, no sudden movements."

I hated having to do this, but it was for everyone's safety. The clones had sown the seeds of chaos in our beloved island, but we couldn't let them win. United we stood. Divided, they would pick us off one by one. While we didn't know exactly what they were after—aside from their obsession with Isabelle's copy and me—we could still strengthen our ranks and get ready to face the full brunt of their impending offense.

Soph took a deep breath as she slowly walked toward me, her hands up in a peaceful gesture. My heart was racing. Her willingness to comply could mean that she was one of ours... but it could also be a ruse to get close enough to try and kill me, just like Richard's clone had done the other night. Only by reaching deep within her soul would I know the truth.

THAYEN

"**D**id Soul show you how to do it?" I asked. Only a few inches remained between Soph and Astra. Voss and Chantal stayed back, and they didn't seem tense—merely worried.

"Just a vague notion of the process," Astra mumbled.

Jericho and Dafne took a few steps to get closer to Astra in case she might need help. I had to admit, a good chunk of our training was seriously starting to pay off. We didn't require being told what to do, like in our early days as recruits. No, we knew exactly where we stood and what our options were, and we were functioning like a well-oiled machine—well, we were functioning as best as we could, considering the circumstances, at least. It gave me hope for the future, especially considering the aptitudes of this newly arisen enemy.

"Where are my clothes?" Dafne asked Voss. His eyes widened, cheeks burning red.

"Crap. We lost them somewhere along the way. I'm so sorry," he replied, then looked to Jericho. "Yours, too.

They were bundled up, we were carrying them around, it got messy, man..."

"Or maybe you're a clone," the fae dragon grumbled.

Voss frowned. "I'm not. Feel free to test me. I've got nothing to hide. But

I also didn't have any way of reaching you. We had a couple of skirmishes of our own. What I do have is a general idea of where your clothes might be."

"I think I remember where you dropped Jericho's," Chantal added. "Once we're tested, we could definitely head in that direction and maybe we'll find Dafne's, too."

"I'll get by with this." Dafne grumbled and motioned at the jacket. "At least until I find something with more coverage. We've got uglier issues to deal with, anyway."

The lack of communications worried me, but I knew I'd see my parents soon enough. The hospital blast had rocked the entire island. I could already hear the sound of running footsteps across the forest floor and down the nearby stone-paved alleys. People were coming from all over—at least those who could leave their posts. Rose and Caleb had been pretty specific in their orders, and there were crucial positions all over the island that needed guarding now more than ever. Our supply warehouses and the command center—the Great Dome—were particularly vital. As long as the doppelgangers' plan wasn't entirely clear to us, we had to be ready for strikes to occur anywhere, not just where Astra and Isabelle's clone would be.

"I need you to stand still," Astra told Soph. "I think it will hurt."

Soph bit her lower lip. "How badly?"

"No idea. I'm sorry." Astra sighed.

"It's okay. Do it."

Taking a deep breath, Astra placed her palm on Soph's chest, just beneath her throat. She closed her eyes, and the daemon princess braced herself for the worst, hands balled into fists at her sides. Astra's skin took on a peculiar pink glow, her Daughter energy seeping through. The light intensified and concentrated in her hand, which gradually sank into the leather, then the skin, the flesh, and the bone.

"Oh, this is weird," Soph managed, beads of sweat appearing on her temples.

"I'm sorry," Astra repeated.

"Don't be sorry, just get it over with!"

Anyone with a pair of functioning eyes could see that Soph was in pain, but she was doing a damn good job of keeping it together. Whether it had something to do with Astra's finesse in digging through her being for a soul or with Soph's daemonic resilience, I wasn't sure, but it was clearly less excruciating than the time the Soul Crusher had checked Isabelle's clone.

Astra pulled her hand back with a gasp. "It's her. I can feel Soph."

"How can you tell?" Voss asked, in awe of what he'd just witnessed.

"It's hard to describe, but to keep it simple… I didn't feel the void I felt in Isabelle's copy," Astra explained. "It's Soph, for sure."

"Well, thank the bleepin' stars," the daemon princess exclaimed and wrapped her arms around Astra, holding her tight for a few seconds. "I'm so glad you're all okay… we heard the boom, the screams from afar. We were still chasing after Chantal's clone, so we couldn't rush here straight away."

I sucked in a breath. "Wait, you've been chasing Chantal's clone until now? That's weird. Did you lose sight of her at any point? Where'd she go?"

"We had our eyes on her the whole time," Voss replied. "And she vanished through one of those shimmering portals about a mile north of here, closer to the witches' sanctuary."

"Did she look okay?" Jericho asked.

"What do you mean?" Chantal said, nervously approaching Astra. "Check me next, just so we're all on the same page," she told the young Daughter.

"Thing is, we fought with Voss and Chantal's clones about ten minutes ago," I explained. "And Jericho did quite the number on your copy. She was burnt beyond recognition, though she did survive and managed to run off."

Voss shook his head, while Astra repeated her soul-searching process. It hurt Chantal on a deeper level, but much like Soph, she kept herself straight and tense, putting up with the pain so the truth could be known. "No, the clone we were after looked okay," Voss said. "Which is weird. Does this mean we have two Chantal doppelgangers on the loose?"

"Oh, good grief," the succubus-fae cried out when Astra was done. "That was invasive on so many levels…" She gave me a troubled look. "Hold on. I'm immune to fire. How did my clone get scorched? Correction, how did one of my clones get scorched?"

"A flaw in the design, most likely," the Soul Crusher interjected, reappearing beside us with Kelara and their ghouls. Stan and Ollie had joined her and the others for food, since Soul had stayed behind with Astra and me. Their expressions as they returned and saw the mess that had once been the hospital bordered on hilarious, though there wasn't anything funny about this whole situation. I'd made a habit of searching for tidbits of humor in the worst of moments—if only in my head—as a coping mechanism, so I was thankful Stan and Ollie looked so weirdly comical despite their shock. "We've got a problem," Soul added. "There was an attack at the terrace. A series of blinding explosions. Kelara and the ghouls were thrown back by the blast."

"Oh, no." Fear stiffened Astra's frame. "Where are the others?"

"I'm not sure. Stan, Ollie and I passed out somehow," Kelara replied. "By the time we came to, everybody was gone. The explosions were more like flashbang grenades, rather than explosive devices, though. Most of the structures along the terrace were okay."

"We're obviously going to investigate this," Soul said, then looked at me. "But I wanna talk about you kiddos first. What did we miss?"

I cursed under my breath. "We need to go check the terrace out!"

"You need to calm down. One step at a time," Soul insisted, his tone clipped. "Your people are strong and resourceful. Considering the lack of dead bodies over there, I find it safe to assume that no one died during those blasts. So, talk to me. Let's get this out of the way."

"Wait, you said there's a flaw in the design?" Chantal replied, quickly adjusting to the Reaper's request. He was right, but I had trouble shaking the anxiousness off. "How can that be? Isabelle's clone had everyone fooled. You Reapers included."

"Either their maker isn't bothering as much now that the cat is out of the bag, or there's a certain lack of information as far as your abilities and weaknesses are concerned," Kelara said. "If the former, it means the clones are now being mass produced, so to speak, with more of a focus on appearance than accuracy. Voss's clone had bladed wings, which are an improvement, if you think about it."

"My what, now?" Voss blurted.

"Long story. I'll tell you later," I said, then looked at Kelara. "What if it's the latter?"

"It confirms what we were already suspecting. That the enemy has very good intel, but not as much as they'd like. And that maybe not all of their DNA samples are good. They can be tainted or incomplete, depending on how they were extracted or retrieved. I suppose we'll find out when we get to the clones' leader. Someone's got to be behind this, for sure. Look at how they're organized, how they're watching us. They know when to strike, where to run, what tools to use against those who fight back," Kelara said.

Voss took Chantal's place in front of Astra. "Check me, too."

"I can do it," Soul offered, but the wolf-hawk shook his head.

"Nope. No. Nuh-uh. Astra's method seems slightly more bearable than what I was told regarding yours."

The Reapers both seemed confused. Astra gave them a wry smile. "I've been practicing on Soph and Chantal. I think I'm getting a good handle on it..."

We all watched as she did to Voss what she'd already done to Soph and Chantal. He whimpered from the pain, a muscle tensing in his jaw, but he kept it together while Astra dug into his chest and confirmed what we were already suspecting. "It's Voss."

"Consider me impressed," Soul replied.

"He could be gentler if he really wanted to," Kelara said, pointing a thumb at her partner. "But you all know he's a high-functioning sociopath. Inflicting pain is like a drug to him."

"Aw. You're too sweet," Soul shot back affectionately.

We briefed Voss, Chantal, and Soph on everything we'd omitted earlier from our clone clashes. They gave us the details of their hunt for Chantal's clone, after which we agreed that we would need a better and more efficient way to recognize one another as our true selves, going forward. Astra's method, albeit less painful than Soul's, still required close contact. Any clone aiming to kill her would jump at the opportunity to pretend to get tested, so we had her safety to consider.

"We need a safe word," Jericho said.

"Oh, I'm not sure you know what that is," Dafne muttered, prompting the rest of us to chuckle, while the fae- dragon frowned, trying to find the humor in the ice dragon's remark. They locked eyes with each other for a moment before she smiled and politely conceded. "But yeah, we need a safe word."

On any other day, Dafne would've had her fun poking and prodding Jericho. The chemistry between them was obvious, though I doubted either was aware.

"Paladin," Astra suggested. "They were knights in medieval France. Much like King Arthur's Knights of the Round Table. It's easy to remember and unlikely to come up in normal conversation."

"And it carries a deeper meaning. I like it," Dafne replied.

Soul cleared his throat. "Has anyone noticed how quiet it is?"

We'd been so absorbed in our conversation that I'd nearly lost track of our surroundings. But the Reaper was right. The footsteps and crackling branches I'd heard earlier were gone. Silence had replaced everything, and it wasn't normal. The hospital had just been blown to bits, and everyone within at least a one-mile radius must've heard the explosions.

"What does this mean?" I asked.

"I'm not sure, but it's suspicious. It makes me wonder where Sofia, Derek, and the others have gone. They were a pretty big group," he said. It made me sick to my stomach to think that something might've happened to my parents or Rose or Caleb or any of those who'd been here with us until an hour ago. "And if we find them, how do we know they're the real ones? If they're hostiles, if they're clones, how in the world will we test them all before the crap hits the fan? Right now, it's just Kelara, me, and Astra who can detect fake souls."

"He has a point," Chantal said. "There aren't enough of us to withstand a large group of clones, especially if they whip out that black spray thing."

The truth of this statement sank in, making my knees feel heavier than ever. "We need to move," I replied. "We have to verify as many of the originals that we come across as possible and get them all to meet us back at the Great Dome. Once we're gathered there with our parents and siblings and close family members, we can organize an action plan."

"We should also split up to cover more ground," Kelara said. "Soul and I can go east with Voss and Chantal and leave Stan and Ollie to keep an eye on the Isabelle clone. The rest of you can head west, where the terraces are, and pick up as many of your people as possible to send to the Great Dome. We can circle back to that hall before the morning and put more heads together for a solid strategy."

"We could do with a Reaper on our crew," I replied.

"You've got enough death magic knowledge to handle yourself," Soul shot back. "Astra can do the soul checking, and she's got Daughter mojo to work with, too. Besides, we're working against a foreign magic, anyway.

Neither ours nor yours seems equipped to handle it."

"Soul and I work better together," Kelara added, then gave me a small coin which she fished out of her pocket. "Consider this a tracking device and an alarm. If you need one of us, just break it, and I'll know where to find you."

"Why aren't my parents here? They should've been here by now... If the terrace was attacked, they would've come to the hospital, looking for me." Astra nervously glanced at the path that led to the restaurant area beyond the greenery.

"I don't know, but we will figure it out," I told her, hiding the charmed coin in a back pocket. "We just need to be extremely careful and stay out of sight. We can't handle large numbers of potential clones for the time being. We can't leave anyone a note about this, either. There could be more doppelgangers roaming through The Shade, so we have to work on a case by case basis."

She sighed heavily but didn't disagree. "Okay. So, we head west and check the terrace first before meeting back at the Great Dome. If our people aren't in one place, surely they'll be in another. Soul's right about the lack of bodies. It's a good sign."

"Yes. We'll do east, including the Vale," Voss said. "We've got this, cuz."

"You're damn right we've got this," Soph replied. "There's no way I'm letting these knockoffs cause any more trouble."

"Paladin" had become a salute for those of us in this initial core group. We hugged one another and hoped for the best as we split into two teams and set off to find others to bring into the fold. I wanted Mom and Dad with us most of all, along with my brother and sister. Not only because they were my family, but also because they were among the most experienced in The Shade in times of crisis.

Since we couldn't communicate in any way, I had to think of where I remembered seeing them last. I felt like we were about to go swimming blind in the ocean, but this was The Shade. There were only so many places they could be, especially right now. Anxiety crept up my spine, piercing through my innermost self and threatening to dismantle my defenses.

But I did my best to shake it off. Mom and Dad were out there. Rose. Ben. My family. I couldn't leave them, and I certainly couldn't allow the clones to cause any more damage to my beloved island. They'd brought the war to my doorstep, and I was ready to fight back. With Astra, Jericho, Dafne, and Soph by my side, I was confident we'd overcome anything the clones might throw at us.

TRISTAN

We took our time surveying the village. It was surrounded by an invisibility cloak of death magic, similar in effect to what GASP had used to conceal sensitive locations but likely different in how it worked and how it could be broken. Unending and I had agreed to keep quiet and stealthy as we looked for a way in.

Her scythe's blade glimmered as she brought it closer to the translucent membrane. The tip pushed into it but bounced back. Everything else around us was quiet and mostly dark, with the exception of illuminated veins on nearby leaves. The jungle was signaling our presence, and it made me feel uneasy as I watched Unending trying to figure out how to breach the protective spell.

"I think I know what this is," she whispered after a while. "I've seen this used before. It's not the kind of magic I'd make with those specific words and sub-words, but I know someone who did."

"Who's that?" I asked.

She looked at me. "Death. I think Death gave Joy the recipe for this."

"Okay. That doesn't exactly come as a surprise. What do we do? How do we breach it?"

Unending took a deep breath and started moving along the edge of the protective shield, carefully watching her steps. "We need to find a weak spot. I remember Death observing a small flaw in its design. The greater the surface it covers, the thinner it gets. There will be portions of it where the magical fabric is delicate enough that I can affect it with my scythe. We just need to find one of those places. The hole will heal itself, eventually. Probably in an hour or so."

I quietly followed as she held the scythe against the membrane, the surface shimmering softly where the blade grazed it. Nervously looking around, I noticed wolf-like animals standing back and watching us. Well, they weren't technically watching us, since they couldn't see us, but they had noticed the shield's reaction to Unending's touch. Their nostrils flared as they tried to capture a scent, but none of them moved. There was something about this place that held them back, likely the death magic itself. I, for one, was thankful that Unending had developed an invisibility spell that no longer required physical contact for the obscuring magic to stay up. We were both unseen without having to constantly touch one another—it came in handy when sneaking around a village of spirit-bending fae protected by a ruthless Reaper. Once my wife revealed herself, she would automatically reveal me, too.

"Here..." Unending whispered, coming to a sudden stop. She put the scythe down for a moment and used her fingers to feel the membrane. It rippled under her touch, and she smiled. "There is a finite amount of energy used to cast this shield, which is why its strength is dependent on its square-mile coverage. Had this place been even five hundred yards smaller, the membrane would've been thicker and more resistant."

She picked up her scythe and whispered a spell against its blade, closing her eyes for a moment. When she pressed the weapon against the shield, I could see the world beyond it shifting, as if a veil had just been raised and we were no longer blind. "This is only a window for us to see through," Unending whispered. "It serves to further weaken this spot, too."

"Oh, wow." I tried to take it all in.

Beyond the protective magic, a quaint and beautiful little world appeared. The houses were round and dome- shaped, made of chalk-like bricks. They resembled igloos, but with windows and open archways for doors. There were white stone pathways that connected the residences, like a network of sorts, not only to one another but also to the village center, where a large square structure rose proudly like a giant watching over its flock.

The plants that grew beneath the protective magic were completely different from the ones in the jungle itself. I had a feeling the greenery of the soul fae was ancient, long since extinct anywhere else on Rothko. The jungle had developed around this place, but there must've been something else about a million years ago. Or three million years ago. Hell, ten million years ago, maybe a scorching desert had dominated this region. Either way, beneath the protective magic, time had stood still.

Flowers that resembled Earth's orchids poked their pink and yellow heads out of clover beds, each arrangement neatly enclosed in white stone pots about three feet wide and four feet long. They filled every inch of empty space between the dome houses and the pathways. Water gushed from fountains mounted in every other yard, and birds sang from the tall, slender trees with spherical green-and-white crowns. This village had been designed to perfection, the soul fae making the most of what little space they had.

They were stunning creatures, I realized as I watched them go about their day. Some were filling pitchers of glass with crystalline water. Others were using ceramic bowls to collect nectar from the orchid-like flowers. The children were particularly joyful about this, flanking their parents, eager to dip their fingers in the golden syrup-like substance.

"Notice anything familiar?" Unending whispered, unable to take her eyes off them.

Indeed, I could see the resemblance. Each of the soul fae carried a tiny bit of the Spirit Bender in their features. The sharp, high cheekbones in particular. The inquisitive eyes were strange, however. They glistened in shades of lilac and mint green, their pupils white. I'd almost forgotten that Reapers' eyes only became like miniature galaxies upon their creation. The Spirit Bender's original soul must've belonged to a soul fae like this, with lilac or mint green eyes... Their lips were pale, and their hair was long and soft, like milky white silk pouring down their shoulders. They wore simple clothes, likely made from cotton-like threads, with various colorful embroidered motifs adorning the necks and sleeves.

They were slender, fine-boned creatures. Easy to break, I thought. No wonder Death had wanted them protected. The soul fae were the most delicate creatures I had ever seen. Like wisps of life that had somehow found a way to survive and experience joy even in the midst of this rugged wilderness. I wondered what they thought of their enclosure. Had they ever contemplated going beyond these death-magic-imposed limits? Had they ever yearned to discover the outside world?

Far past the houses and the square building in the middle of the village, I could see the tops of peculiar trees, unlike anything else I'd seen in the jungle. From that same area, animal sounds emerged—squeaky bleating and husky clucking. They probably had domesticated animals, making them a part of their lives. Had the animals been here as long as the soul fae, or were they more recent additions? I had so many questions, my tongue was practically itching.

"They're peaceful creatures," Unending murmured. "Notice how none of them are carrying weapons."

"Joy obviously protects them fiercely, since they've survived this long," I replied.

"There is comfort and safety here. As much as I'd like to berate Death for her hypocrisy regarding her intervention in the natural affairs of the universe, I have to admit I'm glad she saved them. They're... quite the sight to behold." She paused to give me a sly grin. "I bet you've got a ton of questions, Mr. Anthropologist Extraordinaire."

"You can't even begin to imagine." I chuckled, then grew serious. "Can we get in? I'm glad we can see through the protective magic, but is the membrane weak enough to grant us entry?"

Unending nodded once. "Bear with me, my love. You'll get to talk to them yourself before long."

We needed to speak to them anyway, considering the item we were looking for was somewhere in their village. But I certainly welcomed the opportunity to converse with these creatures, to understand more about their way of life and seclusion. It couldn't have been easy to be stuck here, though they all seemed content with their living arrangements. Nothing about the village spoke of intrusion against the natural elements—as far as I could see, they lived in perfect harmony with their environment. But since Rothko's Hermessi were so ruthless and violent, I could certainly see why Death had taken additional precautions to protect them.

"I'm wondering... if the local Hermessi are so violent, why would Death leave the soul fae here? Why not relocate them somewhere else?" I asked.

"To be honest, I have no idea. But if I were to guess, I'd say Death is a bit of a sentimental. She didn't want to take them away from their home, regardless of its conditions."

"Or maybe she didn't want to take them to another place where others might find them, accidentally or otherwise," I suggested.

Unending chuckled. "Perhaps she just wanted to stick it to the local Hermessi. To prove that they couldn't destroy everyone. That they couldn't go against her. That actually makes more sense."

Unending whispered another spell against the blade, then used it to cut an opening through the membrane. Without hesitation, we slipped inside, the hole slowly closing up behind us. We'd reached the soul fae village undetected, and my heart was racing, a rapid pulse pounding in my ears. Excitement and fear had taken over, making it harder for me to concentrate, but Unending took my hand in hers and squeezed gently.

"It's going to be okay," she said, revealing us both.

The soul fae didn't notice us right away as we walked quietly toward them. Following one of the white stone paths, we reached the nearest igloo-house, where a young woman was gingerly squeezing the orchid-like blossoms to extract their precious nectar, each droplet filling the ceramic bowl in her hand. She had mint-green eyes, her white hair loosely braided over one shoulder.

Unending opened a telepathic connection between us and her, using our thoughts and words to convey our good intentions. I didn't speak their language, but I was suddenly able to understand the young woman and the other soul fae. It was as if a whole new world had revealed itself to me, filling my mind with their warm thoughts.

"Hello," Unending said, her lips fixed in a soft smile.

The soul fae glanced up and finally saw us. She froze, fear marring her beautiful features.

"We do not wish to harm you," I added without actually speaking. "We've come in peace." "Who... who are you?" she asked.

"I am Unending, and this is Tristan," my wife replied. "It is an honor to meet you. A joy to see you and your kind have survived for so long. May your lives be filled with kindness, good health, and prosperity."

The soul fae stood up, both hands clutching the bowl. "We don't have visitors here. Ever. It's strange."

"We wouldn't have dared to disturb you, but there is something in your village that we need. Something left behind by someone a long time ago," Unending told her.

"Someone?" the woman asked, a slight frown settled on her delicate oval face. "I told you, no one ever comes around here."

"He made sure not to be seen," Unending said. Anunit had telepathically given her an image of the Mixer, so she knew what the object looked like. "Would you be so kind as to take us to your leader? We'd like to have a word."

The soul fae thought about it for a moment, then looked over her shoulder, noticing how the others had also stopped what they had been doing. All eyes were on us now, and Unending sent out a mental pulse to ease their minds. "Tell me the truth." The soul fae woman's voice rang loudly in my head, but it had a secondary, unexpected effect. I could feel her grip on my soul.

Only then did I even remember what these creatures were capable of. Unending gave me a startled look. "Whatever you do, don't panic," she murmured.

"Tell me the truth," the soul fae insisted, the pressure in my chest amplifying until I could no longer breathe. "We're looking for the object that the someone I mentioned left here," I said with my mind. "He left it here, and we need it. I swear that is the truth."

"Who was your someone, then?" the soul fae asked.

"The Spirit Bender," Unending replied, unable to fully control herself under the spirit-bending influence. Anunit had been right—these creatures had quite the ability, more than the Spirit Bender, even. Unending was a powerful Reaper, yet this delicate creature was able to at least partially push her. "He hurt me deeply. He hurt the people I love. He caused nothing but harm. Even so, I need that object."

"What for?"

"To catch a Reaper," Unending said. It was partially true, in the end, and it seemed to pass the soul fae's verity test. "To lure her out. She has committed crimes that have led to a command to capture her."

"It's our best chance to get what we need," I added. "I swear to you, we wish no harm to anyone. Just the object."

Seemingly satisfied with our responses, the soul fae let go, and I felt the cords snapping loose. Her power was impressive and a little terrifying, but I understood why she'd used it on us. We were complete strangers who'd just waltzed into her village, and she and her people knew how to keep their little world safe.

"I'm Sissa," she said. "I'm the daughter of our king, Loren. I will take you to him."

"Thank you," Unending replied.

I couldn't believe the speed and swiftness with which Sissa had spiritually beaten us into submission. Unending had an exit strategy for whatever the soul fae were willing to throw at us, but for the time being, we cooperated. There was no need for any kind of offense if we could get what we'd come for. From what I was seeing, Sissa seemed open to indulging our request; otherwise, she could've simply forced us to walk out of this place. I had a feeling she'd not used the full extent of her power, either. It led me to assume that perhaps it would do some sort of damage to our spirits—or maybe it just wasn't in her nature to unleash her spirit bending on anyone. As long as we came across as willing and compliant, the soul fae didn't have reason to doubt us.

I held on to Unending, watching every single soul fae we passed as Sissa guided us to the square building. It didn't take long to identify it as the king's residence. A slender man came out, his long white hair caught up in an elegant bun and a crown of nectar orchids adorning his head. He wore a furry coat over his white cotton shirt and pants, giving off a regal yet eclectic feel.

He stepped onto the porch, eyeing us both with concern. Unending reached out to him telepathically before Sissa could introduce us, conveying the same message of peaceful intentions. He didn't seem impressed, but there was something about his face that I found difficult to read.

"Father, we have guests from the outside world," Sissa said.

The other soul fae were tempted to gather around his royal residence, but Loren waved them all away. "I urge everyone to go about your business. No need for our lives to stop for this." He spoke calmly to his people, and they listened, much to my astonishment. Normally, strangers in an isolated village would've drawn everybody out, but Loren was remarkably effective in keeping them at bay.

Not that I minded. The last thing we needed was more eyes on us. We had yet to meet Joy, and deep down, I was hoping we wouldn't cross paths at all. Chances of avoiding her were slim, but hey, a guy could dream. It was only a matter of time, given our incursion into the one space she had been tasked with protecting. Sooner or later, the ancient Reaper would become aware of our presence.

"That is odd," Loren replied. "You speak directly to my mind. Yet you are not one of us. How can this be?"

"Death magic, Your Majesty," Unending said. "Though I knew someone like you a long time ago."

"What is it you want?"

Unending told him the same thing she'd shared with Sissa. The young woman watched us closely, but she didn't seem threatened or worried anymore. No, now she appeared more intrigued than anything else.

"Do we have such an object in our midst?" she asked her father after Unending described it to them. "I don't remember it."

"What purpose does this Mixer serve?" Loren inquired, looking at us. "What does your targeted Reaper wish to do with it?"

Unending and I exchanged glances. We had to tell the truth. If they so much as caught a whiff of dishonesty, all the soul fae had to do was spirit-bend us into submission. We couldn't afford to get on their bad side. Fortunately, we'd taken this angle into account since before ever setting foot in the village.

"It is used to combine Reaper objects," Unending said, trying to be honest without being too specific. The purpose was to circle around the truth in a manner that did not arouse suspicion, and that required some impressive verbal gymnastics. "The Reaper we're hunting needs it, and like I said, we want to use it in order to lure her out. My master has approved this mission. This Reaper thinks we're doing her a favor. She doesn't know the whole truth."

"And you're fine with lying to someone like this?" Loren asked, raising an eyebrow.

"I am, because it gets me closer to capturing the Reaper. We have laws. We have orders. It must be done," Unending said.

"Interesting. We're normally not appreciative of lying. We cannot really lie to one another," Loren replied.

"I don't like it either, but the circumstances demand it," Unending pressed on. "I believe that we're doing the right thing, even if the methods don't seem right."

Loren thought about it for a while, but he didn't seem convinced. Sissa was smiling at us. We seemed to have won her over. The king, however, was a more difficult customer. "Surely there are other ways to hunt this Reaper without lying to her," he said. From what I could tell, the soul fae obviously valued the truth more than anything else.

"Yes. But she's a slippery one," Unending replied. "She has eluded Death and the others for a long time. This is our best way forward, I'm afraid. And I understand you cherish the truth above all, but the world beyond your village isn't like that. I mean no offense when I say that."

"Father, they seem sincere." Sissa tried to intervene. We'd managed to hide significant parts of the truth, but they seemed to have bought it—or so I thought, until Loren raised a hand to silence her.

"Indeed. But they didn't come here with Joy's approval. They snuck in," the king said, giving us both a grave look. "What does that say about you?"

"We're desperate," I replied. Okay, so he'd bought it, but he was still cautious. A good king, I thought.

The temperature suddenly changed. A cold wind blew through the village, raising the hairs on the back of my neck. A figure emerged from inside Loren's royal residence. She was a Reaper. The Reaper. Joy. As ancient and as powerful as the First Tenners. "You're not supposed to be here," she said from beneath the black mask covering the bottom half of her face. The Reaper uniform she wore was strange, mostly white and so tight on her body that it looked more like a second skin.

She was tall and slender, with bony shoulders and long legs. Her scythe was huge compared to Unending's—a half-moon-shaped disk that reached my height, plus the long black handle. I wondered how heavy it was, considering the ease with which she held it in just one hand. Her hair was short and spiky and bright red, shaved on the sides, and fiery galaxies exploded within those almond-shaped eyes. Symbols had been carved into her scythe— some I recognized, others, not so much. But Unending knew them all, and she didn't look too happy.

"That blade is fully authorized to kill and destroy anything it touches," Unending murmured. "No additional approval from Death required."

"And I will use it on you unless you tell me what the hell you're doing here," Joy retorted, her expression firm and cold. She was the no-nonsense type who wouldn't hesitate to strike unless we answered her questions. It wasn't difficult to understand why Death had chosen her to watch over the soul fae. Heck, she'd been given authority to kill any living creature that dared come near the village—every death that the First Tenners, Seeley, and Sidyan had caused on Visio had been previously and telepathically sanctioned by their maker.

Joy had absolute freedom in this place.

The concept of danger had been more or less abstract to me since Unending and I survived the Spirit Bender twenty years ago. Everything else had been manageable. But as I looked at Joy and acknowledged the lengths to which she was willing to go in order to protect the soul fae, I began to feel the kind of fear I'd hoped I would never experience again. No one was safe with this Reaper, unless Death stopped her in time. Not Unending. Not me.

THAYEN

There was no one at the terrace, like Soul and Kelara had said. The entire alley of shops and restaurants had been abandoned. Chairs had been knocked over. Tables were upside down. Glasses and plates had been broken and scattered across the cobblestones. People had been in the middle of their meals and conversations when some kind of hell had broken loose.

The Reapers were right about the flashbang effect of the explosions, as well. There was some physical damage visible, but nothing to level the whole place. Whatever the clones were using, it was some hi-tech weird magic combo that was insanely effective, since it had knocked out a First Tenner and two ghouls. I did wonder what had spurred people to run off and leave Kelara, Stan and Ollie behind. This must've been wildly violent.

I needed a moment to take it all in.

The obliterated windows, glass spreading like sugar frosting over the stone. The torn linen curtains were reduced to uneven shreds. Small fires still burned here and there, likely the remnants of a fire fae's wrath. Blood had been smeared across the outer walls, but I couldn't see any bodies. Jericho and Dafne did a quick tour of the terrace's restaurants, then came back shaking their heads.

"No casualties," the ice dragon said. "Nothing. No one. Zilch."

"This is weird," I muttered as we made our way farther down the alley. Every single establishment had been hit in a similar fashion. Property damage, interrupted brunches, blood streaked across the cobblestone, mingling with the dropped food. It made me sick to my stomach, and I began fearing the worst. It felt infinitely more pressing than the black spray the clones had used on Astra and me. This kind of dread was impossible to overcome.

"Deep breaths," Astra told me, one hand resting on my shoulder.

I'd been panting, and I wasn't even aware of it.

"What... what is wrong with me?" I managed, breaking into a cold sweat as the horror of it all set in and anchored me into this new reality. I'd been hoping for the best, and that was my biggest mistake.

"I think you're having a panic attack," Astra replied.

Soph came closer, eyeing me carefully. "Slow breaths in and out, Thayen. In and out. One second at a time. As long as there are no bodies, it means no one died, okay? Whoever was here, members of our family or otherwise... they're gone. They fled. They're alive."

"Yeah, but—"

"Yeah, but nothing," she said, cutting me off. "That is the mindset you need. You're leading this group, Thayen, and we're following you because we trust your instincts and your decision-making skills. Do not let these bastard clones tell you otherwise. But we need you to stay strong and conscious."

I nodded once, immediately internalizing her message. I'd given in to the worst side of me. The trauma of what I'd suffered on Visio had come back in an uglier form, sneaking into my consciousness, hell-bent on sabotaging all the progress I'd made over the years. I was a vampire, damn it. I was a Novak and a Nasani, and I had The Shade to protect. Flinching at the first sign of large-scale trouble would be a sign of weakness, and Soph was absolutely right. I was leading this group. I had to pull through, not only for myself but for them, too.

A few deep inhalations later, my surroundings had come back into focus. "What are we looking at here?" I asked, glancing in Astra's direction. "Any odd sensations? Anything out of the ordinary? You're our main weirdness scanner right now."

Astra chuckled softly, then crouched and touched a spatter of blood. It hadn't fully congealed yet. "Nothing particularly supernatural," she said. "Merely a bad vibe. People got hurt here, but they ran away."

"Do we know who was here?" Dafne asked. "Friends of yours? Family?"

"Draven and Serena. Lumi. Kailani and Hunter. Jovi and Anjani. Phoenix and Viola. Rose and Caleb. Kelara and the ghouls had come with them," I said, frowning, then tried the comms channel again. Nothing but empty static. "The tech is definitely off. The comms are completely disconnected now."

Soph cursed under her breath. "If they're not here anymore, they must have gone to safety. Where are the three key spots we can look? They obviously didn't pass by the hospital."

"The Vale is out of the question, since it's mostly human, with civilian structures," I said. "The Great Dome is one possibility. The command center farther north is another. The armory and the training halls would be the third, just off the top of my head."

"Without any way of reaching out to them, we're going to have to check each of those locations," Astra concluded, her gaze darting from the terrace to the other restaurants and shops, taking in all the destruction that had been left behind.

"That was more or less the plan all along," Soph replied, crossing her arms. "Though I would've expected to find more people in this area."

"Come on," I said, unable to stand still for another second. "This place is a bust. Let's hit the Great Dome first.

We'll have to cross the redwood forest, and chances are we'll run into a clone or ten."

Jericho and Dafne flanked Astra, while Soph and I led the way straight into the woods, steering clear of the better-known paths. It was time to act as if we really were in a war zone—until we knew exactly what had happened at the terrace and to our communications systems, and until we found our people safe and sound, we had to assume the worst.

"I'm still miffed that Voss lost my clothes," Jericho muttered.

"For what it's worth, I can imagine what that whole incident was like. Falling, getting up, tumbling around and fighting the clones… your clothes were literally the last thing on their minds," I said.

"And just my two cents here, that robe doesn't look bad on you," Dafne giggled. "You've got legs for days. You can totally get away with this fresh-out-of-the-flaming-shower look." It made Jericho laugh, and it was a sound I didn't even realized I'd missed.

The trek through the wilderness was mostly uneventful. We only caught glimpses of people running as far away from our location as possible. We tried to go after them, but they vanished pretty quickly, and we still had the Great Dome to get to. It was as if the Shadians were fleeing from something or someone, but I couldn't for the life of me understand what. How many clones were out here, and how had they managed to cause such fright in the span of a single hour? It didn't make any sense.

We headed northeast toward the Great Dome, occasionally trying the comms channels again. Telluris was still down, and Astra and I couldn't establish new connections between us, either. "Someone is going to a hell of a lot of trouble to keep us from talking to each other across the island," Soph said.

The darkness of the night reigned supreme, as we only saw glimpses of the starry sky above. It was also chillier than usual, though that wasn't exactly unheard of. The woods were always colder, especially out here, where the northern winds blew uninterrupted. We didn't come to these parts often. The sooner we reached the Great Dome, the better I'd feel.

We walked for another twenty minutes in heavy silence, our minds obviously crowded with all kinds of scenarios. Suddenly Astra stopped, pale as a sheet of paper. "Don't move," she hissed, looking around.

"What is it?" I asked, trying to follow her gaze. I didn't see anything out of the ordinary.

"Remember that tingly sense you mentioned?" she croaked. "I think it's finally kicking in. We need to hide." "Why?" Soph asked, not yet convinced.

Astra grabbed her by the wrist, and we all followed her behind a cluster of massive bushes thick enough to conceal us. "I think it's a portal. I'm feeling the same energy, only much stronger," she said.

"Stronger?" I asked, keeping my voice low.

"When Richard's clone slipped out of this world, I tried to get a better feel for the portal energy, but I couldn't because it was quickly fading. Once it was closed, poof, buh-bye. But this time it's different. My whole body is buzzing."

As soon as she said that, a blinding light emerged on the other side of a nearby clearing. We slowly raised our heads to look and were left speechless by what we saw. For the first time since this nightmare had begun, we'd inadvertently brought Astra close to an opening portal. At least one of Lumi's theories was coming true, it seemed, considering how hypersensitive to this stuff the young Daughter was.

A shimmering gash slit the air, nearly blinding us for a moment. A portal. "Holy moly…" I heard Jericho mumble. They could see it, too. At least I hadn't lost my mind or anything.

Out of the portal came Richard, Hazel, Tejus, Jovi, and Anjani's clones. They looked so calm and casual, as if they'd just gotten out of the car and were about to hit the beach or something. Their GASP uniforms were a searing insult, considering they were frauds. The sight made my blood boil, but it soon froze when I noticed each of them carrying a metal disk. They likely had black spray on them, as well.

I knew Soul and Kelara would want to be here for this, so I reached into my pocket and took out the charmed coin. "Are you sure you want to use it now?" Astra whispered. "If not now, when?" I replied.

They stopped in the middle of the clearing, and the portal closed behind them. Richard's clone seemed to be leading the pack. I wasn't sure if he was a second doppelganger or the same one we'd fought before. Nothing was what it seemed, and everything was different—no wonder my head was a mess. I could barely grab hold of one clone with my glamoring ability, and even that was limited and physically draining without years of practice. There was no way I could handle all of them, especially if they used that black spray on us again. I gave Astra a brief nod, putting the coin back. "We wait until they leave so we can move again. You're right about using the coin. It might be too soon."

"Agreed. And even if we bring Soul and Kelara over here, there's no telling what these monsters will use against us," Dafne whispered.

"We'll use everything we've got," Hazel's clone said from afar, looking right at us. They already knew we were here. Either they'd detected us upon their arrival, or they'd been previously informed of our location, I couldn't tell which. But one thing was painfully clear at this point.

Five clones had set their sights on us, and I wasn't sure we'd be able to get past them in order to reach the Great Dome. Not without a gruesome fight, anyway. We'd seen what they could do, and we had little to no understanding of the foreign magic they were using against us. Every other option we'd had prior to Hazel-clone's remark was now off the table.

"Changed my mind," I mumbled, then snapped the coin, hoping to see Kelara and Soul soon enough. But as the seconds passed, nothing happened. "Ugh…"

"It's not working?" Jericho asked, his voice barely a scratch.

It didn't seem like it. Had something happened to Kelara? There was no time to wonder about this, or any other option to reach out to the Reapers. Our only choice now was to battle these monsters and defend our home. I braced myself for a living hell, determined to get out on the other side of this river of trouble. My parents needed me. My brother and sister. Every single member of the Novak family relied on me and my friends to defeat the insurgents and secure everyone's safety.

Maybe hiding would've been better, but with war knocking on our door, I had to step up.

ASTRA

(DAUGHTER OF PHOENIX AND VIOLA)

There was no sight of Kelara or Soul. Either the coin had not worked, or the Reapers were unable to get to our location. Every second that passed made it clear, however, that we couldn't rely on their assistance.

"I think we can shorten this encounter," Jericho said as the clones strutted toward us. The sheer arrogance that had settled on their faces made me furious. They'd come prepared—I could tell by their abundantly confident attitudes.

The clearing was small, yet wide enough to be used as a battleground. My muscles were tight and hard, tension gripping every inch of me as I prepared myself for the worst. But Jericho's suggestion sounded better than how I'd originally envisioned this scene unfolding.

"What, like go dragon and scorch their asses?" Dafne asked, gaze fixed on the clones.

"It's our quickest way out of here, don't you think? It's not like we can fly away and let them do who knows what they've come here to do. I mean, we could fly away, but what does that say about us?" Jericho replied, a smile testing his lips as he straightened his back and pushed his chest out, a move I doubted he was even aware of as he moved to assert himself before the enemy. He'd picked it up from his father, Blaze—little things like these made me love my Shadian people even more. We'd come out fundamentally different from our parents, but we'd still managed to adopt some of their gestures and personality traits without even realizing it.

"I agree. It's worth a shot," Thayen said. "Just be careful. We don't know what other tricks they've got up their sleeves. The more they fight us, the better prepared they become."

"Say no more," Dafne hissed and slipped out of my jacket. It took Jericho a couple of seconds to take his eyes off her as she turned into a majestic ice dragon with black scales and bluish iridescent streaks down her back. Dafne wasn't big for her kind, but she was fierce.

Jericho removed his robe and shifted, joining her in a full-frontal attack on the clones. Richard's double was the first to get past the dragons and come right at us, grinning like the devil. Thayen bolted toward him, claws and fangs out, but I couldn't let him get close to the bastard. The last thing he or I needed was more black spray in our faces.

I threw out a barrier, and it hit Richard's clone in the side with enough force to knock him over. "Thayen, keep away from him!" I shouted. "We need to stick together and get out of here!"

Thayen started to heed my advice, but Richard's copy bounced back up. Before I could do anything else, they were tangled in a physical fight, growling and throwing punches and kicks in a struggle for survival.

Jericho and Dafne used their respective fire and ice to hold the other clones at bay. Hazel's clone was fast, and she dodged the dragon flames with remarkable agility. Tejus's doppelganger threw barriers that were stronger than my grandpa's real ones. He hurled them at Dafne with enhanced precision, and they hit her like real punches, knocking the air from her lungs. Every time she tried to bite him, he threw another barrier, flinging her head back.

Jovi and Anjani's clones were the first to fall as Jericho's inferno spread out indiscriminately. The fires caught up and swallowed them whole, and they screamed. Thayen fell and cried out in pain, and I could see a dagger in his side. Richard's clone was about to rip into his throat, but Soph darted in his direction.

Before he could finish Thayen off, Soph rammed into him. They landed in a nearby bush, and I rushed to get to Thayen. He needed faster healing than his vampire nature could provide him. In an instant, I was kneeling beside him, my hand pressed against his wound and glowing pink as I allowed my Daughter energy to seep into the damaged flesh and heal it.

"He's way faster than Richard," Thayen grunted as I helped him back up.

Soph was thrown backward, but Thayen rushed to catch her before she could hit the ground and hurt herself. Richard's clone came right out, eager to take the three of us on. I wasn't sure if he was suicidal or simply crazy, but when I spotted the black spray device in his hand, I knew at least one of us would be mentally crippled in a matter of seconds.

Rage filled me to the brim, my temperature spiking as a natural reaction to the damage I knew the clone could do. I allowed this anger to burst out, bright pink light shining from within as I unleashed it all upon him. He stopped, frozen, with only a few yards left between us. As the pink light expanded, he knew he couldn't continue with his attack, so he scrambled backward instead, while Thayen and Soph moved away from me.

"I'll be damned..." I heard Soph exclaim.

Richard's doppelganger was gone. He must've escaped, since there was no trace of his corpse anywhere in sight. Jovi and Anjani's copies had been torched, their forms collapsed in the short grass, reduced to smoking black figures—way worse than what had happened to Chantal's double. But she'd been modeled after a fire fae, supposedly immune to the flames. She'd been disfigured, though she'd lived and run off. I figured these two clearly weren't designed to even survive, much like their originals. Hazel's clone was still standing, but Dafne had managed to sink her enormous fangs into Tejus's double. He screamed in agony. The sound made my skin crawl as the dragon crunched through his bones until there wasn't much left of him. Hazel's copy tried to get back at her, but Jericho slapped her down with his claws and spat enough fire to kill.

The smell of burnt flesh was overwhelming, but I still breathed a sigh of relief when the clearing became safe again. We regrouped—Dafne and Jericho putting their temporary attire back on—and prepared ourselves for the rest of our journey.

"He got you, didn't he?" Jericho asked Thayen, nodding at the blood on his leather uniform. The tear in the fabric was visible, but the wound had already healed.

"I'll be fine," the vampire replied, then looked at Soph. "You okay?

Richard's doppelganger threw you around a bit."

"I know!" Soph grumbled. "Got one over on me, and I have no idea how that happened. You were right, these spooks are getting better and faster. The creep managed to slip away."

"What about the energy levels?" Dafne asked me. "Do you feel the remnants of the portal anymore?"

I shrugged. "Barely. As it turns out, I sense them better when they're about to open in my vicinity, but without a geographical pattern to follow, there's no way of telling where one will pop up next." Pausing, I gave myself a second as a troubling feeling took over. "Oh, no," I managed, quickly realizing what was happening.

"What is it?" Thayen asked. The look he gave me was understandably troubled.

"They're coming…"

"Another portal?" he asked.

I nodded. Without hesitation, he grabbed my hand and pulled me away from the clearing. Jericho, Dafne, and Soph followed. We ran as fast as we could, but I still felt the tear in space, the portal opening behind us.

"Faster!" Thayen whispered. Trees and ferns brushed past us. The wind caressed my face, combing through my hair as we moved, our feet light and our hearts stricken with fear and fury. I glanced over my shoulder and saw the clearing as it shrank behind us. The portal was bright and wider than the previous one.

"Oh, no…" I mumbled, nearly tripping. Thayen was quick enough to react and keep me going, but he couldn't resist following my gaze.

"Crap!"

There were dozens of clones pouring into The Shade. I didn't recognize everyone, but they were all modeled after the island's inhabitants. There were many of them, just like Isabelle's clone had said. They were spreading out, quiet in their infiltration of our precious world.

"What the hell are we going to do about them?" Dafne asked, panting as we put more distance between us and them.

Chills tumbled through me, and I prayed to all the stars that this would turn out to be nothing more than a bad dream. Alas, that wasn't the case. It was real, and it was developing in directions we no longer had any control over. There were too many of them, and they'd caught us off guard and divided. My ability to verify the clones was now more precious than ever. We only had Soul and Kelara to help, and they were on the other side of The Shade.

"We get to the Great Dome," Thayen replied, shifting his focus to the wild path ahead. The redwoods in this area were the biggest, thick enough to conceal us from those we'd left behind. The underbrush was higher too, foliage spreading out like giants, making it easier for us to hide if needed. Developing this wilderness in the middle of The Shade had been the best thing Derek had ever done. With an invasion like this, our forest was basically an efficient line of defense. "And we pray my parents or at least more of our people are waiting there."

Branches broke somewhere behind us.

I turned my head only for a second. It was enough to make me want to scream. Footsteps were amplified. A couple at first, but now… there were at least a dozen clones chasing after us. They'd caught up, and I was terrified, unsure of how we'd get ourselves out of this mess. I recognized Rose and Caleb's doppelgangers. Vita and Bijarki. Dmitri and Douma. "We're so screwed," I heard myself say.

Throwing barriers earlier had taken its toll on me. My legs felt heavy. My body and soul weakened. I didn't have much fight left within me, certainly not enough to take on a dozen clones.

"We can't stop," Thayen said, well aware of the newly emerging threat. "We have to reach the Great Dome."

It was our only option—the hope that our people would be there, and that they would be able to back us against this invasion. The forest was too dense in these parts for Jericho and Dafne to easily move around as dragons, and the enemy would likely take advantage of that fact. Besides, they had foreign magic at their fingertips. I had rapidly depleting Daughter energies and I was terrified.

A horn blew in the distance, low and nasal but loud enough to make my ears twitch. It went on for almost a minute, during which time the shuffling steps of our pursuers subsided. By the time I looked back again, the clones were gone. "Hold on," I said, stopping for a moment.

"We have to keep moving. They'll…" Thayen's voice trailed off as he also realized what was happening. "Whoa. They left?"

"It was the horn," Soph said. "I don't know who's operating that thing or the purpose it serves, but... I think it made them leave."

"Could it be our doing? Maybe Lumi or my dad?" I asked, daring to hope. "I mean, maybe they got to safety and figured out a way to scare the clones off."

Dafne gave me a doubtful look. "Or maybe one of the clones came up with a way to communicate an order to the others while our channels and Telluris are still down."

"We have no way of talking to our people. Meanwhile, they're openly invading The Shade," Thayen concluded. "We'll figure out what that horn is once we find Mom and Dad. For now, we can't stop anymore. Whether the clones have left us alone or not, we have to get to the Great Dome!"

I didn't linger. Despite my exhaustion, I started running again. Thayen, Soph, Jericho, and Dafne followed. We were left with few reasonable options and no means of communication. Just like Soul had suspected, I feared we were now dealing with a second wave. The clones we'd seen in the clearing were part of it. I wondered if that was the only portal that had opened up, or if they'd pushed through other access points simultaneously. If I wanted to lay siege to The Shade, that was how I would've done it. Multiple entries, smaller groups, highly organized incursions.

My only hope was that we'd actually find our people at the Great Dome, and not more of these wretched clones.

KELARA

My head was a blur. I hadn't felt like this since... since Corbin Crimson had trapped me and cursed me with the ghoul sickness. Dread replaced the numbness as my eyes peeled open. I wasn't sure what had happened, but I'd clearly been out of it for a while. Someone or something had managed to turn my lights off.

Everything ached, as if I'd run a marathon. But I hadn't experienced sensations like these since I was alive. It didn't make much sense. I was lying down on my side. The ground felt hard, though there was a patch of grass tickling my cheek. "Ugh..." I pushed myself into a sitting position, my weakened arms struggling to support my weight. Pain persisted somewhere between my temples, making me cringe whenever I moved my head.

My entire circumstance was unusual for a Reaper. I didn't lose consciousness. Not usually, anyway. I wasn't designed for it. But still, here I was, dazed and confused and wondering what the hell had happened. A pentagram with entrapment symbols had been drawn around me in white chalk. The author had pressed hard, causing creases in the rocky dirt, but the traces of white powder were visible.

"No... how..." I managed as the reality of my situation began to sink in.

Death magic had been used to trap me. I couldn't break out of this circle. Fumbling through my pockets, another fact came to light. My scythe was gone.

"How is that even possible?!" I blurted, then stilled at the sight of Soul.

He was unconscious, trapped in a separate pentagram just a few feet away from mine. I was willing to bet all the gold in the world that his scythe had been taken, too. Looking around, I tried to keep a clear mind, to remember everything that had happened. The haze persisted, covering my memories like a thick blanket, with only the remnants of a bright explosion lingering at the center of my consciousness.

We were in the middle of a forest. Not the redwoods, though. No, we'd gone east. Majestic oak trees, as old as I was, towered around us, their branches reaching out to one another, the emerald crowns blocking out most of the sky. Moon rays pierced through here and there, milky beams that touched the forest floor but revealed little else. Thankfully, as a Reaper the light and darkness of the natural world were pretty much the same to me.

"Soul, can you hear me?" I asked, hoping he'd wake up soon.

Yes, there had been a flash. An explosion. Soul and I had left Stan and Ollie to watch over Isabelle's clone. We'd partnered with Voss and Chantal. Where were they? Something broke inside me. The charmed coin I'd given Thayen. He needed us, and we were in no position to help him. I'd promised, and now... because of the pentagram trap, I couldn't even pinpoint his location. "Dammit... Soul!" I shouted.

Nothing. And Thayen's crew was in trouble... The more I thought about it, the clearer the images replaying in my head prior to the bright explosion became. We'd made it all the way down to the Sun Beach, where we'd come across Richard. The real Richard. I'd tested him myself. I remembered him whimpering from the pain my examination had caused him. The feel of his soul in the palm of my hand. He'd been at the terrace when an attack had torn the whole place apart.

Everybody had scattered, he'd told us. Too many clones to handle at once. He'd dealt with the black spray, too. Still shaken up by the horrifying sensations it had caused. We'd agreed to press forward with our quest for Shadians. To keep checking and gathering originals along the way. It had gone smoothly for a while. We'd found Draven and Serena, then Jovi and Anjani. We'd tested them and told them to head straight for the Great Dome, where we'd meet them along with Thayen and the others.

Something happened after they left... a portal. A portal had opened.

I tried to get out of the pentagram, though I wasn't sure why. I already knew it wouldn't allow me to leave. Damned reflexes... the invisible shield around me was impenetrable. Pressing my palm against its clear surface, I felt the hum of energy transferring into my core like a silent threat—a promise that pushing my way through would cause me great pain. Yes, this was old-school death magic, and the only possible culprits I could think of were the clones.

Their knowledge of my craft seemed like a new development, however. It made me think their weird foreign magic wasn't good enough to hold one or both of us down, which was why they'd resorted to death spells instead. But how were they able to cast it? Where had they gotten the scythes? Whose authority did they have? Only Reapers or future Reapers could do this stuff. All the knowledge the Darklings of Visio had used had been destroyed by the Time Master. No one else was supposed to have this ability. There were too many questions and too few answers.

I went back to my fractured memories. We'd left Sun Beach behind, trekking through the woods east of it. Oaks and aspens, just like this one. Hard terrain, rugged and uneven. Plenty of bushes to hide in. And the portal. Yes, the portal had appeared out of nowhere, glowing all white and bigger than Thayen's previous descriptions of it.

Then the bright blast... and nothing.

I found a pebble big enough to make a mark and threw it at Soul. "Wake up!" These Reaper traps didn't have specific blocks on non-Reaper objects, and this was a good time to take advantage of it.

The pebble hit him in the shoulder, and he moaned softly. At least he was still functional, thus helping my nerves unwind a little. I loved him more than anything, and we weren't used to such adversities anymore. Our last scuffle had been with a band of ghouls on Persea, about a year ago. This was something else entirely.

I wanted to reach out to the other First Tenners for help. We obviously needed some assistance. But our telepathic links had been severed as well, I remembered. Not just the comms and the Telluris soul connections of GASP. Again, the reach of this foreign magic baffled me, and we had no one around to answer our most burning questions. I tried to go over my memories again to see if other moments would resurface after the bright blast, but I got nothing. The same black emptiness. The void of a deep sleep.

A couple pebbles later, I finally got Soul to look up and see me. He was as out of it as I had been a few minutes ago, so I gave him a second to wrap his head around our current situation.

"What... what are we doing here?" he asked, trying to get up. He was sluggish and clumsy, as if his arms and legs weren't working together anymore. "What happened to me?"

"The same thing that happened to me, my love," I said. "I think the clones knocked us out and locked us in here."

He froze, giving me a troubled look before he noticed the pentagram used to trap him. "You have got to be kidding me."

"I woke up just like you."

"What do you remember?" Soul asked. I told him about Thayen's coin breaking, then recounted everything I could about the moments prior to the blackout, unable to dig out more from my fractured mind. Thankfully, he had a bit more to fill in the blanks. He frowned as he recounted his own experience. "We were somewhere around here when the portal opened. I felt it. So did you. We quickly realized we were more receptive to its presence during the initial phase, much like Astra. Then they appeared. Clones. Way more than I'd thought were even possible."

"And then we kicked your asses until you couldn't remember a thing." Draven's voice echoed through the woods. He emerged from a nearby oak tree, his dark blond hair dancing in the evening breeze. His hand clutched my scythe, and I instantly knew he wasn't really Draven. A clone, a perfect copy of the Druid I'd last seen at the terrace, long before today's nightmare had begun. "Nice toothpick," he added.

"Don't insult their weapons, darling," Serena's clone said as she joined him from behind another tree. She was carrying Soul's weapon, though she was having trouble with its size. It was much taller and probably weighed more than she did. An ancient weapon belonging to one of the most powerful among the First Ten. At least it had an impact on the clone. That counted for something, though I wasn't sure what just yet. "These are powerful objects we've gotten our hands on."

Soul got up, and I could tell it took a lot of effort, as he wobbled before finding his balance. "What did you do to us? How'd you knock us out?"

he asked.

"A magician never reveals his tricks." Serena's clone giggled.

"Why did you stick around? To rub it in our faces?" I demanded.

Her humor faded. "To give you a warning. Reapers need to stay out of this."

"Wait. Wait." Soul chuckled, shaking his head. "You get the drop on us. You lock us down with death magic you're not even supposed to be capable of wielding. You take our friggin' scythes, and then you have the audacity to tell us to... butt out? Are you serious right now?"

"Consider this your first and final warning," Draven's copy said. "The order comes from high above. Stay out.

This operation doesn't concern you."

Soul pointed an angry finger at him. "Buddy, I will tear you apart limb by limb and beat you over the head with your own arms. You've crossed a line. You don't belong here. Hell, you're not even supposed to be alive!"

"And yet here we are," Draven's copy replied with a cold grin. "We have plans, Reaper. Important plans. Things to do. People to kill. An entire world to change. And you and your undead cohorts need to stay out of our way, lest you learn to regret it. This right here? Consider it a courtesy. We could've done much worse."

That was true. But there was no way we'd ever concede that point. Not after everything the clones had done. "What is your endgame here? How many of you are there?" I asked.

"We are many," Serena's clone declared proudly. "We are—"

"If you say, 'We are unstoppable' I will throw something at you," I said, cutting her off. "We've heard that line before, and it's nowhere near as impressive as you might think. Who sent you here? Who's got a bone to pick with The Shade? Why do you want Astra dead in particular?"

"Come on, talk to us," Soul said. "We might as well chat for a bit before I find my way out of this seal and rip your heads off. I'll make it quick if you give us some intel. Pinky promise."

It made the clones laugh, but I knew Soul was dead serious. He had a sparkling sense of humor and sarcasm galore. He was never the kind who'd take anything too seriously, either. But when the Soul Crusher made promises of death and torture, he always kept his word, with absolutely no exceptions.

"We just need you out of the way, that's all." Serena's doppelganger sighed, rolling her eyes as if this was the last place she wanted to be.

"Where'd you get your death magic knowledge?" Soul asked.

"None of your business. Just sit here, the two of you, like good little corpses and wait it out. This will all be over soon," Draven's clone retorted, then motioned for his partner to join him. They turned and started walking away from us.

Soul was getting restless. "Don't you dare walk away from me!"

He wasn't used to losing his weapon. That scythe was the single most precious part of his existence. The source of his power and an extension of his soul, much like mine. But I had lost my weapon once or twice before. To Soul, this was the worst kind of defeat, and given his galactic pride, I knew he wasn't taking it well.

"Come back!" he shouted. "Hey!"

"Where are the others?" I called out. "The people we were with!"

Serena's clone laughed from afar. "Wouldn't you like to know?" "Hey!" Soul tried again, to no avail.

The doppelgangers didn't listen. They put our weapons away, hidden in their backs, then vanished beyond the trees while I tried to understand what had happened. What could I do to get us out of here? We couldn't be stuck here. Richard, Voss, and Chantal needed us. I only hoped they'd be okay until we could find them again.

"Kelara, we're in serious trouble," Soul said. "We're bloody useless without our weapons."

"I know, my love. But we can't lose hope. We'll figure something out."

"Oh, we will?" he replied, raising an eyebrow at me.

There was no point in both of us being angry beyond control or succumbing to despair. I could hold my own. I could get us out of here. For that, however, I needed a clear mind, and Soul knew it. He took a deep breath and sat down, crossing his legs.

"Okay. But we need to figure it out fast," he said, much calmer. I took it as proof of the trust he'd put in me. It made my heart grow a few sizes, and I would've liked nothing more than to hold him in my arms and kiss him. Unfortunately, this death magic kept us apart. "Those two freaks have plans. You heard them."

"I heard them."

Two clones had bested two First Tenners. They'd locked us in our own magic, and they'd taken our weapons. We were helpless and pissed off. Not to mention embarrassed. But Soul and I were stronger together, even without our scythes. I had zero useful ideas at this point, but something would come to me eventually. The wheels in my head were already turning.

I only hoped we'd untangle this hot mess before any of our living friends got hurt. The clones were enacting somebody's agenda, for sure, and they considered us an issue. An issue big enough that they'd needed to deal with us. That was valuable intel in itself.

VOSS

(SONOFAIDAANDFIELD)

"Hey. Voss."

Chantal's voice sounded so far away. Somewhere at the end of a tunnel, but I couldn't see light, just an endless darkness that had embraced me, refusing to let me go.

"Voss!" It got louder.

An earthquake rocked me until I realized she was shaking me. I felt her hands on my shoulders. What the hell was going on?

"Voss, wake up!"

The darkness vanished as I came to and saw Chantal, a blurry mishmash of soft colors with two turquoise spots where her eyes were supposed to be. I had to blink many times before the image finally came into focus. Yes, it was her. My cousin. And Richard. He'd ended up with us at one point. "Ow..." I grunted, a headache stabbing my brain. "Good. He's awake." Richard sighed. They helped me up, though they looked as startled and as confused as I felt. It took us a while to figure out what had happened, but we all remembered the same string of events prior to a bright explosion.

Soul and Kelara were missing. We'd sent Richard's parents away, along with Draven and Serena. We'd taught them our safe word, knowing we'd use it whenever we met again. A portal had opened, and a throng of clones had come out, among them copies of the very people we'd just said goodbye to minutes earlier. It was all a jumble in my head, but I managed to put all the pieces into a coherent thread as Richard and Chantal shared bits and pieces of their own experiences.

We'd been taken by surprise. "I think we saw the portal open two seconds too late," Chantal surmised, glancing around. "We're still in the oak forest, but... where, exactly? Does any of this look familiar?"

"It's just trees and trees and trees," Richard muttered, rubbing the back of his head. "I may have a concussion.

I'm not sure."

"Try not to fall asleep, then," I replied dryly. "Soul. Kelara. Where'd they go?"

"No idea," Richard said, his brow furrowed. "Do you think the clones did something to them?"

Chantal scoffed, but I could tell she was worried sick about the Reapers. "What could the clones possibly do to entities like the Soul Crusher and Kelara? They're First Tenners."

"They nearly took Soul down with that black spray thing back at the hospital," I reminded her. "Maybe they got to him again. I just... I wish I could remember."

"We were knocked out," Richard said. "Chances are this is all we're going to be able to recall, at least for a while. Our short-term memory is rattled, and it will take time for the brain to fully process what happened. Until then, we need to make a move."

I got up, a new wave of anxiety washing over me and sending chills through my arms and legs. "Wait. Why'd they leave us here? The clones came at us. There was that explosion. All the light... no bodies, see? Except for the three of us. Why? Why were we left behind?"

"Oh dear," Chantal murmured, patting her uniform. "The tablet. The tablet with all our files and directives." "What?" I replied, not grasping the issue as quickly as I would've liked. I blamed it on the throbbing headache that had settled between my temples.

"Check your pockets. There are zero devices left on us," Chantal said. "They took everything, including the healing magic. The earpieces. Our weapons. Everything."

Richard gasped, rolling up his sleeve. "My watch. Damn it, it was a gift from Field!"

"What use would they have for the watch?" I wondered.

"There's a GPS tracker in there that I could activate, but if the comms are down, then likely tracking won't work, either, since they're patched into the same network," Richard explained. "But the watch had sentimental value. This is petty, even for the stupid clones."

We spent another minute or so trying to understand what the play had been. The clones had taken us out, but they hadn't killed us. They'd taken our devices but not our lives. We were on our own—there was no sign of Kelara or Soul anywhere around us. Heck, I wasn't even sure this was where the portal had first opened. The more I looked at the trees, the weirder it seemed, as if we'd been picked up, carried off from the original location of the attack, then dumped here like potato sacks.

"Voss. Should we keep moving and stick to the original plan?" Chantal asked. "Or do we head straight for the Great Dome?"

"If we give up now, we won't have enough people to count on for any kind of retaliation," I said. "The clones are doing something big, and I fear if we go directly to the Great Dome, we risk innocents not even knowing what hits them when the doppelgangers come around."

"We need to sound the alarm, right?" Richard asked with a heavy sigh.

"Yeah. Tell as many people as we can," I said.

Chantal raised a hand as though we were still in class. "One problem, though. Without the Reapers, how do we tell the fakeys from the realsies? I mean, 'paladin' works for the ones the Reapers have already tested, the ones we've taught the safe word, but the rest? Sheesh. Judging by the number of clones we last saw coming through, I'd dare say there are more of them now than before."

"True, but they're coming in without disposing of the originals," I replied. "My guess is they're counting on the confusion they cause to take us down. I think we just need to be careful. Anyone acting weird, even the slightest feeling that something might be off... I don't know, we'll have to be on the lookout."

We'd gone from wondering about Isabelle's doppelganger to a full-on invasion in less than a day, and I feared the growth of this problem would be exponential and fatal to many of those we loved.

Footsteps startled us. We turned around just as Serena and Draven ran out from a cluster of old oak trees and sprawling bushes. Their clothes were dirty and crumpled, partially torn and bloodied. They were both panting but relieved to find us here. "Thank the stars," Serena managed, nearly falling over. Richard rushed to her side and helped her up, while Chantal got close to Draven. He looked like he was about to collapse, too. They must've been through some kind of living hell.

"What happened to you?" I asked.

"Where are my mom and dad?" Richard added, giving Draven a troubled look. "You were supposed to get to the Great Dome."

"We tried, believe me," the Druid replied, rubbing his face. "They attacked us. A whole bunch of them, looking exactly like us." His gaze darted everywhere except to meet mine. "It was weird and horrible. Every magic shot I threw out came back with a vengeance. They look like us, they have our powers, they have abilities and gadgets on top of that… we were overwhelmed."

"My parents?" Richard insisted, fingers digging into Serena's shoulders. Her eyes were filled with tears as she looked up at him.

"I'm sorry, honey…"

"Wait. You're sorry? For what?" Richard demanded, edging closer to panic. I'd seen him like this before, and the last thing we needed was him spiraling out of control. Richard was a strong young man, but just the thought of losing his parents or anyone in his family was enough to send him off into a furious frenzy. He could still function, but he had little to no self-control left.

Something dawned on me. Something we'd overlooked, mostly because of the confusion in our circumstances. "What's the safe word?" I asked.

Draven and Serena didn't seem to hear me at first. Chantal was checking the Druid for wounds, but she couldn't find anything despite the blood on his clothes. And Serena was sobbing, trying to give Richard some truly awful news, only… I wasn't sure there was any truth in this entire scene.

"What's the safe word?" I asked again, raising my voice.

"The what, now?" Draven replied.

In an instant, Richard, Chantal, and I knew what we were dealing with. At least our original plan had worked in this respect. Draven's copy cried out when flames burst from Chantal's hands and nearly burned him to a crisp. He managed to jump back before it did too much damage. I leapt at him, my wings spreading and flapping for that extra push.

Richard tackled Serena's clone. Everything happened so fast. Too damn fast. I found myself kicking and punching the Druid's doppelganger, while Chantal and Richard took on Serena's. The original was a powerful and capable sentry, and her double was just as dangerous.

Draven's copy rammed his fist into my side, and I howled from the pain. He grabbed my hair and whispered something as he jerked my head back in a powerful motion. His palm pressed onto my chest, sending sharp and burning sensations through my ribcage. I tried to fight back, but whatever he'd done to me had rendered me limp. "Voss!" Chantal screamed.

I went down like a tree that had just been cut at the base. Hard and heavy. Unable to stop. I landed on my side, the image twisting before me. Unable to even think about a possible resolve, I could only watch as my friends continued to fight without me.

Draven's clone threw a blue fireball at Chantal. She was trying to reach me when it hit her. She fell, and I wanted to move, to get to her, but I couldn't. Richard collapsed, his face bruised by some of Serena's doppelganger's barriers. She got on top of him, her knees digging into his back. He growled and tried to wriggle his way out, but the doppelganger jammed a needle into his shoulder. Richard said something, slurring his words as he passed out.

"No..."

"We wanted to let you kids go, but we changed our minds," Draven's copy said. "We could use some of you as leverage later."

"No... Don't..." I whispered, my mouth drying up.

He stung Chantal with something that looked like a needle, and she fainted. I was the only one left awake, but I was useless, boiling on the inside as the clones got up and high-fived each other, smugly satisfied with themselves. Their grins were cold, their eyes devoid of any emotion. And yet they looked so much like the real Draven and Serena. It was disturbing on many levels.

"Why are you doing this?" I croaked, my voice weak and scratchy.

"Because we can," Draven's copy replied. "Because it's what we're meant to do."

"Do we take him, too?" Serena's double asked him.

He shook his head. "Nah. He can stay behind and tell the others that there's no point in fighting us. Sooner or later, we'll have them all. We will replace them, whether they like it or not. This world is ours, darling. It was meant for us."

My stomach churned as Serena's copy gave me a brief glance. I could almost spot a glimmer of pity in her eyes as she grabbed Richard's legs and started dragging him away. Draven's copy threw Chantal over his shoulder like a rolled-up rug and proceeded to follow his fake wife. The urgency of this situation overrode whatever Druid magic he'd dosed me with, and I started moving, much to my surprise. I managed to shakily stand.

"Wait!" I called out, my wings flapping uncontrollably but without the strength required to lift me off the ground. All they did was raise the dust around me, pushing me into a violent cough.

Draven's clone looked back at me, a sneer slitting his face. "Stay down. Be a good boy."

"No!"

I wanted to fight. I just wasn't sure how much of their attacks I could still take. My vision was not steady, blurring every other second, making it harder for me to focus. He'd done quite the number on me already.

"Hm. Okay. I've changed my mind, then," he shot back and threw a shimmering ball of energy at me. I barely saw it coming. It hit me right in the head, heat burning through my mind as darkness returned to wrap me in its cold arms.

"No..."

"That's a good boy!" he said, as though I were a dog. "Let's just hope the other two handled the Reapers properly. You heard the bosses... No loose ends. No interference."

"We're modeled after the same material and we're doing all right," Serena's copy replied, her voice muffled in my head. Their exchange made me think that there were more Serenas and Dravens out here—not just these two. But I was useless and definitely their prisoner now.

There was no strength left, only darkness and emptiness as I succumbed to a deep sleep. My thoughts scattered, leaving me helpless, like a fallen leaf lost with the deluge. *No...*

TRISTAN

issa and Loren were not in any way frightened or intimidated by Joy's presence. After all, she'd been assigned to protect them many eons ago. But they didn't look comfortable either, and I wondered why. They didn't seem to like her very much, though they both put on dry smiles whenever she looked at them.

I, on the other hand, was quaking in my boots. I didn't show it. Unending had taught me a long time ago that Reapers took one's fear and used it as a weapon if given the opportunity. Of course, in this case the chances of actual conflict were relatively slim—assuming Joy wasn't some blundering psychopath. Death hadn't been notified of our discovery of this place, nor of our presence. This visit hadn't been sanctioned, and I knew Unending would reach out to her if push came to shove.

"Stay calm," she told me telepathically. "We want to keep Death out of the loop for as long as possible so we can figure out what this place and this particular Reaper are all about."

I agreed. Death had a bad habit of keeping secrets, and risking ourselves in this circumstance felt like a safer bet than just trusting Unending's maker to provide us with the whole truth. We'd learned from experience that Death was picky in what she disclosed, for very selfish reasons.

Joy towered over us both, the light of her scythe casting reflections through her short, spiky fire-red hair. She looked as though she'd been designed for war. Beautiful but with rough features, sharp edges, and a blazing gaze of cosmic wrath. And that ginormous scythe of hers had a chilling effect on my ability to think clearly. "I'm going to ask you one last time," Joy said. "What are you two doing here?"

"Follow my lead, love, please... this whole thing stinks to high heaven. I'm afraid we're going to have to play for both sides," Unending told me, her voice echoing sweetly in my head.

"I trust you. And you know you can count on me," I thought, loudly enough for her to hear.

She gave me a faint smile, then looked at Joy. "Do you know who we are?"

"Yes. It still doesn't explain what you're doing here," the Reaper replied. "You're not supposed to know about this place. About these people."

"If you know who I am, then you must also know what I am capable of," Unending said, revealing her scythe. Its delicate blade shimmered with warning. A promise that if Joy resorted to violence, my wife would respond in kind.

"You may be one of the more well-versed in death magic, sister, but I have a few tricks up my sleeve as well, courtesy of Death herself. If you're here, and since you were able to identify the extent of the damage my weapon can deliver, then surely you understand the lengths I will go to for their protection," Joy said, briefly glancing at Loren and Sissa.

The young princess put on a bright smile, trying to defuse the situation. "There is no need for violence.

Unending and Tristan have come in peace. I know they have because I feel their intentions. I feel their minds." "Yeah, but what if you're not able to properly read them, huh?" Joy interjected. "If they know what you are and what you're capable of, I wouldn't put it past them to use various mental tricks meant to throw you for a loop."

Loren placed a hand on his daughter's shoulder. "She has a point, child. I sense goodwill from them, as well. But it could be a trick."

"Oh, for the love of..." Unending snapped. "I didn't even know you people existed until an hour ago. Frankly, while I find myself fascinated by your species, I have no interest in dealing with you or your abilities. I've experienced your spiritually violent side many times before, and I do not wish to play football with this hornets' nest!"

The king frowned. "That's almost insulting."

"Well, then it's a good thing you never met the Spirit Bender," I mumbled.

"Who?" Sissa asked.

Joy scoffed. "No one you should concern yourself with. He's gone forever, and the world is better for it." She paused and moved her focus back to Unending. "What are you doing here, if not messing with these people?"

"There's something we need. It's in here," Unending replied. "One of Death's artifacts."

"You mean the Mixer." Joy's forehead smoothed. "Don't tell me you're running errands for Anunit. I promised her I would show no mercy if she tried any dumb tricks."

Unending shook her head. "No. We're not running errands for her. That's not what this is about. It should please you to hear that we're actually hunting her. It's a known fact by now that Death wants Anunit more than anything. Tristan and I are using the only workable approach. The Mixer is a crucial part of it."

"You intend to use the artifact as bait?" Joy asked. She seemed intrigued, her hostility gradually subsiding. I could tell from the way her shoulders were dropping that tension was slipping away, slowly replaced with curiosity. "I've thought about it myself a couple of times."

"If Anunit was here, why didn't you catch her?" I demanded, hands on my hips as I adopted a scolding tone. It wasn't difficult to see where Unending was taking this conversation. We were playing Joy from a different angle while also lying through our teeth, but we kept our minds clear and our lips smiling. The shimmer from Unending's scythe wasn't just a sign of activity, I realized. My whole being tingled from the effect of a spell she must've whispered, unbeknown to anyone. "Are you doing something to shield us from the soul fae?" I asked her telepathically.

"Yes. Both Loren and Sissa are trying to read us in deeper detail, but I can hold them off for a while, just long enough for them to miss the deceptive notes in our voices," she replied, then spoke to Joy. "Tristan is asking a very good question, Joy. If you've crossed paths with her, why isn't she already in chains back on Mortis?"

The Reaper looked slightly befuddled. "She was too fast. Resourceful. I underestimated her."

"Then you'll absolutely support us in our endeavor to do what you couldn't?" Unending shot back with a ruthless grin. By the stars, I loved this woman at her softest and her hardest with equal passion. It was difficult to keep up with her sometimes, but the millions of years of existence and experience that she carried within herself were my best reason to follow her lead in situations like this.

Joy had gone from fierce warrior to uncertain guardian. "I will have to verify this with Death. It would be foolish of me to trust you."

"Why, exactly? Have we ever done anything to deceive you, or anyone else, for that matter?" Unending replied, knowing that Death had tried to keep that seal issue under wraps, given her tumultuous ego. In the meantime, she was also reaching out to Death through their spiritual connection without Joy's knowledge. I had no idea what Unending was telling her, but I would soon find out.

"No, but—"

"By all means, consult with Death," Unending said, unwilling to give Joy enough verbal freedom to suggest dishonesty on our part. We didn't want the soul fae to get suspicious and poke even harder at our spirits. The magic Unending used had managed to shield us from intrusion without raising any red flags, by the looks of it. So far, so good. "I'm sure she'll be pleased to hear you've had the Mixer all along. We'll wait."

That was an excellent blow, I realized, as Joy's fierceness temporarily vanished, leaving her looking like a lost little lamb. Silence settled as Loren and Sissa exchanged glances. Around us, the other soul fae were doing their best to go about their business, but they still couldn't help themselves, occasionally stealing curious glances at us. It made me smile as I listened to Unending's voice in my head.

"Before Joy reached out to her just now. I wanted Death to get a heads-up about us having found the soul fae and about me using the Mixer as part of our first trial for Anunit. So, I told her. Our maker was obviously surprised to hear about the artifact, but she didn't hesitate to respond, nonetheless," Unending explained. Joy was in the process of speaking to her maker now, I noticed, as she gazed out into the distance, her lips pressing into a thin line.

"And what was her reply, exactly?" I asked.

"To keep going. Since I told Death that the trials represent our only way to accomplish our side of the mission, we've got her approval. After all, that was our deal. We get what we want out of Anunit, then Death gets Anunit. Fun fact, she didn't react to our discovery of the soul fae, nor did she ask about how Joy had been involved with Spirit and the Mixer... she only said to leave this with her. My guess is she's giving Joy the green light to let us do this properly while also chewing her ass for not disclosing the Mixer's presence in the village from the moment it was brought here."

"Hopefully, it will work. We're playing a dangerous game here," I told her. "What if she decides she doesn't want Anunit to have the Mixer, regardless of our mission? What if she decides to pull the plug on this whole operation and just have us trap Anunit, our family plans be damned?"

"I think we should worry about that later. We have to approach this on a step by step basis and get past Joy first. Death made a point of specifying that Joy isn't the brightest or the most stable of Reapers, but that she is, indeed, insanely powerful and obedient. Loyal to a fault, she said, adding that our family planning issues should not be shared with her. She wouldn't understand, and she'd get frustrated over her inability to understand, and then the powder keg would blow... I mean, I don't know how she made Joy to begin with, whose soul she copied, what abilities she put in... but if she's telling me we have to deal with an unstable Reaper, I know we're better off following Death's lead on this. So, we keep the sharing of intel to a minimum, get the Mixer, and get out. On another note, I am dying to figure out exactly what purpose the soul fae are supposed to serve in this cosmic equation. If Anunit is right, and Death plans to use them to keep us all submissive someday, we obviously need to know about this. We need to prepare."

There were many ways in which this scenario could go wrong. Death could have used the soul fae more than once until now, with minimal effort and damage to all the parties involved. She could have used them against Spirit on Visio before the Darklings' siege. She could have used them against Unending to get her to remove the seal she'd left inside her. But she didn't. Either weaponizing the soul fae against the Reapers was never really an option for Death, or she was waiting for something truly beyond her control to whip them out. These were the only possibilities that made sense.

Either way, Unending and I agreed to keep playing our parts. One way or another, we would get to the whole truth. Anunit was playing games of her own, and we were both determined to make sure she got her just desserts. It all depended on how much intel we were able to get out of this place and how smoothly the Mixer's extraction operation went.

Joy exhaled sharply. "Death says it's fine."

"Meh. Go figure," Unending grumbled. She put her scythe away. "What were her thoughts on the Mixer being here?"

"Death said we will discuss that at another time. She only asked that I cooperate," the Reaper replied stiffly. I figured Death would tear her a new one over this, eventually.

"Shall we consider this a clean slate, then? No issues?" Unending asked.

"How did you know about the Mixer? Anunit? No, you said you were hunting her," Joy muttered, clearly displeased with her current position.

"Spirit told me a while back," my wife said, her mind working like a turbo engine. "I kept it to myself because I knew you'd get in trouble with Death over this. For what it's worth, it's better you told her first."

Joy hadn't been the first to tell Death, but she didn't need to know that. I could certainly see why Death didn't want us to tell this Reaper too much. Something had definitely gone wrong during her creation—it was as if her whole mind wasn't quite... there. She seemed to oscillate between groggy and hyper-alert at times. Adding territorial on top of this unstable pile and yeah, potentially explosive reactions.

"I've got my eyes on you, either way," Joy warned us, but she didn't seem as fearsome as before. Like all the other Reapers, she was accountable to Death, and if the supreme leader had decreed that we were allowed to be here, then so be it, whether Joy liked it or not. Judging by how she'd reacted, I was inclined to assume that she felt powerless at times. We'd breached her little corner of the world. We'd invaded her turf. Whether we were sanctioned to be here or not, it didn't matter. It still irked her, and she had no problem giving us an attitude over it.

"Relax, Joy. We're only here to get a job done," Unending said. "We'll get out of your hair once we have the Mixer."

Sissa seemed content with how the conversation had progressed. "Well, I am glad it is working out. We've been isolated for so long, it's actually nice to meet strangers."

"Yes, it would be a pity if Joy had to kill you both," Loren added, equally pleased with our current agreement. "We will be preparing for supper soon. Would you like to join us?"

Unending and I looked at each other. "I don't see any reason not to," I replied. "Getting to know you and your people better would be an honor. The Mixer can wait until later."

"Absolutely," my wife said, giving Joy a friendly smile. "Personally, I can't wait to talk to you about that enormous scythe of yours. It's truly a work of art."

Joy blinked rapidly, suddenly bashful as she stared at her weapon. "Thank you, I guess."

Much like the soul fae, this Reaper wasn't accustomed to strangers waltzing into her village after slipping through the potentially destructive protective measures she'd put in place. She and the soul fae had only had one another for company, year after year. They didn't go out exploring. They didn't know what the rest of Rothko looked like. Isolation could be hurtful in the long term.

I was actually eager to better understand the soul fae's collective psyche. I also looked forward to getting out of here as quickly as possible so we could move things along with Anunit, but my anthropological curiosity had won this tiny battle, at least for the time being.

TRISTAN

On the other side of the village, beyond the last of the white stone igloo-style houses, a river flowed. It had been here for only five millennia, Sissa had told us. The fountains were independent streams and endless sources of clean water, but the river had been a pleasant surprise. Apparently, a massive earthquake had rocked the entire region five thousand years ago. The soul fae had not felt a thing, protected by the death magic bubble around their community, but Joy had thought it would come as a nice change of scenery to have the newly formed river passing through.

Ever since, the soul fae had made a habit of enjoying a community dinner once a week, with nectar from the orchids pouring freely. Apparently, these flowers had certain natural properties that enhanced the senses. "From their description of this stuff, it sounds a lot like the succubi's spiced rose water," I said to Unending as we gathered around a massive campfire built beside the rocky riverbank.

The people were bringing fruit platters and bowls of nectar, sharing them around the fire. Unending and I stayed with Loren, Sissa, and Joy. Clusters were forming—even at this low number, the soul fae couldn't exactly all talk over dinner. Groups were bound to happen, and it illustrated the depth of their interpersonal relationships. The soul fae I'd seen in familial packs earlier were identically gathered around their fruits and nectar, few of them crossing over to other groups. It told me that they weren't only isolated as a community. Sure, they got along, but they mostly kept to themselves and their families, plus a close friend or two at most.

"It's always like this?" I asked, looking at Sissa.

"Like what?"

By now, we'd learned a bit more about their history, at least as far as the past couple thousand years were concerned. The soul fae kept an archive of documents, carefully preserved in the caves beneath the village with a little help from Joy, but they didn't dwell too much on the distant past. Even so, two millennia were enough for me to get a better idea as to what kind of people they were and how their society functioned.

Any violent inclinations or tribal skirmishes were swiftly put out by the Reaper. Peace was more or less obligatory. Few had been the instances of murder or theft, as the soul fae had made a habit of reading one another's intentions. They had trust as a currency, trading favors and thoughts for other goods. Some of them were better at working the land, while others were excellent craftsmen. The society itself was healthy, and Joy served as an enforcer—not only against any outside forces, but also against any elements within that could cause chaos or create disruptions.

"I don't see a big gathering, exactly," I told Sissa. "I was expecting you'd all sit by the fire and expand your conversations to the whole village, not just the family clusters."

"Oh. I don't know," Sissa replied. "We're fine like this. The dinner itself serves mostly to have us all in our collective company, but no one expects us to bond beyond the friendships we've already formed."

"Yes. And it's a little strange," I said, then looked to Joy. "Have they always been like this? Normally, people in settings with bigger crowds enjoy shuffling through and talking to as many others as they can throughout the evening."

"Parties. You are basically talking about parties." Unending chuckled.

"And festivals. Symposiums. Any large gathering where people break away from their familiar circles and interact with acquaintances or even strangers," I said, trying not to smile.

Joy raised a skeptical eyebrow, watching the fire burn, its orange tongue licking at the night sky. "They've always been like this. They're shy, if you ask me."

"We're very sociable," Loren replied, frowning. "Just with a limited number of people."

"Good grief, a whole village filled with introverts." I couldn't help but laugh. "No wonder you've been living here so well, uninterested in going out and seeing what the rest of this world has to offer." It was interesting, to say the least, since introverts were the happiest in their safe spaces, with barely a family member or two around. The soul fae showed some similarities to the Amazonian tribes I'd studied decades ago. "Your bloodlines are strong, though," I added. "I see you place great value on such ties."

Sissa nodded. "We do. Family is everything to us. We think the same. We feel the same. We would never hurt one another. The same cannot be said for the others. I suppose it's why we stick to our... clusters, as you call them." "Don't get me wrong, it's not a bad thing," I replied. "It's eerie but not unseen or unheard of. I'm simply expressing my fascination."

Unending had telepathically tried to find out more about Joy's relationship with Spirit, but the Reaper had dismissed her request, saying it belonged in the past. She clearly didn't want to talk about it, and I wasn't exactly shocked. Spirit must've charmed her, and she must've felt foolish and ashamed upon learning of his machinations. It was a sensitive topic.

An hour went by as Loren and Sissa told us more about their village and what they remembered from the earliest pages of soul fae history. Joy didn't do much talking during this time, focusing mostly on watching Unending and me like a hawk. Every movement I made sparked her interest. She followed each of my wife's wandering glances. Death may have told her to stand back and assist us, but Joy wasn't done being suspicious of us. She didn't have much reason for this. It had to be instinct.

I couldn't taste any of the soul fae's fruits—wonders of their gardens and orchards. They looked like sublime crosses between peaches and apples, but they came in the wildest variety of colors, from bright yellow to rabid pink, neon purple and lime green. They smelled amazing, with faint notes of citrus lingering in my nostrils long after I'd put the fruits back in the bowl.

The nectar, however, was something I could ingest as a vampire, though only in moderation. A few sips were enough to virtually open me up to the universe itself, my senses suddenly exploding and stretching beyond their natural limits. My head felt as light as a feather, yet I could hear the wings of a butterfly-like insect flapping half a mile away. I could see the microorganisms that dwelled around the crude green bulbs of nearby orchids—tiny beings with too many legs and caterpillar bodies. I could smell sweat of the wolf-adjacent creatures that Unending and I had seen in the jungle before we'd entered the village. The animals were circling the protective layer, unable to get in. It was an interesting fault in the magic's design. Smell was the one sense that was constantly underestimated.

"This is insane," I managed, gently leaning into Unending. She couldn't drink or eat anything at all, since she no longer had a living body to nourish. She and Joy were the only ones untouched by the nectar's effects, and they watched us as we smiled and softened under its sweet influence. "I mean, amazing, but insane."

Unending whispered into my ear. "Better than the spiced rose water you mentioned?" In a sense, she was vicariously living through me, listening to my thoughts and impressions of everything I tasted.

"Different would be the key word. Similar, yes, but also different," I replied, clearly not making much sense. "I think the effect is much stronger and concentrated on each nerve ending in my body. The succubi's concoction serves to relax one's muscles, to elevate the mood and such. This nectar is more of an amplifier than anything else," I added, then described each of the sensations that had taken hold of me.

Joy shook her head slowly, the corner of her mouth twitching slightly with stifled amusement. "You're all so fragile."

"What do you mean?" I asked.

"One minute you're alive. Then you're not. I suppose it's the charm of life itself. Experiencing every sensation to the fullest. Tasting everything. Feeling everything. And then, poof. You're gone. No more fruits. No more nectar. No taste left. No sensation but for the emptiness of lingering between life and death. A wisp. Nothing more," Joy said. There was sadness in her voice as she spoke. As if maybe she wished she could experience life again.

It got me thinking. "When you met Anunit, did she perhaps offer you a resurrection deal in return for the Mixer?" I asked. "It's what I would do, given her talents and how badly she wants that artifact."

"She did, actually." Joy's stern gaze settled on the roaring campfire. The sound of wood crackling made my ears twitch. It felt as though I were right in there, the flames caressing my skin. It was a false sensation, of course, since all fire did was consume everything in its path. It was the nectar's effect on me, playing with my brain. "I turned her down. Living is not for us Reapers. Not even for a minute."

"Don't you miss your old life? Even a bit? The taste of food? The crisp sweetness of water?" I said. "Even as a vampire, I sometimes long for my human days when I could experience certain things that are now forbidden for my kind." The only joy I still had once in a while was that I could be in the sunlight, provided that I was under Unending's invisibility magic. I couldn't feel its warmth on my skin, but at least I didn't experience the fear of burning under it.

Joy sighed. "I never lived. There is nothing in a life for me to miss."

This left Unending speechless. "Wait, what do you mean?" I asked on her behalf.

"I'm a copy of a soul like the other First Tenners. I have faint memories of a life, but I never went through the process myself," Joy said, raising her chin as she looked at us. There was a mixture of sadness and resignation in her voice, as if she'd already given this plenty of thought and reached the safer conclusion that she was better off not finding out what living was all about.

"How is that? I mean, Death made ten of us," Unending replied. "I understood you were as old as us, but she... why did she make you, if not to be one of us?"

"I was created specifically for this purpose," Joy said, glancing around. "To protect the soul fae, no matter what. This is my only objective. The sole reason for my existence. Death once told me she wanted to make sure that no one would ever try to get to the soul fae and use them against her. I almost failed in that respect when I allowed the Spirit Bender to come in so he could see them. My weakness nearly cost me my job. My everything."

Unending looked at me, visibly troubled. "Death never told us. None of us knew you were out here," she said to Joy. "Please, believe me when I tell you that we would've come to visit. We would've liked to meet you much sooner than... well, now."

"Death made you. She kept you here in isolation, unable to leave Rothko," I said, and Joy nodded slowly. "How have you not lost your mind? I mean, the soul fae... no offense, of course," I told Loren and Sissa before shifting back to Joy. "The soul fae, they live and they die. They move on. You've been here since basically the beginning of time. The same planet, this same world for so long. How have you remained sane?"

Joy shot me a sly grin. "Who said I was sane?"

And we were now back at what Death had told us about her. At least she was aware that she wasn't the poster child of Reaper mental health. She was in a good mood, though, and that had to count for something. The last thing I wanted was piss her off and lose control of this situation—with or without Joy, we couldn't afford to scare or make the soul fae feel threatened or betrayed in any way. I could see why Unending had stressed over us being careful.

"I'm truly sorry." Unending sighed. "Had I or my siblings known about you, about these people... we would've gladly offered to keep you company, or to take turns, even, so that you could get some time to yourself, to visit other worlds..."

"Death never intended for any other Reaper to find out about the soul fae. Not the common ones, and certainly not the First Tenners," Joy said. "She was always adamant that this had to remain solely between us."

"But why?" Unending asked.

Sissa agreed. "I'm curious, as well."

"Would other Reapers wish to harm us?" Loren interjected, his white brow furrowed, one elbow resting on his knee as he sat cross-legged between Joy and his daughter.

"Soul fae can control spirits," Joy said. "Whether they belong to the living or the dead, it matters not. And if the Reapers should ever try to rise up against Death, she expects the soul fae to protect her."

Unending scoffed. "She was right..."

"Who?" Joy asked.

"Death," my wife was quick and smart to lie. "She anticipated a day when she might be too weak and become vulnerable to internal attacks. The Spirit Bender wasn't extreme or dangerous enough, at least in her mind; otherwise, she would've used these people against him. I think she expects something much worse to happen someday."

I understood the gravity of these words. Yes, Anunit had been right to suspect this purpose for the soul fae. I wondered how a rebellion of Reapers big enough to push Death into this worst-case scenario would unfold. If the horrors that Spirit had perpetrated on us and thousands of innocent Reapers weren't enough to warrant summoning these creatures... what did qualify?

Joy didn't seem to have an answer. The soul fae were just as clueless. The only one who had a better idea of what to expect would be Death herself. But maybe she wasn't the only one, after all. Something had pushed Anunit to such a theory, and we needed to find out what, exactly. Because if Death was still vulnerable in any way, we had to know. We had to prepare for the worst—the balance of the universe had to be maintained at any cost.

TRISTAN

"What is the extent of a soul fae's abilities?" I asked. "I know they have the Spirit Bender's powers, but—"

"Oh, no—they're more than that," Joy said. "The soul that was used as a matrix for him was one of the weakest. Frankly, I think Death also watered his formula down considerably. Remember, Spirit had to cut you with his scythe for his influence to work."

She was right. We'd already noticed that particular aspect. Unending and I exchanged nervous glances while Loren and Sissa watched us with genuine curiosity. Everything we'd been discussing with Joy up to this point probably sounded like gibberish to them, since they'd lived in complete isolation, having met no other Reaper besides their guardian. And Joy kept her cards close to her chest.

"Sissa, tell them what you can do. Actually, no. Show them," Joy told the young princess, who straightened her back and shifted so she could sit cross-legged. "Spare no boundary whatsoever."

I held my breath for a moment as Sissa set her sights on me. "No holds barred?"

"None," Joy insisted.

"Is it an overreaction on my part to admit I'm a little uneasy about this?" I asked, chuckling nervously. I had plenty to hide, and I didn't want Sissa to dig around in my head. Unending wasn't sure how much her mentally protective magic could push back without arousing suspicion from these creatures, since obviously we knew less about them than we'd originally thought.

"Deep breath, my love," Unending said through our telepathic connection. "Don't give them reason to poke around where they're not supposed to."

"I mean, not that I have anything to hide, but... I managed to elude the Spirit Bender's manipulation. Losing control over myself honestly terrifies me," I added aloud, making Loren laugh lightly.

"Worry not, young man," he said. "Sissa would never be intrusive or disrespectful. It's not our ethos."

All I could do was hope for the best. Sissa's eyes glimmered gold while looking at me, and I felt something tickling my skin. It covered my entire body, seeping through the flesh and deep into the bone. I couldn't fight it. The force was too strong and dominant, unwilling to yield or soften its hold on me. My soul was in the palm of Sissa's hand, and she started to squeeze—slowly, at first. Just enough to make me gasp as I realized I was no longer in charge of myself.

"Tell me your biggest fear," she demanded, and I was unable to ignore this request. The compulsion was like a tidal wave crashing into me, dismantling each of my defenses. I noticed that giving in was much easier than resisting as far as the soul fae's power was concerned. It hurt less.

"My biggest fear..." I managed. "Is that I'll wake up one day, and Unending will be gone." I was honest. Losing my beloved was what scared me the most. We'd become so close, so deeply bonded over the course of twenty years, that an existence without her seemed impossible. Unthinkable. A true hell on earth.

"That's so sweet." Sissa sighed, her smile radiant with warmth.

Joy scoffed, leaning on her elbow. "You can do better."

"I'm trying to ease him into it," the young princess replied. On one hand, I was amazed by the firm hold she had on me. On the other hand, I was still very much terrified. Sissa focused, her gaze locked on mine, and I felt pressure gathering somewhere in the back of my neck. "Stand up."

I had no choice. Jumping to my feet, I took a deep breath. My body was not mine. My will was gone. I was defenseless, hers to do with as she pleased. I tried to imagine what this sort of power could do in a war. The Spirit Bender on his own had been terrifying enough, but the soul fae didn't even need to touch me in order to control me.

"Holy crap," I whispered.

Unending didn't move a muscle. She didn't take her eyes off me, either.

"Bow before me," Sissa said.

I bowed, astonished by how easy it was for her to do this to me. "This is unbelievable," I replied. "I'd thought Spirit was a force to be reckoned with. Whew…"

"Enough," Unending cut in, looking at Sissa. "Please, let him go."

Joy laughed. "Scared she might damage your boy toy? Imagine what any one of these soul fae could do to you or the other Reapers."

"Tristan is my husband. He deserves more respect," Unending shot back.

"You're a Reaper. You shouldn't even be married." Joy sighed, shaking her head slowly. Sissa listened to my wife's demand, and I felt her hand letting go of my soul. Freedom seemed like mere seconds away, within inches of my grasp. I let out a heavy breath just as the last of Sissa's spiritual tendrils left my body, and I couldn't stop a smile from taking over my face.

"There. I am sorry if it felt… invasive," Sissa told me, lowering her gaze.

I took her hands in mine in a gesture of goodwill and bowed once more, this time of my own accord. "Not at all, Your Highness. It is truly an incredible gift you have."

Sitting back next to Unending, I welcomed her arms around my neck as she glued herself to me and covered my cheek and temple with soft kisses. "Are you okay?" Her mind spoke to mine. I gave her a faint nod. She looked at Joy. "The world changes. The rules evolve. Two of my fellow First Tenners are an item, bound forever by the golden thread of love. There are three couples I know of, personally. It is rare among us for love to find a way, but it does. I'm sorry you have never had the chance to experience that for yourself."

Sissa sat next to her father. Joy couldn't bear to look at us. It didn't take me long to figure it out. "You were in love," I said. "Weren't you?"

"You're talking nonsense," the Reaper muttered. She wasn't trying too hard to deny it, but it's difficult to hide a broken heart, regardless of one's living status. Her kind had already proven they were capable of profound and complex emotions.

"Oh, dear. You're right," Unending told me. "Spirit. Or am I not even close?"

Joy got up, cursing under her breath. She put a hand to her chest and pulled out a shimmering gold chain, its last link broken. "No, no, you're onto something," the Reaper grumbled. "And this is what he left me with."

The chain looked just like the one that Unending and I shared, only Joy's was broken. I had never seen a broken chain before, but I knew what it meant—it was the sign of a shattered heart. A love that only she felt, unrequited and empty.

"This could only form if the love, the bond itself, was mutual," Unending said, staring at the golden links. "You and Spirit were once a couple. A true pair of souls..."

"Yes. And then he left, and the chain broke one day. He'd fallen for someone else, I suppose. If you thought Reaper couples are rare, I'm guessing Reapers falling out of love with someone is some kind of rainbow unicorn. He came back, but I already knew he was looking to use me again, so I sent him away, and not with the kindest words. All I have to remember him by is this," Joy said, then walked off into the night. I watched her figure disappear between the white stone igloos, the orchids swaying in the evening breeze.

"It's a delicate subject, I suppose." Unending sighed.

Loren waved the concern away. "She'll get over it. More than once, we've talked about it. About the love she felt for someone who's long gone. Tomorrow, when the sun comes out, she'll come back, prickly and surly as always."

"She's extremely emotional." Sissa giggled. "A pleasure to read, if I'm honest. I'm never bored with Joy."

"Off her rocker would be more accurate," Loren said. "She scares me sometimes. That volcanic temperament. By the stars, if she gets the wrong idea into her head, it is downright impossible to make her see the truth. I've had to bend her spirit a couple of times to calm her down, though she doesn't remember it."

"Why? What did she do?" I asked.

"Oh, she worked herself into a frenzy. Cooped up in the village, with a broken heart and no other Reaper to talk to... I've always believed Death could've organized some shifts to secure our protection, but no. It all fell on Joy. She snaps a lot. It's out of her control, I'm afraid, but our abilities serve us well in that respect."

Unending stilled, giving me a dark look. It was so brief, I barely noticed it before she turned and smiled at the king and princess. "Please excuse us for a moment," she said. "My husband and I need to discuss something in private. We'll be right back."

We got up and left Loren and Sissa by the fire. They didn't seem offended, choosing to turn their attention to the enormous fruit platter that had been sitting in front of them for the better part of an hour. I followed Unending across the village and all the way back to the edge of the protective spell where we'd entered.

"What's wrong?" I asked.

"Anunit is here," she said, her tone clipped. "She reached out. Telepathically."

"When?"

"Just now." She sighed. "Said she needed to talk to us. It's urgent."

I frowned. "Couldn't she just tell you? You know, while she was on the line?"

"I have no idea," Unending said. "Let's just see what she has to say."

Already nervous, I looked around and over my shoulder, worried that someone might see us. "Do you think we should turn invisible? For our own safety," I suggested.

"We can't," Unending replied. "I think Joy put blockers in place the moment she realized we were inside. We'll have to be careful, my love."

By the time we reached the invisible membrane, I was inching closer to the edge. It had gone surprisingly well with the soul fae. Even Joy had sort of warmed up to us, and I feared we could easily screw it up if we weren't careful. But Anunit had demanded our presence. She'd taken risks herself by coming so close to the village just so she could speak to us. Then again, like I'd told Unending, she could've communicated her issue without even approaching this place.

"Something doesn't add up here," I warned her.

"We'll find out soon enough," Unending replied, carefully looking beyond the protective shield. A figure emerged from the dark jungle, where the night reigned supreme and heavy, keeping every celestial body's light away. Anunit was here, and my stomach felt heavy with lead. "What couldn't bear waiting?" my wife hissed, pressing her palms against the death magic spell. The motion served to help the Reaper see us both through the shielding membrane. The spell was definitely easier to influence from the inside than from the outside.

"Ah. That's pretty cool," Anunit replied with a flat smile. "Didn't know you could do that."

"Talk, Anunit," Unending warned her. "What was it that you couldn't communicate telepathically?"

The Reaper crossed her arms, stopping a few feet from the edge. "I wanted to check whether you were both okay. I haven't heard from you since we parted ways."

"Are you kidding me?" I snapped. "We're dealing with your damn trial, Anunit. What the hell is wrong with you?"

"I take it you've met Joy?"

Unending cleared her throat. "You cannot be serious."

"What? I like danger," Anunit replied dryly. "Plus, I wanted to be here when you got the Mixer in case Joy decides to go all wrathful on you two."

"You want to be here in case we're obliterated by Joy? You failed to mention the capabilities of her scythe, by the way," Unending shot back. "Or the fact that she's not as powerful as a First Tenner, but rather technically *a* First Tenner!"

The Reaper shrugged. "I needed you in there. The less you know, the better. Trust me. So, where is it? Where's the Mixer? I can take it off your hands now."

"We don't have it yet," I said. "We were in the middle of getting to it when you insisted on bringing us out here.

Seriously, do you ever think before you do something?"

Anunit shot me a sharp grin. "Always. Well, then. I'll be right here waiting. Please, go fetch my Mixer so we can move on to the next trial. I honestly don't have much more time to waste on you two. If you want a living body and a chance at making babies, Unending, this is how you do it."

"There's no point repeating yourself like this," I murmured.

"I was right to doubt you." Joy's voice shot from behind like a bullet aiming for the back of my head.

Unending and I spun around just as Anunit disappeared. What sort of games was she playing? Had she lured us out here for the sole purpose of discovery? Because I doubted we could stop Joy from descending into a frenzy— both Death and Loren had been clear on how easily she could blow up.

"Believe it or not, there's a solid explanation for this," Unending tried, though I could tell from the strain in her voice that we were springing for a long shot here. "I did tell you that Anunit doesn't know we're hunting her."

Joy brought her scythe forward, massive and threatening, its blade glowing a cold and unforgiving white. "I'm not buying it. You're too friendly, and it sounded to me like Anunit is doing you some kind of favor. Getting you a body? That's her specialty! Unending, you lied to me. You're consorting with a criminal," she replied. "Wait until Death hears about this."

"Death knows! She's the one who sanctioned this!" Unending replied.

"No!" Joy screamed, her eyes bulging with rage. "No! Did Spirit send you to get the Mixer? Are you lying to Death, maybe? I wouldn't put it past Spirit to get you and Anunit to do his dirty work for him!"

I gasped. "Spirit was destroyed. I thought you knew that!"

"He had tricks up his sleeve! He's not really gone! He can't be!" Joy was spiraling out of control, and the speed at which she was falling apart was unnerving. I wondered how much worse her issues had gotten since Spirit's departure and betrayal.

"We destroyed him twice," Unending said. "Once, twenty-one years ago. And the second time on Visio, where he'd left a backup of his soul. He's gone, Joy. He's gone forever."

Joy didn't put the scythe away. If anything, she was only getting angrier, if not hateful toward us. I wasn't sure how we'd be able to navigate this unexpected conflict. "Because of you. Because of you, I'll never see him again."

"Oh, Joy…" I sighed. "I thought you were over him."

She revealed the broken love chain again. "Does this look like I'm over him? It needs to be complete again. It needs him, and you… you took him away…"

How had we gotten to this point? I was utterly baffled, no longer able to even follow this fractured conversation. The only thing that I knew clearly was that Death would need to have Joy replaced in the village, because she had lost her mind in isolation. Maybe Death hadn't tried all that hard when she'd made Joy... but this Reaper needed comfort and special care more than anything else right now. And we needed to get the Mixer—this had suddenly become a dangerous challenge, since neither of us could stop Joy from lashing out.

"We can still try reasoning with her," Unending told me through telepathy. "But she looks a bit lost right now.

Or... we can do something more... extreme."

"Like?" I replied in my mind.

"Trust me?"

I sighed deeply, giving her a small smile. "Always," I said out loud.

Joy bolted toward us, light flashing from her scythe's enormous blade. Unending disappeared and caught the Reaper from behind, one arm clenched around her neck. She drove her scythe into Joy's side. The scream that followed made my blood curdle—but it was short. Too short to have been heard beyond the village's outer circle of white stone igloos. Unending had worked her magic, and Joy was on the ground, hurt and unconscious.

Panting, my wife offered a wry smile. "Well, this is not how I expected this evening to turn out, my love."

"Will she be okay?" I asked, my pulse racing.

"Yes. She'll be sore and pissed off, but yeah. I'm afraid we need to move much faster now, however," Unending replied. "I'm not sure how long she's going to stay under. I've never done this to a First Tenner before, and if Joy is as powerful as one of us, we might only have minutes."

I moved away from the protective shield and took her hand in mine. "Then we need to acquire the Mixer fast." "We'll deal with Anunit when we hand the artifact over. She's got some explaining to do for this deliberate mess. I don't even know how I'll reason with Death about this incident. I injured her precious guardian of the soul fae," Unending said.

Inching closer, I pressed my lips against hers. It was a tiny moment of peace and sweetness in the heart of madness, and we both needed it. "We'll figure it out together. Let's just get what we need and vamoose. Joy will want our heads on pikes when she wakes up."

We rushed along the stone paths, taking advantage of the fact that most of the soul fae were still by the riverbank. Loren and Sissa had the Mixer, and we needed to get them to cooperate without arousing any suspicion. Joy's lights were out, but for how long? I wasn't sure. Time wasn't on our side anymore; that much was an indisputable fact.

I wondered how our odds of success had shifted over the past five minutes, but I decided against dwelling on it too much. The stakes were incredibly high now that Unending and I were pretty much on our own, skating across unknown and dangerous territory. We only had each other to rely on.

THAYEN

We managed to confirm a few more originals on our way to the Great Dome, but we had yet to fully understand what had happened at the terrace alley near the hospital. With all our communications down, our access to information was severely limited. At least we took some comfort in knowing we'd cleared some of our people, but it didn't feel like much of a victory. We needed a better way to identify and keep track of each other with the sudden spike in clones swarming through The Shade.

Astra had done a brilliant job of memorizing the names of everyone she'd tested. The word "paladin" was now the single most important key to our safety, though we were nowhere near breathing a collective sigh of relief. It was also a short-term solution. We knew we needed something more reliable in the long-term.

The night stretched over the redwood forest, long shadows keeping us company as we headed toward the Great Dome. I could see the clearing ahead and the portal's slender silhouette, the moonlight bouncing off its stone frame with iridescent flickers. As we drew closer, the hall emerged with its brass-like skeleton and enormous glass panels. I remembered how hard Dmitri, Jovi, and Phoenix had worked to renovate it about five years ago. Of course, Corrine and Ibrahim had helped with magic, but most of what we referred to as "the new Great Dome" was due to the labor of those three.

"We need to be careful," Jericho warned as we walked. "There's no telling what we'll find there."

I had to agree. "We've spent most of our journey in the woods, away from Shadian structures. At this point, even a house could be a hot spot of danger. My biggest concern is how many shimmering portals might have opened since this morning. We don't even have an estimate for the number of clones potentially among us."

"Thayen... something's wrong," Astra interjected. The color had drained from her face as she stared ahead. She slowly raised a hand to point in the direction of the Great Dome. "Look."

We all followed her gaze, stopping for a moment as threads of smoke became visible. Some of the glass panels on the east side of the structure had been shattered. A fire had burned inside, I realized. Knowing that it was my parents' favorite council meeting spot, a sense of urgency came over me, my legs moving before I could formulate an intention to run.

"Thayen, wait!" Dafne called out. I'd left everyone behind.

Bolting through the woods, I reached the Great Dome in the blink of an eye but found myself breathless. From afar, the signs of damage and the traces of what had obviously been a violent attack weren't evident. From where I stood, however, it was painfully clear. The portal we'd used to reach the Supernatural Dimension and the In- Between had been disabled. Its misty form was gone, and I could see the nearby trees through its stone frame. The symbols had been scratched off, too.

By the time Astra, Jericho, Dafne, and Soph caught up, my heart was pounding as I stormed into the Great Dome. For a moment, I feared the worst at the sight of bodies on the ground, until I realized they were all alive and breathing. "In here!" I shouted, then rushed to my father's side first. He'd taken a blow to the head, but his wound had already healed. He was groggy—still halfway between conscious and asleep—but he was okay. I checked him from top to bottom before moving to my mother, who was on the floor next to him. Astra was already verifying their souls, apologizing for the physical discomfort. It would never be any less weird, but it was a necessary measure, and no one seemed to mind.

Mom had also suffered some crippling hits, but nothing she couldn't recover from with her vampire nature. "Mom, talk to me," I said, gently slapping her cheeks until her eyes popped open, and she saw me.

"Thay, honey!" she cried out and instantly reached out to hug me. I held her close for a moment while Dad groaned and managed to push himself into a seated position. Astra put a hand through his chest.

"I'm sorry about this," she murmured. He squirmed as she pulled her hand back, smiling. "It's you, all right..." "Ouch... Good to know," he replied, then looked at me, while Astra moved to check Mom next. "Son... where'd you come from?"

Soph, Jericho, and Dafne were already helping the others wake up. The attack had caught Corrine, Ibrahim, Claudia, Yuri, Liana, and Cameron in here. For a second, I wondered why they'd been gathered inside the Great Dome, since they were all practically retired. Xavier and Vivienne had been told to stay on Neraka, where they'd been visiting with the Manticores. Lucas and Marion, on the other hand, were nowhere to be seen.

"What happened in here?" Soph asked, loudly enough for everyone to hear. Gradually, the Shadians gathered themselves and stood, stretching their arms as they tried to overcome the headaches they seemed to have. "Clones?"

"Yes. And much to our shame, we got our asses handed to us," Ibrahim grumbled, rubbing the back of his neck, a pained expression on his face as he looked around. The council table had been shattered, and it looked like at least half the chairs had been used as weapons. The floor was covered with tiny shards of glass, and a draft was persistently blowing through the broken panels on multiple sides of the structure.

"How many of them?" Jericho asked, one hand resting on Cameron's shoulder as he checked him over to make sure he was okay. "They did quite the number on you, I see," the young dragon added, pointing at the dried blood covering half of the vampire's face.

Over in the corner, Dad fumbled through a box filled with medical and magical supplies that had survived the skirmish. He gave cloths and bottles of potions to Corrine, who quickly started using them on what injuries remained on her and the others. Most cuts and bruises had already healed, but Liana was still holding her side, blood pouring from a half-opened gash. She pressed the potion-imbibed cloth onto the wound, hissing from the pain. "Bastards. I'll torch them all, I swear. Every last one of them, including the two who had the audacity to look like my husband and me."

I gave Mom a startled look. "You were attacked by your own clones?"

"Yeah," she nodded. "That was the terrifying part. They stormed the Great Dome and mingled into the skirmish. Everything happened so fast, we didn't even know who we were fighting—our friends or their disturbingly perfect copies."

"They knew we were in here," Dad added, looking around angrily. "They counted on our confusion, and it worked. I hesitated more than once, not knowing whether I was about to tear out Ibrahim's throat or his clone's, and it blew up in my face."

Jericho cursed under his breath. "That means they were highly organized. Targeting this place because they knew who'd be in here. They were banking on confusion, and they got it."

"If they keep this up, if they intensify their attacks in this particular manner, I'm afraid we won't survive," Corrine said, her brow furrowed as she finished patching the last of Ibrahim's wounds. "There are more of them now, and it's only going to get worse."

Astra nodded slowly. "Dozens more, if not hundreds. We saw one portal opening up about a mile south of here, but I'm willing to bet breaches occurred across the island."

"What's their endgame? Are they still just coming after you, love?" Liana asked Astra.

"I don't think so," I replied, looking at the Daughter. "They tried coming after us and after Isabelle's clone, too, but they also attacked the terrace and the shop alley. The hospital was destroyed, as well." We spent a few minutes sharing what we'd learned thus far, including our fighting experiences with the clones and their peculiar devices. The more Corrine heard, the more concerned she became, becoming restless and pacing the room.

Mom and Dad gave us all the details of their battle, in a bid to share as much useful intel as possible. But we didn't have a lot to go on, just a confirmed suspicion that the clones were up to something bigger. Their scope extended beyond freeing Isabelle's doppelganger and killing Astra. They'd moved to an invasion of The Shade itself, focused on sowing confusion, on throwing us off their tracks, and on causing physical damage.

The conclusions I'd begun to draw were starker than I'd hoped. We weren't yet defeated, but it didn't look good for our world. These clones—whoever they were, whatever they were, and wherever they'd come from—were bent on upending The Shade's peace and order. They'd accomplished too much in a narrow timeframe, and I worried more damage would be done before we even had the chance to really fight back.

"Dad!" Astra gasped as Phoenix staggered into the Great Dome. He looked dazed, blood trickling from his temple. He bumped into the doorframe before dropping to his knees. Astra was quick to reach him, her hands glowing pink as she healed his injuries, then made sure it was actually him. The more she used this ability, the smoother it seemed to go—for her and for the person being tested.

"Phoenix..." Mom murmured, joining the Daughter. They helped him back up. "What happened to you?"

"Where's Viola?" Dad asked, a frown casting shadows over his eyes.

"We were on our way here," Phoenix replied, catching his breath as Astra's healing began to affect him. "Viola, my mom and dad... they attacked. Clones of us. I don't know how my wife and I got separated. We were suddenly fighting one another. Then we were fighting the clones. It got so confusing, so fast..."

Dad gave me a sideways glance. "I see they've found their favorite strategy."

"Where's Mom?" Astra insisted, gripping her father's shoulders, desperation sharpening her voice as she waited for a better answer than what Phoenix had to offer.

"I don't know. I woke up on the ground, my head throbbing. I realized I was closer to the Great Dome, though I'm not sure how I got there. There was no sign of her, or of Mom and Dad," he said. "I looked for them."

My mother hugged him tight, and he softened in her embrace while throwing his arm around Astra. He held them both close, his eyes shut, as he took a moment to gather himself. Silence settled over the room. It felt heavy, like stacks of iron pushing down on my shoulders. It made my heart sink, my stomach shrinking as I tried to process everything.

Dad looked at me. "How did you five make it all the way here?"

"We stayed close, and we're using a safe word," I said. "We'll share the word with you. Paladin. It's how we're able to keep track of the originals in this place, at least for the time being."

"However, we do need more," Astra replied. "This is woefully overwhelming, and I'm afraid I'm not enough under these circumstances."

"We had Soul, Kelara, Voss, and Chantal with us, but they headed east. They should be on their way here by now," Jericho added. "Or so we're hoping. Kelara gave Thayen a way to reach out in case we needed them, which we did, but it didn't work. Either that, or something happened. But we agreed to circle back to the Great Dome eventually and then decide where we'd go afterward. They know the safe word, too. We're hoping they'll still show up…"

"The idea was to give it to as many originals as possible, to make sure we didn't bring any clones into the fold later down the line. Without a clear idea of what the enemy is planning, we didn't know what else to do." Dafne sighed.

Soph nodded once. "At least we're confirming some people along the way. When we meet them again, we'll be able to confirm them without Astra shoving her hands into their chests."

"The idea being to not let Astra get close to a doppelganger posing as one of us, yes. I understand. Very good thinking," Dad said approvingly with a slight smile. "Well done."

Some of us were together again—I was grateful to have my parents back—but Astra was understandably terrified, wondering about her mother and grandparents. Phoenix promised her they would eventually find them. "For the time being, we need to stick together and move forward," he said.

"Speaking of sticking together, why were you all gathered here?" Soph asked, trying to steer the conversation away from Viola's unknown whereabouts. Mom had already suggested that she was out there, much like Hazel and Tejus, trying to figure out where to go next. The clones had done a marvelous job of breaking them up, but they hadn't defeated us yet.

"We were trying to ascertain whether it's time to enable the covert ops," Dad said. "Given these trying times, I figured Hansa and Jax could get the protocol going."

"Wait, covert ops?" I replied. "What covert ops are you talking about?"

"A long time ago, after we destroyed Ta'Zan, Sofia, Hansa, Jax, and I sat down and put together a task force," Dad explained. "It was kept secret over the years, with only a few aware of its existence. The agents remain dormant until needed. Once the protocol is activated, they will begin implementing secret defense measures throughout The Shade. We designed the program in case of an invasion. We didn't want another Ta'Zan to come along and think he can destroy us."

Corrine smiled. "It's actually brilliant because maybe ten people know about it, all of us elders. Not even Ben or Rose were ever made aware of its presence."

"Not for a lack of trust, mind you," Mom interjected. "We just felt it was safer to have it classified. Given what we're dealing with now, I'm sure you see the benefit of such secrecy."

"I most certainly do," I replied. "But with our comms down, how will you be able to get the protocol going?

How are the agents activated? And who are they?"

"And what does the whole operation actually entail?" Astra added.

Dad took a deep breath and let it out slowly. "The lack of comms isn't an issue. It's a visual signal, and it will be launched by Corrine. It will be visible for an entire day from any part of The Shade. As soon as the sleeper agents see it, they will be activated. It's a complex work of magic, courtesy of Corrine and Ibrahim here..." He paused to look at Astra. "Once they're activated, the agents are to report here to the Great Dome for further instructions. Hopefully, by then we'll have another Reaper or two coming in to help us. You'll be overwhelmed otherwise. The operation itself was never fully defined, since there were so many possible scenarios to consider. In this case, verifying originals is paramount, so that's what we'll focus on."

"It's really a defense protocol," Mom added. "It's the best we can offer to counter the current threat."

The more I thought about it, the more concerned I became. Yes, it was the best we could do, but it wasn't enough. The clones were highly prepared and ridiculously well organized. They had weapons and devices unknown to us, capable of shattering our defenses and reducing many of us to bumbling messes. "We're not prepared for something of this level or amplitude," I said. "I mean, who could see it coming, right? Without additional testing capabilities, how will the Shadians differentiate between originals and clones? This will inadvertently impact the civilians."

"I'll launch the covert ops signal. That way we'll have forces headed this way. Maybe the clones don't know about this protocol," Dad replied. "Meanwhile, you need to go out and catch or destroy as many of these clones as you can. You need to keep verifying Shadians with Astra and sending them over here. If we form a defense cluster around the Great Dome, it'll keep the clones away. I doubt they'd be foolish enough to attack us where we're strongest."

"That sounds reasonable," Liana said, hooking an arm through Cameron's. "Meanwhile, my man and I will go find Lumi. Hopefully, we'll get the original and not a doppelganger who tries to pulverize us both. Lumi has a way of reaching out to Nethissis. More Reapers are needed, and I see no other way of getting the word out to them."

I agreed. "I'll keep the team as it is, if they're willing." Glancing around, I noticed Jericho, Dafne, and Soph were grinning like devils. They weren't just willing. They were eager to join me in what came next. I looked to Astra. "We need you. Can you do this?"

"Yes. Derek is right. We have to verify more people and increase the defense circle here. We'll have something safe to come back to this way." She took Phoenix's hands in hers. "You have to stay here. When Soul and the others come back, use them. Maybe get Kelara to stick around and send Soul with another small team to gather additional originals. And if we find Mom, I'll make sure she stays with us, okay?"

Phoenix took her in his arms, hugging her tightly as he hid his face in her bright pink hair. "I will, honey. And you take care of yourself out there. Come back to me. You and your mother…"

Time wasn't our friend, but at least we hadn't run out of options. Bracing ourselves for the worst, we bid our elders farewell and headed out, determined to restore the balance in The Shade. Behind us, a thick pillar of orange smoke rose, billowing toward the moon. It glowed from within, like a magical beacon that would easily be spotted from anywhere on the island.

"The beacon," I muttered, taking a second to admire it.

"It's starting," Astra said. "The war we never thought we'd have to fight."

"Well, I'm the kind who gets bored easily," Jericho replied. "At least I'll have plenty of entertainment along the way."

Dafne chuckled. "You really have found a positive side in all this."

"You're a silver lining, too," Jericho shot back with a wink. It made the ice dragon blush as she looked away, and we left the Great Dome behind.

I had no idea how this would end. But I had one hell of a team to work with, and everything to lose. The clones were up to something. My glamoring would come in handy, provided we managed to take one or more of these fiends alive. As we headed north, back to where Phoenix said his group had fought with doppelgangers, I hoped we'd find Viola, Hazel, and Tejus soon. I hoped we'd get more intel and understand what the enemy wanted. I hoped we'd all survive.

But Astra was right. This was a war we were walking into, and we were blind. I dreaded what would happen once the conflict spilled into the civilian areas. The panic. The suspicions that would lead to tragic accidents. We had to move fast in a thickening darkness over which we had no control.

ASTRA

(DAUGHTER OF PHOENIX AND VIOLA)

*D*ad knew I would stop at nothing to find Mom. I was scared, but I also knew she wouldn't be easily defeated. A Daughter had some weight in this world, and deep down I doubted the clones would be stupid enough to take her. What truly horrified me was that they might push to kill her instead—but at least I knew that hadn't happened yet. I would've felt our spiritual connection become severed. No, Mom was alive somewhere. I'd find her.

The redwood forest seemed quiet, perhaps eerily so. My senses were going haywire, proof that more shimmering portals had opened in this area. Everything was wrong. It was as if each particle in the air had turned into a needle, pricking my skin.

"Thayen..." I managed, breaking into a cold sweat as we continued to head for the northern edge of the redwoods. "Thayen, there were portals open here."

"Portals? Plural?" he asked, giving me a concerned look. Our trek came to a halt as the others gathered around me. I had trouble breathing, overwhelmed not only by the sensory supercharge but also by my own emotions. My dad had barely made it out of an encounter with clones. My mom was missing. My grandparents, too. Damn it, the more I thought about it, the more it sank in, wreaking havoc in my soul. "Astra, come on.

Take a deep breath." Thayen encouraged me as he placed his hands on my shoulders. "In and out. In, count to three, then out, count to three."

I followed his advice, inhaling until my lungs could bear no more. I held it in for one, two… three seconds, then slowly let it out. One… two… three. A few more rounds of this, and the sharp pain in the back of my neck vanished. My skin no longer felt as though it had been set ablaze. I was coming back to something more stable, and I had Thayen to thank for it.

"Yes, portals." I resumed my earlier statement under Dafne, Jericho, Soph, and Thayen's watchful eyes. "Multiple. I think we're looking at way more clones than our worst-case scenarios so far."

Jericho frowned. "They're probably spreading out. And I doubt they're all looking to attack the Shadians; otherwise, we would've heard plenty of commotion already."

"Sparky's right," Dafne said, drawing a raised eyebrow from the dragon-fae. "I think they have specific targets and missions for this invasion, and not all of them are about a weaponized offense."

"We should stick to our to-do list, then," Soph said.

"Yes. It's still our best way forward," Thayen replied. "And since we are heading north, we should certainly check the Vale. It's mostly human, and I wonder if the clones have any interest in it. To this point, they've attacked the hospital because of Isabelle's clone, the terrace alley where some of our GASP officers were gathered, and the Great Dome where the GASP founders were meeting. I'm not sure about other places yet, but I can definitely see a pattern."

Resuming our fast walk through the redwood forest, I began to see what Thayen was conveying. "They're attacking GASP objectives, right?"

"We're the primary armed force here. The defenders. If they want to attack The Shade, they take out the military spots first," Thayen said.

There were only theories and spoken fears for us to contend with, and we had these for company on our way to the Vale. Naturally, we were tense and on edge by the time we got there. It looked peaceful. Quiet. Too quiet, much like the woods. As if The Shade itself had caught on that something awful had happened, and something worse would soon come.

The humans were mostly out and about, clustered closer toward the town center. The streetlamps flickered in the darkness, their amber light cast over the cobblestone streets. Houses rose ahead, lining the sidewalks with manicured gardens and open windows. It was nice and warm outside, like every other summer evening. The cafés were open around the central plaza. Beyond, I could see the schools and the administrative buildings silhouetted against the dimly lit starry sky.

If this were any normal day, I would've liked nothing more than to stop by the ice cream shop and spend forty- five minutes simply trying to decide which flavors to get. Simpler times were long behind us, however, and nothing our eyes registered could truly be trusted.

"It seems okay," Dafne said quietly. "Though I don't know as much about the humans' social life as I probably should."

"Since you're half human yourself?" Jericho chuckled.

She shrugged. "Yeah. I spend most of my time in the Black Heights. My parents are there. My whole ice dragon clan is there."

"Just because it seems okay doesn't mean it actually is," Soph warned. "They could all be clones just waiting to pounce on us."

At first look, no one was paying attention. People were just walking up and down the street, stopping by shops, laughing, exchanging greetings, and forming groups to head into town for the night. But Soph had a point. It could be an act. Or maybe the paranoia had finally gotten to us. There was no way for me to tell without checking each of the humans, and that involved way too much contact for my safety.

"We should definitely head to the armory behind the training halls sooner rather than later, and grab some pulverizer weapons," Soph said, eyeing the passersby. "I know we never used them on the island, but clearly times are changing. How many do you keep in the armory?"

"About a dozen. But if the covert ops have instructions to use pulverizer weapons in case of an invasion, there might be more stored elsewhere. Listen, let's do a tour of the Vale and see what it's like, first," Thayen suggested. "We'll pay attention to every single gesture. Anything that's out of place, we check it out."

"And if they seem normal?" I asked, wondering if it would come down to me to verify everybody from the Vale. I was already tired, and I didn't even want to know what toll such an operation would take on my rapidly depleting energy levels.

"We select a group of humans and bring them into the loop so they can keep an eye on things around here, then head for the armory and grab the weapons. Soph's right about them," Thayen replied. "If crap hits the fan here, at least a handful of the humans will know what to expect, and they'll head straight for the Great Dome to join the central defense circle."

That made plenty of sense. We took the main street leading to the town plaza, where a gushing water fountain marked the very center of the Vale. Spending some time in the area, we paid attention to the smallest details, like Thayen had advised. Nothing seemed out of the ordinary. If anything, I was beginning to feel as though this was the last place the clones would think of hijacking.

Recognizable figures emerged from one of the side streets as we walked toward the northern edge of the town. Voss, Chantal, and Richard spotted us, their eyes widening with surprise. My heart skipped a beat, thrilled to see some familiar faces again. Soph was just as excited, but Thayen stopped her before she could raise a hand to wave at them.

"Careful," he whispered. "Safety protocols first."

"Right. You're absolutely right," Soph replied.

Thayen put on a smile, and we mirrored his expression as we looked to Voss, Chantal, and Richard. I felt terrible playing this part, but it had to be done. We'd learned enough about the clones to know that they were most adept at blitz attacks.

"We were just on our way to the Great Dome!" Voss said as they reached us. He tried to shake Thayen's hand, but the vampire stepped back.

"Safe word," he demanded.

"Dude, we picked Richard up along the way," Voss replied, seemingly in no mood. He was angry. "We lost Soul and Kelara. We got separated in a clone attack. Don't you want to hear how that went?"

"Safe word, then we can talk," Thayen shot back, his claws already extending.

Voss shook his head slowly. "Fine. Have it your way." A split second later, his wings burst wide, each feather replaced with stainless steel blades. We were dealing with clones, and the war had just spilled into the Vale.

"Did you hear him?" Chantal's copy sneered, mimicking Thayen in a derogatory mumble. "Safe word. Safe word. Like that'll do you any good."

The fires of Eritopia burned through me, insatiably pink and furious, as my skin began to glow. There wasn't much left in me, but I was willing to put it all into this battle. I took a step forward, which was enough to make the three clones flinch slightly. "Remember what Derek said," I told Thayen. "We should try to take out as many of them as possible."

Richard's clone bared his fangs at us, growling.

"We'll need one alive so I can push my glamoring further," Thayen said.

"Fine by me," Jericho muttered, fireballs bursting in the palms of his hands as he assumed an attack position.

Around us, the humans of the Vale realized that something bad was about to go down. Some were quick and wise enough to move back and slip through the adjacent alleys in a bid to distance themselves from the impending brawl. Others gathered on the edge of the sidewalk, foolishly curious.

I waved my hand and released a wide barrier, enough to push them back and send them a message. A few of them stumbled and nearly fell over, but soon they all understood that this was the worst place for them to be.

And as Richard's double pounced, I unleashed my Daughter powers. I'd had enough of these clones. I'd had enough of the madness and the mindless violence.

TRISTAN

drenaline coursed through my body, making me unable to sit still for more than a second at a time. Unending and I had left Joy unconscious and under a death magic sleeping spell that was bound to wear off at some point. Anunit had pushed us into a conflict with the extremely volatile guardian Reaper, and while we'd yet to understand why she'd chosen to show up in the first place, we knew she was waiting beyond the shield. We had to deliver what we'd promised.

In order to do that, however, we needed Loren or Sissa to take us to the Mixer. It was inside the village somewhere. "I feel so guilty right now," I muttered as we cautiously headed back to the riverbank. The campfire was roaring, and the soul fae were still gathered in their familial clusters, laughing and eating and drinking. Loren threw his head back at something his daughter had just said, and his face lit up when he saw us.

"Tristan, Unending!" he exclaimed. "Welcome back!"

"We'll be okay," my wife replied before she gave Loren the broadest smile she could muster. "You seem to be having a good time. Forgive us for stepping away. We just had some private matters to discuss."

Loren waved her fabricated concern away. "Worry not, please. Have a seat. Sissa was telling me about her cousins' attempt to leave the village yesterday. I had no idea they'd even tried it."

We sat down beside the king and his daughter. I was already restless—squirming and constantly looking around—until Unending nudged me in the ribs, reminding me of how important it was that we play it cool. It wasn't in my nature to deceive or to lie, particularly to seemingly good people like Loren and Sissa. But we'd made a promise, and we intended to follow through no matter what.

"How did that happen?" Unending asked, doing a remarkable job of sounding calm and casual. I was terrified of even opening my mouth.

"Well, they were curious. We all are, up to a point," Sissa replied, the shadow of a smile dancing across her face. It was quickly followed by a resigned sadness. "But we grow out of it. My cousins are still young and somewhat foolish. Despite the warnings, they insisted on seeing what's beyond the shield."

"What did Joy have to say about that?" Unending asked. The mention of the Reaper's name made me shiver. Any minute now, she could be headed back here, and I didn't want us to stick around much longer. If we had convinced her that Anunit had been foolish and that the mission was still focused on taking the Mixer, we might get away with it. But Joy had simply lost it upon hearing of Spirit's double demise—whether it was news to her or not, it didn't really matter. She was falling apart at the seams and looking for people to take it out on. The soul fae would bend her into submission. Unending and I were just punching bags, at this point. My wife had a plan, though, and she was a smooth talker, so I trusted her to lead this conversation in a more favorable direction.

Sissa giggled. "Joy isn't keen on words in general. She just smacked them and sent them back to my father to tell him what they'd done. But they were too afraid of him, so they came to me for advice. Apparently, they tried to use knives to tear holes in the protective shield."

Loren burst into laughter. He doubled over with tears in his eyes. "Silly children... Like cutlery was going to help... By the heavens!"

"Well, they learned their lesson," Sissa replied, trying not to chuckle, though her cheeks were as red as roses at this point. "I hope you'll forgive them, Father."

"There's nothing to forgive. Have you forgotten the time you tried to get out?"

Unending raised an eyebrow. "Something tells me the apple didn't fall far from the tree, Your Majesty."

"What?" Loren stared at us, slightly confused.

"Like father, like daughter?" I said, going for an expression that might've been more familiar to him. The king put on the proudest grin.

"You're damn right," he replied. "I think every single one of the more curious among us has attempted to leave this place without fully understanding the repercussions or the dangers we face out there in the world. In time, we all learn our place and accept our fate. We're safer here. The young ones are always stubborn, so it doesn't come as a surprise when one or more of them try to do what we once attempted."

"I see. That makes sense," Unending said.

Sissa smiled at her father. "You were just as mischievous?"

"Didn't you hear Tristan? Like father, like daughter. Where do you think you got your rebellious streak from?" Loren shot back.

I glanced over my shoulder, checking to see if Joy had come to. There was no sign of her. Just white stone igloos and blossoming orchids and delicate, narrow paths that zigzagged through the village. The night had fully settled, and the stars were shining down on us. The smell of burning wood filled my nostrils, and the sound of it crackling a few feet away tickled my ears. It was nice and peaceful here, but I knew it wouldn't last. This... all this was an ephemeral illusion of peace and comfort because Anunit was still out there. Her presence—though unseen—applied enough pressure to keep me on edge.

As I covered Unending's hand with mine, I hoped she would see the urgency in my eyes. "Your Majesty, would you perhaps mind showing us the artifact?" she asked the king, and I knew we were finally headed into the last stage of our stay among the soul fae. "As much as we enjoy your company and your wonderful hospitality, my husband and I must keep moving. We're trying to catch Anunit before she flees to another location. Time is of the essence."

Loren and Sissa exchanged glances. "I think Joy should be present for this," the king said.

"She doesn't have anything to do with it," Unending replied, maintaining a faint smile. But Loren was not so easily persuaded.

"It's a death magic artifact, and Joy has asked to be a part of any operation that involves the Mixer. This happened telepathically, long before we sat down for dinner. Personally, I don't care about who sanctioned this entire endeavor. Out of respect for Joy, I'd like for her to be involved in the hand-over."

Unending nodded slowly. "I see. Completely understandable, of course. However, I only wish to see it. I'd like to better understand what it is about it that has Anunit so interested. You can hand it over to me when Joy comes back. If you'd like, I can reach out to her telepathically."

"By all means, please do," Loren said, then got up. "Fine, let us return to my chambers. I keep it there. It's the safest place in the village, as every inch of it is warded with death magic."

"Even if—by some miracle—a Reaper like this Anunit you speak of did breach the protective shield, she would never be able to get the artifact out of my father's house," Sissa added.

Unending looked at me. "Joy obviously didn't want anyone to try anything funny. I suppose she'll be the one to break the wards when it's time to hand it over to us." She moved her focus back to Loren. "I've let her know that we're looking to leave soon. She should be with us shortly."

"That's good. In the meantime, let us go," Loren said.

We followed him back to his house. Sissa stayed by the riverbank, per his request, to entertain the rest of their extended family. She wouldn't be needed for the showcase, and I breathed a sigh of relief, since I certainly didn't want her involved in everything that would soon follow.

"Have you told Death about what happened with Joy?" I asked Unending through our telepathy.

"Yes. She hasn't been able to reach Joy, or Joy isn't answering, which might be because I knocked her out," she replied. "We still have a green light."

"Will that get Joy off our backs?"

"Hopefully. You've seen the ego on that Reaper," Unending said. "Combined with her precarious mental state... I shudder to even think about it. We need to be quick about this, either way. It's just the two of us against Joy, since Death coming here would trigger Anunit's alarms, and we'd lose that little devil before we're done with her. We can't drag the soul fae into our skirmish with Joy, either. Another Death directive."

"So, get the Mixer, one way or another, then get out before Joy finds us still here," I replied. "Sounds like the kind of mess we're used to..."

Tension gripped me by the throat, but I kept my cool as we made our way down the stone path and stopped outside the main entrance to the king's quarters. Loren turned around for a second and smiled. "Welcome to my humble abode," he said, then went inside. We joined him in what appeared to be a small lobby, barely ten feet wide and long. Pottery artwork adorned the walls, mostly white and blue against the pale gray paint. The details on each piece were absolutely exquisite—the soul fae must have worked on these with slim and sharp tools, likely the size of toothpicks.

Some depicted casual scenes of the soul fae plucking fruits from the orchard or squeezing nectar from the orchids. Others gave glimpses of group celebrations and the building of houses. A few portrayed creatures I had never seen before. "What are these?" I asked, compelled by my own curiosity.

Loren followed my gaze and smiled. "Monsters from our ancient mythology." He pointed to one particular creature with giant horns and hooves for feet. It looked a lot like the goat hybrids I'd found in Greek mythology. "This one is a Pashin. He steals the dreams of children, and they grow up to be bland and empty vessels." He then showed me an octopus-like monster. "And this is the Soul Eater. Each of its limbs can enter one's chest and pluck out the spirit to eat it."

"Okay. Wow..." I murmured.

"Yes, I'm afraid we have scary stories passed down to us across many generations," the king replied, slightly amused. "They're all children's tales, however. None of this is real. I've certainly never seen a Pashin or a Soul Eater."

"Maybe they date back to an era before you were all enclosed here," Unending suggested. "These could have been dwellers of Rothko before the mass extinction that nearly wiped your people out."

Loren shrugged. "Perhaps. No one can confirm this, so I'd rather consider these tales part of our folklore and nothing else. There is a basement beneath this house where the most ancient of our texts are preserved. The artists who made these ceramic pieces were given access to the original writings for inspiration."

He walked us through a couple more rooms, including a lounge area with plush and furry sofa-style seaters and a wider chamber featuring a dining table and wicker chairs. Despite being the king, Loren seemed to be a fan of simplicity. There was nothing to denote opulence, and I figured living in a small village had played a fundamental part in this. No one here cared if he had fancier linens, and they didn't have any precious metals to mine for, either. From what I'd been able to gather thus far, the soul fae had been making do with what their isolated patch of land had to offer.

We reached a small wooden door on the eastern wall of the dining room. Loren produced a key from around his neck and showed it to us. "The first of many wards," he said, unlocking the door. As soon as he opened it, a cold draft burst out, sending shivers down my spine.

Ahead, pitch-black darkness awaited.

"I must admit, the simplicity of your home is impressive," Unending replied. "Of all the kings I've met in my long lifetime, you are the most modest."

"It's all I know," Loren said. "From our ancient texts, I understand that there was once a hierarchy for our people. The upper class, the middle class, the lower class. The first had fortunes and land titles. The second had functions and homesteads, thriving on what the earth gave them. The third lived mostly in poverty or servitude. I've read stories about our glorious kings. Fair princesses and valiant warriors. That's all that is left of our civilization. Memories imprinted on thin pieces of stone and crumbling sheets of paper. But I have no need for riches or a palace, when our world is so small. Besides, wealth does not define me. It's my ability to lead the people and make sure they understand why we belong here and nowhere else that truly counts. Everything else is... nothing."

"That makes sense," Unending replied. "Your role is important, but it doesn't require the artifices of monarchy to set you apart."

"My bloodline is my wealth." Loren chuckled. "Now, come on into the basement. I bet you're going to love it."

We went down a narrow set of wooden stairs. Each step creaked as we descended into the underground, and I nearly lost my breath upon realizing exactly how big this place was. It wasn't an average basement. At first glance, it seemed as big as the village, with tunnels going in different directions and stretching for at least two or three miles, if not more, judging by the protective shield's arch width.

Shelves covered the walls on both sides of each corridor, and there was barely a spare inch anywhere. Rolled-up scrolls, leather-bound manuscripts, stone and clay tablets, stacks of yellowing papers—everything the soul fae had written over the years, according to Loren, since before the great extinction. Stories and poems. Philosophical ramblings. Novels and novellas. Religious texts. Legal documents and yearly reports from what had once been the palace's administrative wing. There were sketches, too, and illustrations, compendiums of mythology and legends of every nation of the soul fae.

These tunnels were all that remained of a civilization that had once spanned continents, each of its people renowned for their ability to bend spirits. This planet had been merciless in its destruction, and I really couldn't blame Death for choosing to save them.

"Here..." Loren muttered as we headed south down a dimly lit corridor. This one was different from the others. Its shelves were loaded with various objects—most of them mundane, such as candleholders, reading glasses, shoes and pots, porcelain drinking sets, trays, and other items used on a daily basis by their ancestors. "This is the reliquary of times gone by. It has historical value, more than anything else. It's the only place where you'll find jewelry, by the way. The real stuff, not what we weave with leather strings and river pebbles. Look."

He stopped by one of the shelves where several decorative boxes had been stored. Dust covered them, but I could still make out the mother-of-pearl inlays and brass edges. Loren opened one to reveal a stunning set of earrings and a matching necklace. The rubies stood out because they were considerably larger than similar jewels I'd seen and were a vivid, bloody red. I couldn't look away. The gems were framed by tiny diamonds and mounted on white gold. They looked old, parts of the facets chipped away. The original sheen was gone, and rust had settled in the tiny nooks between each element, but they were still beautiful. Still eye-catching.

"How did these pieces survive for so long?" Unending asked. "We're talking millions of years here. Even metal changes its properties over such a period of time. Why hasn't everything in here turned to compressed carbon?"

Loren smiled. "Death was kind enough to cast a spell on this place when my ancestors built it. The magic slowed time to such a degree that it seems as though it has stopped altogether. Eventually, maybe in a billion years, what you see in this place will be nothing but dirt. In the meantime, my people will start remaking and rewriting everything so that when the originals fade away, our future generations will still know what this is and what it means."

We continued down the corridor until we reached the far end. A multitude of death magic symbols were scribbled on the wall, and Unending couldn't help but run her fingers over the runes. "These are the wards you mentioned. Aside from the key, that is," she murmured.

"Indeed. But only a part of them. Death had the ceilings and the floors inscribed, and Joy added spells of her own. I doubt there's an inch in this place that hasn't been warded, all for the sake of protecting the objects within. No one can walk out of here with the Mixer, that much I can tell you. Not even I." Loren searched through one of the bottom shelves and took out a box, barely the size of a shoebox. "This is it..."

Gingerly lifting the lid, he showed us the contents. The Mixer was nothing like how I'd imagined it. It was a ring-shaped object, about as wide as a regular bracelet, and I wondered how it worked in bringing multiple scythes together. The interior of the band was etched with a multitude of death magic runes, every inlay filled with some type of black crystal. The exterior was smooth gold, matte, lacking the usual metallic sheen. It was an odd thing, but its craftsmanship was out of this world.

"The Mixer," Unending whispered, her galaxy eyes widening as she beheld the object, barely a couple of feet from her reach. Loren put the lid back on rather abruptly, nearly startling her.

"When Joy comes back, I will happily hand it over. Until then, and assuming you're not the biggest fans of large gatherings such as the one currently unfolding along the riverbank, would you two like to come upstairs? I believe I have more ceramic art you might be interested in," he said.

We nodded and allowed him to lead us back into the house, but just as Loren reached the wooden door, Unending tapped her blade against his shoulder. He dropped like a log, face down on the floor in a deep sleep. "I am sorry about this, Your Majesty," she said, then looked at me. "We have to hurry. I need to find the wards that keep the Mixer from leaving this place."

There was very little time to do that. Loren wasn't the problem, of course, but rather the Reaper we'd knocked out earlier. The Reaper with the strength of a First Tenner who'd snapped upon seeing Anunit—though her incontrollable rage had very little to do with our mischievous runaway. Joy was going to cut our heads off unless we got what we came for and left the village before she woke up. Or maybe Death would manage to hold her back. We'd had trouble reasoning with Joy before, however, and she'd absolutely lost it this time around.

"Joy's issues stem from isolation, right?" I asked. "Or some design faults, too?"

Rushing down the creaky wooden steps, I swallowed the nervous lump in my throat. The first trial was proving to be more difficult and more dangerous than we'd expected, and it was Anunit's fault. If only she'd stuck to telepathic communication. I worried she'd done this on purpose, but I couldn't understand why she would gleefully sabotage her own operation.

"Yes. And I doubt she'll let us go without a fight. Hence our need to hurry before she comes to," Unending said. "Death's order is usually enough to hold a Reaper back, but you saw her earlier... completely unhinged. I think the isolation, like you said, plus some sloppy Reaper design work on Death's part might have screwed with Joy's spiritual circuits."

"I still don't get why Anunit insisted on showing up. She was basically the catalyst for this hot mess."

"Me neither." She sighed.

We were missing some information, and I was determined to fill in the blank once we got out of here. That was our greatest challenge at the moment—retrieving the Mixer and escaping from the village before Joy's wrath caught up with us.

THAYEN

*J*ericho and Dafne stood by, ready to intervene if needed, but Astra unleashed what I assumed was the little Daughter energy she had left, dropping to one knee right afterwards. It burst out as wave upon wave of glimmering pink waves that crashed into the clones before they could touch us. She was back up a few seconds later, though I wasn't sure she'd have much fight left in her. Richard's doppelganger fell backward hard, crying out from the pain her power had inflicted. "Don't say I didn't want to help." Jericho sighed, crossing his arms.

Voss and Chantal's clones managed to duck, dodging the worst of the hit. They bolted toward Astra, but Soph and I were quick to stop them, launching into combat without hesitation. "We really need one of them alive!" I shouted, as Chantal's clone tried to burn me to a crisp. Dafne knocked her away with a swing of her leg, and the clone landed at Soph's feet.

"I got it from here," Soph said.

I spotted Astra close by. She had reached Richard's copy, her hands flashing pink like an intermittent beacon. Her arsenal had definitely been close to depletion, but she wasn't done tormenting him—not after everything he and his ilk had put her through. Astra grabbed him by the throat, the pink glow sinking into his skin. He screamed in agony as the energy spread and covered him whole, while she became paler with every passing second.

One of Voss's bladed wings nearly slit my throat open. It was time to try something new, as the circumstances no longer allowed for more classical combat. He'd already whipped out his black spray bottle, eager to use it on me. I hadn't tried my glamoring on a moving target before, but what other option did I have?

I needed to get to Astra before she hurt herself. I could hear Richard's clone's screams turning into tortured gurgling as the pink flames consumed every inch of his flesh and bones and skin. What she was doing to him was the stuff of nightmares, and I knew she had to be extremely furious to resort to such gruesome methods. Astra had always been the peacemaker, yet the clones had brought out the darker side of her.

"You're not going anywhere," Voss's double hissed, then tried to spray me with the black stuff. I put both hands out and released the mental lassos I'd been brewing. I felt the connection forcibly establish. The sharp tips pierced his being and took hold of the fake soul he had inside. He stilled, horror settling across his face as he realized what was happening.

"On your knees," I ordered him, my voice low and cold as ice. My skin tingled, anger heating up my insides, making my stomach tighten into a fizzling clump of anxiety and rage. "On your knees!" I snapped, and Voss's clone was forced to kneel on the ground.

Soph had her foot on Chantal's clone's throat, boot pressing hard until I could hear the bones snapping. The daemon princess looked at me, one eyebrow raised. "You said keep one alive. Voss's cheap-ass copy is one. We don't need her, do we?"

I shook my head.

Chantal's clone opened her palms, fireballs forming in angry shades of yellow and orange. She was about to torch Soph, but she wasn't as fast as she would've wanted. A split second later, her spine was crushed, and the fire fae knock-off was dead. With Voss's double under my surprisingly effective control, I was able to briefly check on Astra again. Nothing was left of Richard's doppelganger except for a small pile of black ashes.

Astra was on all fours, taking deep breaths, heaving whenever she had to exhale. "Soph, help her, please!" I said, then shifted my focus back to Voss's clone. I heard Jericho and Dafne as they got closer to Astra, as well.

She wasn't on her own, and that gave me some comfort.

The veins on Voss's clone's throat throbbed angrily, but he couldn't do anything against my firm hold on him. Soul had been so on the money with this ability. It was getting easier with each turn, to the point where I could feel the clone's fears rumbling through me like a bad stomachache. He was terrified. He'd never expected to be in this position.

"Tell me why you're here," I demanded, one ear twitching as I listened for movement and words between Soph and Astra. Most of the humans of the Vale had run away already, but I could still hear the occasional rush of footsteps nearby. They'd been scared off, yet there were the curious ones who just couldn't resist, especially considering the sudden silence that had followed after Richard's clone's bloodcurdling screams.

Voss's copy sneered, defiant despite my influence. "Screw you."

"Tell me why you're here!" I amplified my ability, imagining thousands of daggers that I could use to pierce his skin and break him into little bits and pieces. It worked. Voss's clone grunted, sweat dripping down his face as my glamoring cut through him.

He crouched from the pain, but he was resisting. I could feel the walls around him struggling to stay up, though I was pretty close to breaking them all down. Jericho scoffed. "Push him, Thayen. You can do it."

"Tell me why you're here!" I snapped.

"Ah!" Voss's clone whimpered. Finally, the sound of defeat emerged. He was a resilient bastard, but I was motivated to succeed. "Isabelle. We're... we're all here for Isabelle."

"Why?" I asked, briefly stealing a glance at a troubled Soph. Astra was looking better, one arm draped around the daemon's shoulders. At least she was upright, though the purple bruising on her hands was difficult to ignore. She'd worn herself out. I doubted she could still help us in the clone verification process, but I was thankful she was okay. "Why?" I repeated the question, eyeing Voss's copy carefully.

He muttered a curse under his breath. "She has something we need. Something she's... something she's been working hard to get for the past couple of months."

"Wait... what do you mean months?" I croaked, my blood running cold.

I'd opened up a can of worms, and I wasn't sure any of us could face what was coming. I was already beginning to regret asking. Simply knowing that Isabelle's clone had been around for two months presented a series of nightmarish scenarios along with a plethora of difficult questions. The most important one was raised by Astra.

"If she's been around for two months, why did she wait so long to try and kill me?"

"Answer her question," I commanded Voss's clone.

He was on his knees and panting, my glamoring influencing him physically and ripping through his resistance. Admittedly, I'd allowed myself a streak of meanness, focusing my ability on him like a concentrated laser beam. I wanted to tear him apart from the inside, but not before we got as much intel out of him as possible.

"Damn you..." Voss's clone blurted. "I don't know what it is. We only know it as the Object. We have orders..."

"What orders?"

Jericho came to my side. "What if he's lying about this... Object?" he whispered.

"I'm not lying!" Voss's double cried out. "Only Isabelle knows what it is. That was the whole point, so no one who got caught would snitch!"

The more the doppelganger spoke, the more questions I had. "What are your orders? Speak!"

"Argh! Sow the seeds of chaos! We were ordered to either go after our originals or attack key military points across The Shade," he replied. "The orders keep changing... we're told to go to one place, then another. We're all waiting for a green light to go after Isabelle."

"Don't call her Isabelle. She's not Isabelle, just as you're not Voss!" Astra retorted, strength returning to her wavering voice.

"Well, I am Voss. And she is Isabelle. Just not your Voss. Not your Isabelle," the clone shot back, baring his teeth in an aggressive grin.

I tightened my hold on him, ripping a groan from his throat. "What's your next move? What were you doing in the Vale? How many of you are there? Who's leading you?"

Voss's clone sighed heavily, tears streaming down his cheeks. "You can't do this to me."

"I can. And I am. Talk."

"No! No, I can't! No!" he shrieked and started toward me. It happened so fast, I didn't even register the amount of willpower it must have taken for him to break out of my hold. Either that, or I hadn't had a good grip on him to begin with.

He lunged at me, his bladed wings spreading wide. But Jericho torched him before he could even get close enough to use those sharp feathers. The fire swallowed him whole, and he screamed in agony, but it was too late. He collapsed into a charred pile of molten flesh.

"I had to," Jericho said. "Those wings were a problem."

"I know… it's okay."

Astra moved to stand beside me. "Thayen, you heard him. Their prime objective is Isabelle's doppelganger.

Whatever she spent two months impersonating our cousin for has got to be extremely important."

"Oh, it's important, all right. This freak here managed to free himself from my glamoring. He chose suicide by GASP instead of telling the truth," I replied.

Before I could formulate another thought, the horn sounded again. This time, it was much louder. Heavier, too. It pressed directly on my brain, sending throbs of pain through my skull, inflaming my temples and sending my senses into overdrive. It rang for about a minute, during which time no one dared to move.

"I think it's a signal," Soph concluded. "Look…" She pointed somewhere behind us. We all turned around to see some of the humans slipping out of the side alleys and running into the redwood forest. They were headed south.

"Those aren't Vale humans," Dafne said, her brow furrowed. "They're doing the same thing as the clones. As soon as they heard the horn…"

"So, there were copies inside the Vale, too. Why didn't they jump us?" Jericho asked, shaking his head slowly. "I swear, this is getting more confusing with every minute, and I'm not sure we'll pull through unless someone starts talking."

A sense of urgency came over me as I watched the human clones disappear between the giant redwoods. "We need to go back to Isabelle's clone. If she's their ultimate endgame, not an actual invasion of The Shade, then we have to secure her. Now!"

We started running once more. The clones had worn us out. They'd successfully sown the seeds of chaos, pushing us to doubt one another. Some of our people were missing, but if Isabelle's clone was their prime objective, then I dared hope that our friends and loved ones would return to us eventually.

Something had to give in this hot mess, because I wasn't able to make much sense of it. What had Isabelle's doppelganger taken? And who'd ordered her to take it? We had no idea what their ultimate goal was, but at least we knew where they were all headed.

Deeper in the woods, we saw more clones running in the same direction. I froze on the spot, realizing the full scope of this monstrous operation. They had no interest in attacking us this time around, but they were beating us to the finish line.

"Jericho," I said, trying to think of a faster way to reach the hospital before the swarm of clones. "I think we need to ride on your back, buddy. They'll get there before us if we go on foot."

Jericho didn't need to be told twice. A moment flittered past, and he'd burst out into his dragon form, roaring as Soph, Astra, and I climbed onto his back. Dafne seemed hesitant, giving me a weary look. "I could fly out with you," she suggested.

"Come on, we don't have the time, hurry!" I replied, and she ran up Jericho's tail, climbing behind Astra. With one flap of his wings, the dragon took off from the small clearing, sending a storm of dried leaves and twigs swirling beneath him.

I felt suddenly very small as we breached The Shade's starry sky, and Jericho began his short flight back to the hospital area. There were dozens of clones out here—at least—all of them headed in the same direction. My heart was strained, yet I couldn't give in to the fear that had been circling me like a hungry lion.

We still had work to do.

THAYEN

*R*iding Jericho had been the best idea. The hospital area was clear except for Stan and Ollie, the ghouls we'd tasked with guarding Isabelle's clone's warded room. We landed with a thud in the middle of a clearing. Dafne was the first to slip right off, helping Astra down. The Daughter was slower than usual, but considering she'd just depleted her energy by torching Richard's copy, it was a miracle she was still standing and not halfway into dream world.

Soph and I were the last to jump off Jericho's back after a brief survey of the wide clearing. The smoking rubble was the same as we'd left it. A remnant of what had once been The Shade's hospital. I remembered coming here as a kid, fresh off Visio, to get my physical checks and immunization shots. Shayla, one of our witches, had opened an office on the third floor, where I'd stop by once in a while to discuss the many nightmares I'd had for years after I'd moved here. Visio continued to haunt me for a long time before I felt like I truly belonged here.

It was all gone now, and there had been no time to fully process what this building had meant to me—not to mention the other Shadians. Taking in a deep breath, I walked over to Stan and Ollie, leaving Astra with Soph, Dafne, and Jericho for a moment, though I could still hear the dragons bickering in the background.

"Oh, for heaven's sake, put some clothes on!" Dafne said.

"I would if I had any!" Jericho replied.

Soph giggled, a sound followed by shuffling and crunching. Looking over my shoulder, I saw her extract a medical robe from a nearby pile of crumpled and still-smoking textiles and rubble. The garment was similar to what we'd found for Jericho earlier, only this one had been half burnt. There must've been a supply locker here before the flames. "It'll do," Jericho grumbled, snatching it from Soph's hand. "Thanks."

"Hey, fellas," I said to Stan and Ollie. Their big black eyes sparkled with recognition as I approached them. "Have you seen your Reaper partners since we last saw you?"

Both ghouls shook their heads, letting out simultaneous low growls that sent shivers down my spine. I didn't have to speak ghoulish to understand that they were concerned. Peeking through the glass panel of Isabelle's clone's room, I found her still sitting at the table, her hands cuffed and her expression just as sullen as before. I pressed on the two-way speaker button mounted near the glass panel so she could hear me. "I see you're still here."

"Took you forever," she muttered.

"We ran into some of your friends," I replied.

The doppelganger grinned coldly. "Yeah, I heard the signals. They're coming for me. You know that, right?" "What is it that you got from this place? What is it that you had to spend two months pretending to be Isabelle to get?" I demanded. "We thought you'd replaced her just a few days ago. Not months."

My blood ran cold as I wondered where the real Isabelle was. Where she'd been kept for so long... and if she was even still alive. I was genuinely afraid to ask her clone about it. There was little patience left in me to deal with her games and riddles. I was determined to get the truth out of her, one way or another, but time wasn't on our side. Not with who knew how many copies racing toward the hospital as I stood here and watched Isabelle's double giggle in her seat.

"Wouldn't you like to know?" she replied.

"I most definitely would."

Jericho drew my attention. "Thayen, we have to go. Soph can already hear boots on the ground. At least dozens, maybe even more than a hundred."

I gave him a quick glance, training my ears on the sounds around us. I heard the distant rumble, too. Thuds and twigs breaking. Dried leaves crumbling beneath the soles of their boots. Short breaths and swishing past the redwoods. They were less than a mile away and coming in fast. If we didn't move within the next five minutes, the headway we'd made by flying with Jericho would have been for nothing.

"As much as I would love to stick around and glamor you into submission," I said to Isabelle's clone, "there's no time, and I have no intention of letting you go with your knockoff buddies."

I released the speaker button, then looked at Stan and Ollie. "You two should head out and find Soul and Kelara. We know nothing of their group's whereabouts, and I'm starting to get seriously worried. The comms are still down, not just for us but for the Reapers, as well. I have no way of reaching out to them."

"Thayen, we have to take her somewhere safe, as far from here as possible," Astra said. "Stan and Ollie need to know where we're going. We might as well regroup there when they do find Soul and Kelara's crew."

"Right. You're absolutely right," I replied, thinking for a moment. "Crap, where are we taking her?"

Dafne raised a hand. "Might I make a suggestion?"

"Of course," I said.

"The Port." Dafne sighed. "The underground cells, to be specific. Not everybody knows about them, and I figure it'll buy us some time because it's such a maze down there."

"That's a really good idea," Jericho agreed. "Especially since the clones are using intel from the originals, though I'm not sure how they're getting it—"

"Probably magic," Dafne said, cutting him off.

"Yeah. Makes sense. The Port is definitely our best bet. Not everyone can navigate those tunnels. Most in our generation have never even been down there," Jericho said.

I nodded once. "The Port it is, then." Pressing my palm against the charmed reader on Isabelle's clone's door, I listened for the lock's click as it gave me access. "Don't try anything stupid," I warned her as I unhooked her cuffs from the table-mounted ring and yanked her upright.

"Wherever you go, I go." Isabelle's doppelganger chuckled. "At least this way I get to watch you die in pain, cousin."

"I'm not your cousin. You're not Isabelle," I hissed and dragged her out of the room and away from the hospital's piles of scorched rubble. It would take forever for me to shake off the charred smell of this place.

"We need to move. Now," Soph said, her voice wavering. "Something is coming."

"You're damn right something is coming," Isabelle's clone replied.

Before any of us could even take a step toward the Port, we were frozen on the spot. A high-pitched sound cut through my brain. I gasped, bucking under the sudden pressure. I had never experienced pain like this before, and I wasn't the only one. Jericho snarled as he fell to his knees, clutching his head with both hands. Dafne screamed, her legs shaking, but she fought against the agony, stubbornly remaining upright.

Soph bared her fangs, looking somewhere behind us, while Astra whimpered and wobbled. The daemon held her close, and I followed her gaze. Something big was coming. I could see its enormous figure treading through the forest and knocking the redwoods aside like they were nothing more than matchsticks.

"Dad?" Jericho managed, blinking rapidly as he looked at the giant dragon. It seemed familiar, yes, but I couldn't shake off my unease at his presence. "It's Dad!"

"Oh, no... it's not." Isabelle's copy chuckled.

The creature stormed into the clearing, making Stan and Ollie jump back. He certainly looked like Blaze, but the sheen of his black scales was strange and unnatural. The glow in his eyes was a tempestuous green and certainly not what I remembered Blaze looking like in dragon form. Most importantly, his jaws unhinged and released a storm of fire upon us.

The heat was unbearable, but I managed to grab Isabelle's clone and get away from the flames. Jericho burst into dragon form and fought back with fires of his own, while Dafne and Soph grabbed Astra and joined me on the edge of the clearing. Behind us, clones were coming. I could see them. Jericho and his father's unsettling doppelganger battled, clawing and biting at one another.

For a second, I worried Jericho might lose. The fake dragon knocked him down with his massive tail, then spat fire. The flames covered Jericho, and I held my breath in anticipation. But my friend bounced back, untouched by the blaze—after all, fire dragons were immune to fire. Then I remembered what had happened to Chantal's clone when Jericho had burned her. It was a long shot, but it was worth trying.

"Jericho, use your fire on him!" I shouted.

He gave me a confused look, as if wondering what the hell I was talking about, until it hit him. He huffed and growled, his head slowly turning to face the incoming attack from his father's doppelganger. His lower jaw dropped, and a stream of fire erupted with the pressure and power of a fireman's hose. It hit Blaze's double smack in the face, and the creature howled in agony as the inferno spread over his form and seeped through his scales. It forced the creature to move back long enough for Jericho to lower his head so that we could climb onto his back.

I held on to Isabelle's clone and proceeded toward him. Another high-pitched sound erupted. This one was stronger than the last. So strong, in fact, that it made my ears hurt. I felt blood trickling down my neck as I fell face first into the warm leaves on the ground.

"Thayen..." Astra cried out. It was followed by the thud of another body collapsing.

Isabelle's copy wiggled in my arms, but weakness spread through me, and I feared I might not be able to hold on to her much longer. I heard Jericho's tortured howl and the rushing footsteps from yards away, getting louder.

But I had lost control over myself. My head hurt beyond belief. Sweat burst through my skin and drenched my clothes, swiftly followed by shuddering chills as darkness wrapped its arms around me. I knew nothing of what would come next. I only knew I couldn't change the outcome. Not in this state.

ASTRA

(DAUGHTER OF PHOENIX AND VIOLA)

The blackness that had taken over my eyes dissipated, and the image came back into focus. For a second, I wasn't sure where I was or what had happened, but my senses were fired up and pumping adrenaline through my veins, forcing me to sit up and pay attention.

The high-pitched sound persisted, louder than earlier, and despite the crippling pain, I was too angry to give in. I'd come too far to let these bastards take me. No, this had to end. I had to do something. Dafne and Soph were both on the ground, writhing and moaning in agony. Thayen was out cold, and Isabelle's clone was trying to get out from under him. At least he'd pinned her down during his fall. Jericho roared and shook his head in a bid to stop the pain from buckling his hind legs, while his father's clone was thrashing, still fighting the flames that had melted off parts of his scaly armor. Thayen had been on point with his advice—the clones weren't all perfect. The fire fae and the fire dragons who were supposed to be immune to flames were anything but.

Boots thudded dangerously close, the high-pitched sound amplified by their vicinity. I forced myself to look behind us, just in time to spot a couple of familiar clones emerging from the redwoods. Jovi and Anjani. Others would join them in a matter of minutes, but it was the cubic object in Anjani's clone's hands that caught my eye. That was the source of the sound. I could see the air rippling around it. Whatever that thing was, it had been designed to torture us.

"I've had about enough of this crap!" I muttered, my throat burning as I raised a trembling hand. Jericho shifted back into his humanoid body and scrambled into his half-torched robe, grunting from the pain. I had a feeling he was taking it better than in his dragon form for some unknown reason.

The succubus's copy laughed as she fiddled with the control, increasing the high-pitched sound's volume to the point where I couldn't focus anymore, the pain so sharp it sliced through my brain. With one last push, one final drop of energy I had left, I sent out a barrier. It smacked into her, and she fell back. The cube hit the ground with a clang, and the sound stopped. Jovi's double rushed to grab it and aim it at us again, but Stan and Ollie appeared in front of him.

He stilled, realizing what was about to happen. The ghouls pounced and tore him apart, limb from limb. He screamed, and then it was quiet, but Stan and Ollie weren't done. I looked away as they did the same to Anjani's copy, blood spraying outward as they disemboweled her on the spot. I managed to pull myself back up.

"Thayen, wake up!" I shouted.

Voices murmured through the surrounding forest. The clones were coming, and there were more of them than I could even count. Jericho grabbed Isabelle's clone just as she wormed out from under Thayen, and Dafne rushed to get the vampire back on his feet. He blinked and shook his head as he came to, and I gripped him by the shoulders, giving him a shake for good measure.

"You with us?" I asked.

Thayen nodded. "I think so... What happened?"

I pointed to the bloody pile of body parts that Stan and Ollie had left behind. "They happened. It was that device," I said. One of the ghouls grabbed the cube and brought it over, but Soph took it and smashed it into the ground.

"We really don't need this," she said, wiping the blood from her ear. "Jeez, I can barely hear anything..."

It would take a while for us to fully heal, especially since I'd used the very last of my energy to stop Anjani's copy from turning our brains into literal mush. Jericho pointed up. "Flight is our only option."

"Do it," Thayen said. Isabelle's clone kept laughing. "Laugh it up. You're coming with us."

"Am I, though?" she shot back. "Look around you, idiot. You're surrounded."

Jericho slipped out of his robe and tossed it over to Dafne, who looked away one second too late. He burst out in full dragon form and lowered his head once more. We could all hear the clones shouting at one another as they rushed toward the clearing. Only seconds remained before this whole place would be swarming with their wretched kind.

Within seconds, we'd climbed onto his back. I held on tight, though I knew how heavy we were on a dragon his size. Jericho sprayed all the fire he could conjure around him, turning clockwise as he raised a curtain of orange flames around us. Some of the clones walked right into it and screamed as the blaze licked at their skin. Most, however, stayed back and yelled orders.

The dragon clone had collapsed, parts of him reduced to charred flesh and crackled bones. Jericho exhaled sharply, releasing a cloud of black smoke, then flapped his wings and got us off the ground. Seconds later, we were up in the sky, having left a ring of fire behind. The flames started eating through the redwoods, spreading fast, but they'd done a decent job of keeping the clones at bay.

Isabelle's copy didn't look very happy, back under Thayen's control with her hands still trapped in charmed cuffs. "Bet you didn't see that coming, huh?" I said, and she rolled her eyes.

"We're headed for the Port, right?" Dafne asked. She glanced down at the ground once in a while, keeping Jericho's rolled-up robe under her arm. The night sky was illuminated by the flames, and the smoke rose to swallow the stars and the moon of The Shade's nocturnal spell. None of us were comfortable with setting the redwood forest ablaze, but we'd had no other choice. I was too weak to do much else.

It was a miracle we'd made it out of this mess alive once again. On top of that, we'd taken what the clones had been aiming for this whole time. We had Isabelle's copy, along with whatever she must've stolen from us—I figured it had to still be on her somewhere, but we'd figure that out later. First, we needed relative safety more than anything else.

"Yeah, the Port," Soph replied, cringing from the ear pain she was still dealing with. The wind blew in our faces, slightly cooler than usual, drying my sweat and brushing through my hair. It had a soothing effect as Jericho flew east, far from the fire ring.

I knew Stan and Ollie were capable of looking after each other. With their ghoulish abilities, they could easily sneak past the clones that had come for us down there. And they would soon go look for Soul and Kelara. We needed the Reapers, now more than ever.

"You're not going to win this," Isabelle's clone said.

"I need you to just shut up for the time being," Thayen replied dryly. "Your voice is the last thing I want to hear after that audio torture."

The doppelganger laughed lightly. "Don't you understand? They won't stop until they find me. They will kill each and every one of you until they have what they came here for."

"And what is that, exactly?" Dafne asked, her tone clipped. "What did you take that is so damn precious to your clone buddies?"

"Like I'd be stupid enough to tell," Isabelle's double muttered.

None of us were really comfortable, crowded like this on Jericho's back, since the dragon was smaller than his father and others from his species, but at least he was strong enough to hold us. Despite his clear discomfort, Thayen found enough energy to grab Isabelle's clone by the back of the neck, pushing her down until the side of her face pressed into Jericho's scaly nape.

"You either shut your mouth, or you start talking," he snapped.

"Why don't you make me, huh?" she replied, then burst into mocking laughter. "You can't, can you? Batteries depleted? You're getting soft, buddy. No way you're getting out of this alive."

Every word she said made Thayen angrier and angrier until he unleashed his glamoring on her. I was sure he would've liked to compel her in a more controlled environment and not on the back of a dragon, but Isabelle's doppelganger did have a way of bringing out the worst in us.

"Where is Isabelle?" Thayen asked.

The clone whimpered under his influence, and he tightened his grip on the back of her neck, too, just enough to make it hurt.

"Where is Isabelle?" he insisted.

"Argh... stop!" she cried out. Jericho growled, his body rumbling beneath us. "Stop, Thayen! Please!"

Thayen wouldn't yield. "I'll stop when you start talking. Where is Isabelle?"

"She's alive… she's alive…" the clone managed.

"And the object? What is it? Where is it? Where did you get it from?"

"I can't…" she mumbled, unable to keep her eyes open anymore.

I carefully leaned to the left so I could get a glimpse of her face. Blood trickled from her nose. Thayen was bleeding, too. He'd pushed himself too far again. "Take a break," I told him. "You're wearing yourself out."

"I won't stop until she tells us everything we need to know!"

"Damn it, Thayen, I'm too weak to help any of you right now. We need you at full power, and the more you push yourself, the worse off you'll be!" I replied. "Please. Stop. We know Isabelle is alive, and we can get more out of this bitch later, once we reach the Port."

"She's right," Soph chimed in. "You've done enough already. We have to save our strength until we get to safety."

Thayen sighed, releasing Isabelle's double from his grip. She exhaled sharply and muttered a curse, but she didn't dare say another word. None of us were pleased with how it had turned out, but we had to be grateful for still having her in our possession. The clones could've taken her away. We could've lost her…

The fight wasn't over. The war had just begun, and I doubted we'd won a single battle. But we'd managed to make it this far. With the Port in our sights, I could only hope we'd unravel this mystery before it killed us and all the people we loved. These were dangerous times, and we had to get Isabelle's clone to talk. Once we knew what she'd taken from us, what that object really was, we'd have a better idea about what the enemy was truly planning.

They'd been brazen enough to infiltrate The Shade. They were determined to kill me. I was sure the problem wouldn't end with the clones retrieving what she'd stolen. I had no idea where my mom was. I didn't know if Derek and my dad and the others were okay. I couldn't even imagine where the other Shadians were or how they were holding up in the face of this bloody onslaught.

I could only move forward with Thayen, Soph, Jericho, and Dafne by my side and hope that we'd reach a safe spot soon. There was still so much work to be done and so little time. Our home had been plunged into chaos, and I had a feeling it would be up to us to pull it back to the surface. It was an overwhelming thought, but it also served to keep me on my toes.

I needed to stay sharp.

KELARA

Soul and I had been sitting here for about an hour, maybe more. Time seemed to flow differently when a Reaper was stuck inside a death magic pentagram. I'd tried everything, including reaching out to other Reapers, but our telepathic connections were still off, courtesy of the annoyingly resourceful clones. I'd tried tapping into my bond with Death, as well. No luck on that front.

"I feel incredibly stupid right now," Soul muttered, sitting with his legs crossed. We'd seen dozens of clones rush by. Some stopped to grin at us or tease us for our inability to leave. He'd promised each one a disturbing and bloody death, but that hadn't made him feel any better.

We were trying to figure out how Draven and Serena's copies had gotten the drop on us. That bright explosion must've done more than just blind us. Then again, blitz attacks were designed to disarm a target. In that sense, the clones had definitely done the job right. It was just so embarrassing for the both of us—prime fighters, First Tenners, Reapers with special abilities renowned in our world for all the amazing things we could do. Yet we were stuck in here, unable to get out, our weapons removed.

"It's the fact that they took our scythes," I said. "That's what hurts the most. Because you and I know we would've gotten out already if we still had the blades."

"Yeah. There's only so much death magic entrapment can accomplish when a Reaper still has a scythe."

We'd tried everything in our power to leave. Nothing had worked. We'd gone through all the stages of Reaper grief, too. At this point, Soul and I were resigned to our fates, waiting and hoping that someone might come along and break the circle from the outside. Without our scythes, external interference was pretty much our only option.

But the forest had been quiet for more than twenty minutes. Not a single breath. A misstep. A clone. Absolutely nothing. We knew nothing about the rest of The Shade, either, though we'd been assuming the worst. I was hoping Seeley and Nethissis might come around, or at least the Time Master. They'd made a habit of checking up on us more often than the others, mainly because their business kept bringing them back to The Shade lately.

Sighing deeply, I looked around again. Nothing but trees as far as the eye could see. Trees and lush shrubs. Grass on the forest floor with specks of pink and purple wildflowers. Beautiful patterns on the underbrush leaves. A squirrel foraging through a bush for food.

"We're going to be here for a while," Soul said. "So... how's your day going so far?"

I couldn't help but laugh. He wore a broad smile, the kind that said, "Hey, we're screwed, but my sense of humor ain't dead yet," and it made me want to reach out and hug him and shower him with kisses. But that wasn't an option, and I felt a pang of sadness poking me in the stomach.

"No, no, don't pout, my love," Soul said, his smile gone. "We'll get out eventually."

"I just hope we get out before the whole island is blown to bits and pieces."

"You care about them, huh?" he asked, slowly narrowing his galaxy eyes as he studied my expression from five yards away. "The living of GASP."

I nodded. "Yes. Don't you? They're good people. You know they would do anything they could to help us."

"Mm-hm... just don't tell my siblings. They'll think I've gone soft."

"They already think that," I said, drawing a scowl from him.

"How so?"

"Well, we're a pair. Dream and Nightmare keep making bets about who's really wearing the pants in this relationship, if you know what I mean." I giggled. It made him scoff, but I could see he was trying hard to keep a straight face.

A low growl made me turn around. I nearly squealed with joy when Stan and Ollie emerged from the woods, their noses pressed to the ground as they sniffed out our tracks. "Fate smiles upon us after all!" I exclaimed.

The ghouls lit up when they saw us. They rushed to greet Soul and me, but the pentagrams' magic pushed them back. "Sorry about that, buddy," Soul said to Stan. "We're trapped in here."

"But you can help!" I said, carefully eyeing Ollie, who was now circling me, whimpering and anxious because he couldn't reach through. Every time he tried to touch the invisible shield, it zapped him with painful electrical currents, making him snarl. "No, not like that, buddy. Our scythes. The clones have our scythes. You can track them, can't you?"

Stan and Ollie exchanged concerned glances before they gave us a double nod.

"Good. Draven and Serena's clones had our weapons the last time we saw them. If you can track the scythes, you can find those bastards and try to retrieve them for us," Soul said. "This is powerful death magic they've put on us. You can't help otherwise, since you belong to the same realm."

Within seconds, the ghouls bolted somewhere northwest of here. I watched them for a while, until their bony figures disappeared between the trees. Silence settled over our little spot in the woods as Soul and I looked at each other. It was getting harder to keep my spirits high, but I needed to stay strong for whatever might come next.

"Now, we wait," he muttered, giving me a playful wink.

I had a feeling he was working on his own resolve, just as I was. That was the trouble with powerful and potent beings like us. We were fierce and difficult to defeat, yet utterly useless without our scythes. The clones had managed to point out some serious design flaws, but this wasn't the time or the place to do something about it. Sure, the Spirit Bender had almost kicked our asses more than once—in retrospect, however, there was really only one of him. In this case, we were dealing with at least dozens of creatures made solely to stir confusion and equipped not only with all forms of known magic, ours included, but also with spells that were simply out of this world.

It sounded awful to even think such things, but I would rather have dealt with Spirit than with these fiends. Spirit was a familiar enemy. He had limitations. I wasn't sure what weaknesses we'd find in the clones, and whether it would be enough to stop them.

Soul and I spent another maybe twenty minutes talking and trying to keep ourselves from succumbing to anxiety and despair. He was doing a surprisingly good job of nudging my mood in a more positive direction.

"Do you think Sidyan and Lumi will ever be an official pair?" I asked him. We'd been dishing and gossiping about the Reapers in our close circle of friends, and the bond between a Reaper and a living swamp witch had been the subject of constant fascination for the past two decades, at least.

"I think Sidyan would like that," Soul said. "Lumi's the one holding back."

"Really? I could've sworn it was the other way around."

He shook his head. "Sidyan even spoke to Death about sanctioning their relationship. She moaned about it at first, but given the changing trends in our society, I think she just gave up trying to enforce those antiquated rules. It's definitely Lumi who's keeping him at arm's length."

"Why, though?" I replied. "I know she loves him..."

Soul offered a dry smile in return. When he realized it wasn't enough of an answer, he sighed and gave me his lengthy opinion. "I think she's afraid it might end badly. Think about it. She spent thousands of years locked in that Nerakian basement. She was tortured and demeaned. Lumi has some serious trust issues. Sure, she's friendly and loyal to GASP, and she will tear down mountains for her disciples. But in the end, the path to her heart is wrought with trouble and distrust. I don't think she's got any control over it, however. She probably wants more out of this relationship with Sidyan, yet she can't bring herself to fully trust that things might be okay for them in the end. If you look around now, you can certainly see what I'm talking about."

"Yeah, this clone war is certainly unexpected."

"And a good reason for Lumi to stay focused on the job. For what it's worth, I think we'll see Sidyan again soon.

He can't stay away from her for too long." He chuckled.

Someone cried out. Soul and I looked for the source, observing commotion in the distance. Two people were running toward us in a loose zigzag pattern. Behind them, I could see Stan and Ollie getting bigger as they drew closer.

"You have got to be kidding me," I managed. We didn't move, but I could feel myself tensing with anticipation. Our ghouls had accomplished something incredible in a short period of time. They'd found Serena and Draven's clones, and they'd succeeded in chasing them all the way here. I had no idea how they'd done it, but I was damn proud of them. "Yes, Stan! Yes, Ollie! Bring them over, boys!" I shouted, feeling a huge grin stretch across my face. Soul shifted slowly, getting in position on the edge of his pentagram enclosure. By the time I looked out again, Draven and Serena's clones were only yards away, nearly stumbling as they tried to escape the wrath of our ghouls. I'd have expected them to be more frightening and less frightened, but as I noticed a missing arm on Draven's clone,

I realized that Stan and Ollie had been pretty aggressive in their approach.

Draven's doppelganger's face and chest were covered in deep gashes, blood dripping as he ran faster. But Ollie pounced and rammed into him. The sheer force of impact pushed him right inside my pentagram. To my surprise, the marvelous loopholes of Reaper trapping pentagrams had struck again—normally, non-Reaper related items and beings remained subject to the laws of physics, regardless of the pentagram's rules. A Druid or a Druid's clone or any living creature could still get in. But Draven still had my scythe on him, so he shouldn't have been able to come through. Yet he did. Draven fell so hard and so fast, he didn't even see it coming. I caught a glimpse of Stan doing the same to Serena's copy, propelling her directly into Soul's arms.

It quickly turned into a fight to the death as I tackled the Druid's clone, kicking and punching as fast and as hard as I could. He snarled when I caught him in a head lock, pinning him down with my full body weight. I tightened my grip and yanked with all my strength until his spine broke, before he could shift into a snake and slither out of my hold. "Argh..."

His body softened, and I heard the last breath he gave. There was no sign of his spirit anywhere, though. How could there be, if he didn't have a real soul? Then again, Thayen had been able to glamor them. I hadn't seen any clone ghosts so far, and it was an interesting pattern to observe, but also a disturbing discrepancy. While their fake souls were meticulously crafted to fool even a Reaper, partly susceptible to glamoring, none made it into our realm. None survived beyond death...

Soul celebrated when Serena's clone finally expired. "Hell, yeah!" my beloved snapped, gripping his weapon with both hands. Beaming with pride, he shot me a devilish grin. "Grab your gear, sweetie. We're going clone hunting!"

The blade of his weapon shone white as he aimed it at a nearby tree. His lips moved as he uttered a telekinetic spell. It shot into the trunk and severed it at the base. The whole thing came down with enough weight to crash right into the pentagram that had held Soul in place for too long.

"For your information, the traps they put us in were glitchy," I said briefly. "Our scythes got in while on the bodies of the living doubles."

"Heh. Go figure," Soul replied. "Happy accident?"

I found my scythe under Draven-clone's body. Rolling him over, I retrieved my weapon and did the same number on another tree, forcing it to come down and disrupt the pentagram's outer circle, breaking the magic.

"Maybe. I think we'll need to be careful in the future, nonetheless. The mere fact that they know death magic, with incomplete, faulty spells or not, is enough of a problem already. They might figure more out. We obviously don't know enough about them... Anyway!" Breathing a sigh of relief, I threw my arms around Soul's neck and pulled him close. We kissed, closing our eyes for a moment, thankful to have escaped from the clones' traps.

Draven and Serena's clones were dead, and we'd gotten our weapons back, but this was nowhere near over. I looked to Stan and Ollie. "Boys, you've earned yourselves a snack," I told them, pointing a thumb at the doppelgangers' bodies. "Have at it."

"We have to find Thayen and the others. Voss, Chantal, Richard. We don't know what happened to them," Soul said, his brow furrowed.

"We're free now, my love. We can cover enough ground," I replied.

"Yeah, that's all nice and wonderful, but we still can't summon more Reapers to help. The situation is clearly getting out of control here."

Behind us, Stan and Ollie were ripping pieces out of the clones, feasting on flesh and bones with satisfied purrs. It was an absolute mess, and it made me sick to a stomach I no longer really had, so I chose to focus on Soul instead. Even in death, there were things I just couldn't bear to look at.

"One step at a time. You're right, we need to make sure the others are okay first. Astra, in particular. She's been the clones' target from the very beginning," I said.

We knew what we had to do. Hopefully, our friends would have made significant progress while we'd been stuck out here. Whatever came next, I sure as hell wasn't willing to let the clones win this war—because this was a war, and they'd picked the wrong people to wage it against.

KELARA

With Stan and Ollie by our side, we zapped to different key points across The Shade. First, we checked the terrace area near the hospital again, then the hospital itself, and I found myself speechless at the destruction that had occurred. The silence was almost unbearable, a symptom in the aftermath of great violence.

The ground had been burned black on a wide radius. There was nothing left of the hospital, save for the room where Isabelle's clone had been. "Soul, she's not here anymore!" I said, alarmed.

"I think Stan and Ollie leaving their post to come for us was a dead giveaway," he said, then nodded at the ghouls. "Look at them. They're calm. I think it's a good sign."

"A good sign of what, exactly?" I scoffed, motioning around us. "Look at what happened here. How is any of this okay?"

Soul chuckled, irritating me with his calmness. "None of this is okay, but the fact that Isabelle's clone isn't here, coupled with Stan and Ollie's relaxed demeanor, should tell us something. I'm willing to bet she's with Thayen and the others. I think they came back for her; otherwise, our ghoul buddies here would be fidgeting and snarling and whatnot."

I realized that he was almost certainly right. "You're right," I said, then looked to the ghouls. "Did the clone leave with Thayen's crew?"

They both nodded, their lips moving as they hissed and struggled to make their thoughts understood. I caught snippets of what they were trying to tell us—they'd lived as mindless beasts for so long that they lacked Herbert's eloquence, though we could still communicate, albeit in simpler terms. I gave Soul an alarmed look once Stan and Ollie were finished with their choppy account.

"Clones galore," I sighed, then pointed to the clone's room. It was intact—the only thing to have survived the inferno that had swallowed this place whole. Redwoods had been burned to a crisp, reduced to piles of ash. Smoke was still rising from the embers, and there were throngs of footprints scattered all around. I walked over to the edge of the charred disk, analyzing a piece of burnt wood. "The fire that caused this was at a very high intensity. We're talking dragon flames," I added.

"Probably Jericho. And I'm guessing that thing over there was a dragon clone," Soul replied, pointing to the opposite edge of the blackened area, where a smoked pile of bones had survived the scorching blaze. "I mean, it looks like a dragon from here, but his species is supposed to be immune to fire. Considering the clones aren't all perfect, maybe their maker didn't know about the flame-retardant capabilities... I don't know, I'm just guessing here."

"No, no, no, you're onto something," I murmured, rushing toward the dragon corpse. The closer I got, the clearer I could see its skeletal features, its wing bones shattered from the high temperatures of Jericho's fire. "You're right, and the ghouls confirmed it. A real dragon would never die from... well, dragon fire. Just like the water fae can't drown. Creatures of one element can't usually be killed by that element."

"That, in turn, tells me that whatever went down here ended with Jericho and his group escaping," Soul said, while Stan and Ollie nodded once more. "I don't see any drag marks, just a whole bunch of confused traces. Hordes of clones probably spun around here, trying to figure out what to do next."

"Still guessing?" I chuckled, giving him a sideways glance. Meanwhile, Stan and Ollie got to sniffing the entire area, all the way to the burnt edges where fresh grass was still growing. "Hey, what put the fire out? I don't see any wet patches anywhere. No trace of water."

Soul shrugged. "Does it matter?"

"Maybe. If the clones are capable of putting out a dragon fire, then why'd they bother? Why didn't they just let it spread and burn?" I replied.

My question seemed to trouble Soul, but he didn't have an answer. "I don't know."

The ghouls moved toward the center of the burnt clearing, their deformed nostrils flaring, their black eyes darting in different directions as they registered every scent that had been left behind. There was something wrong about this place. The pieces of the puzzle weren't clicking in the right spots. We were missing valuable information, and I loathed making assessments with incomplete knowledge.

"Soul, it's worth asking this question, though, don't you think?" I said, eyeing him curiously.

"What question?"

"About putting out the fire. If Thayen's group managed to get out of here, likely on Jericho's back, then why did the clones bother to stop this place from burning to the ground? Why not just go after them?"

"Maybe they did go after them," he said, and Ollie growled softly in support of his argument. "See? They went after them."

I sighed deeply. "Yeah, but time would have been of the essence. Especially when their target was flying. I'm sorry, I'm repeating the same issue, I know... but it's bugging me."

"We'll figure it out eventually. For now, I've got a better question for you," Soul shot back, hands resting on his hips as he walked toward me. "Where'd everybody go? The originals, the clones... where are they?"

"We should try the Great Dome next," I replied. "Thayen did say they were headed in that direction when we first parted ways. And if that doesn't yield anything, we should check the witches' sanctuary and the treehouse residences. Maybe the Shadians figured out they were being invaded and went into some kind of self-imposed lockdown."

Soul nodded once. "I think I remember Lumi or one of the senior officers—Rose or Caleb, I don't remember which one—saying something about underground bunkers being accessible from pretty much anywhere on the island. Then there are the Black Heights. I know the dragons will happily welcome refugees in times of crisis. It's just the two of us, Kel... we don't have time to check every damn spot in The Shade, so we'd best focus on what we can do."

"Finding Thayen," I said. "Yeah, you're right."

"One step at a time, remember?"

Stan groaned softly, looking up at the moonlit sky. As if his feet had suddenly caught fire, he jumped and vanished into the air. Soul, Ollie, and I quickly followed, leaving the ground and taking to the skies in our subtle forms.

Below, the black disk looked smaller and less significant. The redwood forest was dark and quiet, the wind blowing through its branches and making the leaves rustle. The smell of smoke persisted, but the skies were clear. Lights glimmered in the distance, in different areas of The Shade. Soul was right: we didn't have the time or the resources to verify the entire island. Not without the Time Master to help us.

One thing was clear, however.

The clones had caused enough trouble to throw the whole of GASP for a loop. We stayed close to Stan as he pursued the aerial traces left behind by Jericho in flight. We bounced through the open air, the redwoods' crowns inches beneath our feet. I was nervous and anxious, but I knew we couldn't let our friends deal with this on their own.

Thayen and Astra needed us right now. To be honest, getting to the bottom of this mystery would've satisfied my own restless curiosity. Who were these doppelgangers? Who'd sent them? What were they after? It bugged me that even after all this time, we still had so many questions left unanswered, while the clones pranced around The Shade like it was their domain. It irked me beyond belief.

Somewhere far ahead, I saw a dot moving. A creature with its wings flapping, headed toward the Port. "Soul, I think we're getting closer."

We had to be careful. Zapping across greater distances, we barely had time to look to the ground and see if the clones had passed through. We didn't know what they were planning or where they were headed. We only knew they wanted Isabelle's clone alive and Astra dead. That was the very core of the issue, and the only place in this entire mess where Soul and I could actually make a difference.

So we kept chasing after Stan, who'd caught a solid trace of Jericho. We kept going, in a rush to find our friends and help them fight back against creatures that didn't belong here. Hell, these clones didn't belong anywhere. Their mere existence was a troubling abomination, and I was looking forward to being able to communicate with Death again—or to at least send her a message. She needed to know that someone had been fabricating fake souls. She had the power and the authority to help us investigate on a much broader and more effective scale.

But first and foremost, we had to get to Astra and the others before it was too late.

THAYEN

For a second, I actually dared to think we'd make it safely to the Port.

Jericho suddenly tilted hard to the left, nearly throwing us off his back in the process. I wanted to ask what the hell was wrong with him, but then I saw the ice shards narrowly missing his belly.

Someone was firing frozen projectiles from the ground.

"Thayen, they caught up with us," Dafne breathed.

I looked down, my blood curdling at the troubling sight. At least five dozen figures were running on the ground, chasing after us. I recognized some of them—Ben and River, Hazel and Tejus, Dafne, Lethe, Heath, to name a few—all of them clones. All of them focused on us. The air rippled from the multitude of barriers the sentry doppelgangers launched upward, and Jericho was forced to bank right. Dafne cursed loudly enough for the whole island to hear.

"Damn these bastards! They copied me and my dad!"

"Not that well, apparently. None of them are flying!" Astra replied. With no time to wonder how that had come to happen, I only took it as a much welcome fluke.

"Hold on!" I shouted. "It's going to get bumpy!"

Jericho roared and released a heavy rain of fire below. I watched the flames spread and engulf some of the clone clusters. Screams tore across the clearing, but some of them managed to slip into the woods ahead. We weren't done with them, and I knew they'd try harder to get to us.

The horn blew a third time, prompting me to look over my shoulder.

Astra was pale, her eyes wide with horror. Soph kept glancing down, her brow furrowed while her red eyes scanned the forest, catching movement here and there. "They're hot on our heels," the daemon said.

"Jericho, you need to go faster," Dafne urged.

He growled in protest, but he made the effort nonetheless, his wings flapping frenetically while the ice dragon prepared to dismount and take flight on her own. "Where are you going? We need to stick together!" I warned.

"We're too heavy on him!" she said. "I can fly on my own. If nothing else, I can help keep some of those creeps back!"

I didn't want to split up, especially right now, but even I had to admit that we were terribly overwhelmed. If Dafne could help, it made sense to let her, so I nodded my assent. "Be careful," I added for good measure.

She took off her jacket, and I looked away, only hearing the rustling of fabric as she handed her and Jericho's garments over to Soph. "Hold on to these," Dafne said. "I'm going to need them."

"Oh, cool. I've got enough to start a grungy Shadian fashion line," Soph muttered.

The ice dragon chuckled and jumped off, bones crackling as she shifted in freefall. Her wings spread wide, and she descended closer to the treetops, huffing in her search for clones. Jericho was moving slightly better, I noticed, since he had less weight on his back. But it still wasn't enough. A barrier caught up and punched him in the gut, throwing us to the side.

Astra screamed, but Soph caught her by the wrist before she tumbled off. The Daughter dangled midair, but the daemon had a firm grip, pulling her back up and helping her throw one leg over Jericho's spine to properly mount him. I'd nearly lost Isabelle's clone, too, but I'd locked my arm around her waist in a bid to keep her as close as possible and hoping I wouldn't end up losing her along the way.

I heard Dafne roaring somewhere close by, along with the whistling of water gushing through the air. She'd unleashed her special ability, something she didn't use very often, since it wore her out faster than the usual ice shards. I managed to look back just in time to see her spewing a powerful jet of water over the trees. As soon as the liquid hit the first leaves, it instantly froze, glazing everything in a thick layer of ice.

"Thayen, watch out!" Astra shouted.

But I didn't see it until it was too late—a fireball the size of a melon crashed into Jericho's side. The impact was explosive, yet it wasn't the actual flame that undid us, but the force of the strike.

Astra's scream tore me apart on the inside. I couldn't catch her because I was falling, too. Hitting the ground would hurt. It would disable us and leave us at the mercy of the clones. Jericho spiraled down, clearly dazed as he struggled to regain his balanced flight. More fireballs were propelled upward, all of them aimed at him.

Isabelle's doppelganger was just below, shooting toward the ground at a crippling speed. I tried to reach out, to grab her by the ankle, but I wondered what good it would do. How would I stop us from crashing?

We were about to penetrate the forest's thick tree crowns, and I braced myself for the impact. It would hurt.

Badly.

Astra's scream was cut off. Dafne had caught her and Soph, determined to reach the Port. Jericho managed to get under Isabelle's clone and me, and we landed on his back with a thud. I held on tight, my legs straddling his scaly back. My grip was so strong, it made my muscles sore. But we'd made it, damn it. We'd survived an aerial attack and—Jericho's snarl obliterated my last thread of hope. Something silvery poked out from his wing.

"This is getting annoying!" Isabelle's clone snapped from her position pinned under my body on the dragon's back.

Ahead, we watched as a long and slender arrow shot from below and struck Dafne in her wing. The dragons cried out, and we all fell. I shot through the branches, snapping some of them off. The cool air filled my lungs as gravity pulled me down. Instinctively, I grabbed whatever I could as I plummeted, but everything broke under my sudden weight. I got cuts and bruises on my way down, though I did manage to slow my fall—enough to soften the force of a landing that would've crushed me otherwise.

I couldn't breathe for a good minute. Finally, my lungs filled with precious air, and my ribs ached, sending waves of hot pain through my torso. "Gah..." I managed, wiggling my toes and fingers first to make sure my spine was still intact. We only had seconds before the clones would reach us.

"For cryin' out loud!" Isabelle's doppelganger moaned from a few feet away from me. I raised my head and found her on her back, twigs and leaves poking out from under her. One stick had punctured her side, and blood was seeping into her blouse like a crimson rose unfolding its petals.

A loud thump made me jump. Jericho had landed about ten yards to my left, the metallic arrow stuck in his wing. He roared from the pain, shifting back to his humanoid form to better deal with his injury. The arrow had gone through his bicep. Dafne wasn't too far away, either. I could see Astra and Soph getting to their feet. The ice dragon must've softened their fall.

Rushed footsteps echoed in the night, and I knew we had a battle coming. The problem was that we were all injured in one way or another. I doubted we could hold our own against the incoming hostiles.

"Astra. Soph. You okay?" I called out, pushing myself into a standing position. As soon as I straightened my back, I felt my spine crack. It wasn't broken, but it had taken some damage. I needed at least half an hour to get back to full strength—wishful thinking, since I could already see the bastards coming, silhouettes dashing left and right between the old redwood trees.

Half a mile behind me, the Port waited.

Isabelle's clone's snicker got on my nerves as she stood and pulled the stick out of her wound. "You're so screwed."

"It's not over yet," Jericho replied, gritting his teeth. He used his fae fire to melt off half of the arrow. I ran to his side and helped pull the rest out of his arm. He snarled and released a slew of expletives while I used the incandescent end of the arrow to help close his wound and cauterize it at the same time.

I caught a glimpse of Astra doing some healing on Dafne's shoulder, her hands glowing pink as she struggled to breathe. There was no energy left in the Daughter, yet she kept pushing herself in order to help others. Soph had draped Dafne's jacket around her, and she was running over to give Jericho his garment, as well.

The fire dragon grabbed it and quickly got dressed. Soph and I positioned ourselves in front of Isabelle's double. "There's no other way," the daemon breathed. "We have to fight them."

"I don't have enough strength to do another curtain of fire," Jericho said, flames bursting in his hands. "But I can still torch a clone or two."

Astra helped Dafne up. The ice dragon's injuries had not fully healed, mainly because Astra was spent, but at least the bleeding had stopped. They reached us at the same time as the clones, and the air thickened with hostile tension as the creatures surrounded us with devious grins on their faces. Nausea caused knots to form in my throat, but this was it. This was our only option.

My claws and fangs were out, skin tingling as I got ready to use my glamoring ability in combat. I'd yet to perfect the technique of casting my influence against a moving target, but I would have to try.

"How's Dafne?" I asked, my gaze fixed on Hazel and Tejus's clones. They were slightly closer than the others. What were the odds I could glamor them both at once? Slim to none, I figured, as Hazel's clone threw a barrier out.

Astra gasped and launched one of her own. The air ripples clashed and burst into a soft pulse that nudged us all back.

"I'm currently useless," Dafne said, and Soph handed her one of her spare long knives.

"You can still slice one of these bastards," the daemon princess replied.

The ice dragon smiled at the sight of the blade. "Damn right."

"Jericho, I hope you've got enough fire left in you to show these knockoffs that they made the biggest mistake of their pathetic lives when they decided to invade our island," I said.

Isabelle's copy giggled. "I like how you're still hoping to survive this."

She was cuffed, and Dafne moved to grab her by the back of the neck, long knife ready to cut anyone who dared approach them. "Shut the hell up already," the ice dragon muttered. "I'm getting tired of the sound of your voice."

"You're woefully outnumbered," Isabelle's clone retorted. "Might as well give up now and hand me over.

Maybe they'll kill you quickly."

"I see about a dozen of them left," I said, eyeing our adversaries as they inched forward, gradually closing the circle around us.

"Guess again, nimrod," Ben's double replied. More of them emerged from all around us. They'd been wearing red glasses and using invisibility magic. They must've been part of the posse from the beginning but stayed hidden from sight. Jericho had missed them, since he hadn't been able to see them. My blood ran cold as I realized we were dealing with many more clones than I'd thought, and each was armed with a disk shield and a black spray bottle... and who knew what other dirty tricks up their sleeves.

We had limited space to work with due to the redwoods. Dafne couldn't use her ice shards while in humanoid form, and Jericho's arm would take some time to heal. Astra's batteries were low, and only Soph and I were slightly better equipped to fight. It didn't look good, especially since we couldn't even call for help.

Ben's clone threw out his hands, flames crackling from his open palms. He started throwing fireballs at us, and we had no choice but to duck. Dafne kept Isabelle's copy close. "I'll keep her away from them," the ice dragon said. Among the doppelgangers, there was a version of me. It made my blood run hot and cold at the same time, since this was the first time I was seeing a mirror image of myself. To say that I was creeped out would've been an understatement. He came out from the swelling crowd, grinning as he approached me, eager to fight. I got into an attack position, shifting my bodyweight from one leg to the other. He started running, his feet light as he glided across the short distance. Something glowed just behind him. A split second later, he'd been cut in half, blood gushing as his torso and legs fell in different spots.

Kelara emerged from between realms, her scythe crimson red and dripping.

The clones exchanged confused glances, but they had no time to figure out what was happening as Stan and Ollie started tearing through them. Growls and spine-tingling howls mingled with horrified screams. Somewhere to our left, a gaping black hole opened, and an unseen force threw some of the doppelgangers inside before it closed. An interdimensional pocket. The Soul Crusher was here, too.

"Sorry we're late." Kelara sighed. "There were some... issues along the way."

"Better late than never," I said, hope daring to blossom in my heart.

The clones still outnumbered us five to one, and they intensified their attacks. Astra used whatever sentry abilities she still had functional to keep some of them at bay, but they were getting closer, so I moved to protect her while Dafne stayed close to Isabelle's clone. Soph teamed up with Kelara, and they started zigzagging through the doppelganger crowd, slashing left and right before the clones could use their black spray on them.

Stan and Ollie were doing a horrifyingly good job on their own, able to switch from subtle to visible forms, catching their targets on the wrong foot at every turn. Soul was decimating the clone population with a mixture of death magic and modified interdimensional pockets, dooming those he tossed inside to a gruesome demise. He'd told us once that if he closed such modified pockets with people still in them, they would be crushed into nonexistence, their souls forever lost. Of course, there weren't any real souls to worry about in this instance, but I still shivered at the thought. I could tell these were modified pockets because of the screams that came out of them before they vanished.

"We're trying to get to the Port," I told Kelara, then dodged Ben's clone's fireballs and bolted toward him just as he took out his black spray bottle.

Dafne cried out. I ducked and drove my clawed hand into Ben's clone's chest. I felt his heart between my fingers, and I tore it away from the ribcage. The doppelganger fell, stunned by what had just happened, then gave his last breath. I threw his heart on the ground before turning to look for Dafne. More clones were coming for me, but that wasn't the biggest of our problems.

Isabelle's copy had gotten the drop on Dafne. They were both down, and the clone was using her charmed cuffs to strangle the ice dragon. Soph was too far away. Astra was fighting off Hazel and Tejus's doubles, utterly overwhelmed. Jericho tried to get to Dafne, but Field and Astra's clones rammed into him, and it quickly turned into a bloody brawl.

I scrambled away from the other hostiles and ran toward Dafne. Her eyes had rolled into her head, and I wasn't sure how much longer she'd last. My heart was racing, as I dreaded the thought of losing anyone in this fight. I threw my hand out, releasing what felt like an invisible lasso. It hit Isabelle's clone in the chest, and I had her under my glamoring control.

"Stop!" I shouted, but it didn't seem to be working.

Claudia's copy slipped past the others and pounced on Dafne and Isabelle's double. All I could see was a mixture of arms and legs flailing, and I wasn't sure what was happening. By the time I reached them, Isabelle's clone was dead, her throat slit, and Dafne was trying to get out from under her. Claudia's doppelganger had already stepped back, wearing a deranged grin as she admired her bloodied hands. She was holding something.

A small cubic object, perhaps the size of a die, caught the moonlight on its surface. The object...

I tried to take her down, but she whispered "Morfuris" and vanished, leaving me stunned for a few moments. Per GASP protocol, we'd been taught to always carry a red lens on us in case it might be needed. I dug through my pockets and fished one out just in time to see Claudia's clone running away through the redwood forest, headed straight for the Port.

"Put your red lenses on! We have to stop Claudia's copy! She took something from Isabelle's clone!" I shouted. It was happening so fast, I didn't even have time to fully process Isabelle's clone's death or my friends' injuries. My only reaction was to chase after Claudia's double. She had something—the one thing that all the other clones had been working so hard to retrieve.

I couldn't let the monsters have it, no matter what it was. So I ran. I ran as fast as my legs could carry me, following someone who'd been modeled after one of the strongest and most resourceful vampires I'd ever had the honor of knowing.

ASTRA

(DAUGHTER OF PHOENIX AND VIOLA)

It was as if an invisible force had taken over each of us as we each slipped our red lenses on. The moment we saw Thayen running off into the woods after Claudia's copy, we understood that our fight here had ended. Whatever Isabelle's clone had had in her possession, it had been transferred to Claudia's, and we could not let it leave The Shade. The enemy had gone to great lengths to get it, and we'd be foolish to let them have it.

The thought was collective in our small, frazzled group. One by one, we moved away from the fighting and started running after Thayen. Jericho and I helped Dafne up—she refused to be left behind, even though Stan and Ollie had kept some of the clones away from her. I saw Soul throwing my grandparents' copies into one of his interdimensional pockets before he moved on to other "elders" of The Shade. Soon Soph was hot on our heels, bolting in the same direction.

We left Kelara's group to handle what was left of the hostiles, though we were still outnumbered. I didn't regret the decision, and I knew Kelara wouldn't blame us for it, either. She hadn't seen Claudia's clone running off, but she'd heard Thayen. She understood how important this was.

As we went after Thayen, watching Claudia's copy a few yards ahead through our GASP-issued red lenses, a peculiar thought occurred to me.

We'd gotten strangely accustomed to killing the clones of our friends and families. Knowing that they were a deadly enemy didn't take away from the fact that they'd been modeled after the people we loved most. I would've expected a more disturbing feeling to linger at seeing my grandparents or even Isabelle's doppelganger get killed. At least a bit of nausea, some uneasiness while my brain processed the physical similarities. But there was nothing.

I wasn't sure why it irked me. Maybe it was the violent nature of this situation that had forced me to push my feelings aside. All I knew was that the clones were bad, and they had to be captured or eliminated without hesitation, no matter whose appearance they'd stolen. On any other day, I might've said easier said than done, but here... it was strangely easier done.

"Dafne, wait up!" Jericho gasped as the ice dragon got closer to Thayen, who was maybe ten yards behind Claudia's clone.

"You're going to need to move a lot faster if you're going to keep up with me," Dafne shot back. I could've sworn she was smiling, though I couldn't see her from this angle.

Claudia's clone pulled something from her pocket as she kept running. She yanked the top off and threw it over her shoulder. By the time we saw it coming, it was too late. The canister hit the ground and exploded in a puff of black smoke. Thayen covered his mouth and nose with his arm, but Dafne and Soph weren't as quick. They both took deep breaths, and I knew they wouldn't be able to keep running unless we helped them.

Holding our breath, Jericho and I moved faster and caught up. Dafne's grayish eyes were filled with tears, and she was seconds away from a heartfelt scream. Jericho scooped her up and threw her onto his back, firmly crossing her legs around his waist as he took off running. I didn't have much strength left in me, but Soph needed my help.

I reached her just as she was about to collapse, my hands glowing pink as I cupped her face. Incandescent veins spidered across Soph's cheeks. I pushed myself beyond my limits and healed as much of her broken mind as I could. It was the only thing I could think to do, considering I'd experienced enough of that black spray to understand that she needed emotional healing more than anything else. I had to move fast.

"Listen to my voice, Soph," I said. She whimpered in my hold, tears streaming down her cheeks as I held her up. "Nothing you're feeling right now is real. Listen to me!"

Finally, she found the strength to meet my gaze. "It hurts, Astra..."

"I know, and I don't have the strength to fully heal you, so I need you to do some of the work for me. Just listen to my voice," I said, fatigue taking over and turning my limbs into boiled spaghetti. "Listen to my voice and understand that you're under the effect of foreign magic. You have to push through. Please."

Soph nodded rapidly, her eyes widening as she took deep breaths, gradually coming out of the emotional hallucinations the black spray had inflicted upon her.

"We have to keep running. We have to stop Claudia's clone from getting away," I reminded her. "Can I count on you, Soph? Can I count on you to follow my lead on this?"

She nodded again. "Yes. I think so... yes..."

"Okay. Let's go."

I took her hand in mine and somehow found enough air in my lungs to suck in a breath and start running again. There were other clones following us—the mongrels must've slipped past Kelara's crew, but they were still far enough away to not pose an immediate threat.

We caught up with Jericho and Dafne. The dragon fae was considerably slower with her on his back, but at least she was conscious and remarkably calm, considering the nightmare she'd inhaled. I imagined it had something to do with Jericho's presence. She had her arms around his neck, her cheek pressed against his as she worked on controlling her breathing while he ran.

"You're imagining it," Jericho said to her. "Just focus on that. It's a lie. It's all a lie. You're okay, and we're going after Claudia's clone."

"It's a lie," Dafne repeated after him. "It's all a lie."

"Way to go, Jericho!" I exclaimed as the four of us sped down the widening forest path.

Thayen was about forty yards ahead now, still on Claudia's clone's heels. As long as we had her in our sights, there was some hope left that we would succeed in stopping her. My legs hurt. My thighs were burning. But I couldn't give up. We were so close.

"Come on!" Thayen shouted, briefly looking over his shoulder at us. "She may be like Claudia, but she's not Claudia!"

The faster he moved, the closer he got to her.

We left the woods behind. The giant redwoods watched us as we made our way onto the beach. Farther to our left, where the ocean met the sandy shore, the Port rose with its stone structures. Beyond it, the lighthouse beamed in the night, rivaling the moon itself beneath the sea of stars.

A shimmering portal opened at the base of the nearest Port building—a shipyard warehouse that hadn't been used in ages. Adrenaline spiked through me as I understood what Claudia's clone's next step was. She planned on taking what she'd gotten from Isabelle's doppelganger back to wherever they'd all come from.

"Don't let her get away!" Jericho shouted to Thayen.

"Obviously that's what I'm trying to do," Thayen shot back, clearly frustrated and possibly tired from the constant running and fighting we'd had to deal with for what felt like an endless number of hours.

But Claudia's double managed to get away, jumping through the shimmering portal. We ended up a few feet from it, its energy rushing through my body like an electrical current, jolting me back to life.

"Crap!" Thayen muttered, unable to take his eyes off the glowing gash. "We can't... we can't let her have whatever she took!"

"Then we have to go in after her," I said, though I had no idea what had given me the courage to say such a thing. I only knew that the simple proximity of the portal was downright rejuvenating, as if all the energy I'd wasted healing and throwing barriers and fighting back against the clones was finally coming back to me. It was as if someone had plugged me into a socket, my batteries refilling faster than I could even comprehend.

Thayen gave me a troubled look. "Go in there?"

"What have we got to lose?" I replied, the urgency pressing against my chest. "If we stay here, they'll keep coming for me. They won't stop, Thayen. Whatever Isabelle's clone took, I'm sure it's only the beginning."

"Gah, this hurts!" Dafne cried out, and I quickly touched her face to heal her. She was still under the black smoke's influence, though she'd been doing an incredible job of keeping it together. The pink glow in my hands seemed brighter. My earlier theory about my "batteries" recharging was true. "Oh, keep it coming," the ice dragon said as my healing began to work on her traumatized mind.

I moved to Soph next, finishing what I'd started earlier, while Thayen gave me a confused look. It demanded an explanation, and he'd certainly earned it.

"It's the portal," I told him. "It's not just that I can sense it when it's open. It's recharging my energy levels for my Daughter powers. I'm not sure how to explain it, but I'm feeling a lot better now than I did five minutes ago."

"Astra's right," Jericho said, his brow furrowed as he looked at the shimmering gash. "We have to go in there.

Now."

"What if we can't come back? What if we find our death in there?" Thayen asked.

Soph raised her chin in defiance. "We're cowards if we sit this one out. And you know it. Claudia's clone took something from us. It was important enough for her people to come through and wreak havoc in our world. We cannot let this stand."

"Damn it!" Thayen snapped and walked right into the portal.

We only had a few seconds left, at most, before it would close. There was no room for hesitation. One by one, we went through, and the sensation was like nothing I had ever experienced before. Chills danced across my skin, mingling with hot sparks as I felt the shimmer envelop me from head to toe. My soul buzzed, and my heart swelled to the point where I feared it might burst from my chest.

It only lasted for a few seconds as I walked through a peculiar sea of diamond white. I closed my eyes as I approached the exit. I couldn't see it, but I could feel it. As soon as I stepped onto the other side, my words were lost.

Thayen, Jericho, Dafne, Soph, and I stood on the beach. The Port was just ahead. This was The Shade. For a moment, I thought maybe we hadn't made it through. I thought the portal had closed, and that we'd only advanced a few feet across the sand.

"It's not our Shade," Thayen mumbled, his eyes wide as he looked around. I followed his gaze and understood exactly what he meant.

This was The Shade, sure... but not ours. The air seemed different. Denser. Heavier. The black sky lacked stars and the moon, yet moonlight seemed to come down from somewhere. The ocean lapping at the shore was blue, but a strange blue, almost gray, as if the world had run out of pigment. The same could be said of the sand. It was meant to be golden, but it inched closer to silver. The green of the nearby redwood forest was faded, too, and I had trouble wrapping my head around what I was seeing.

"Holy crap," Soph said, gasping as she reached the same conclusion.

This was the other world, the place the clones had come from. Our people weren't the only things that had been copied. Someone had made a Shade. A slightly different Shade, but a Shade nonetheless. My skin pricked as the whole concept unraveled inside my head. The synapses were making all the right connections, yet I couldn't believe the sight before my eyes.

"Guess we're suing for copyright infringement, huh?" Jericho muttered, making Dafne snort a brief chuckle as she rested her head on his shoulder. She was tired, and I couldn't blame her. My healing had only stopped the nightmarish visions and feelings caused by the black smoke. It didn't replenish her physical energy.

This was beyond strange. It was troubling on so many levels, and it still didn't make sense. We had new questions to deal with—the primary one being about this Shade's creator. Who had done this? What kind of power had it taken to pull off something like this?

The shimmering portal closed behind us, and we were officially stuck here, at least temporarily. We'd have to find our way back later. But Claudia's clone was somewhere nearby, and we had to stop her before she and her people took us down. We were walking into strange and unknown territory. Ironically enough, this territory was The Shade.

KELARA

By the time we were done with the clones in the woods, Thayen and his crew had already left. I'd heard him shout Claudia's name, and upon seeing Isabelle's clone's body on the ground, it didn't take me long to put two and two together.

"Considering the amount of effort they put into retrieving Isabelle's double, I'm thinking she had something they needed," Soul said, frowning at the sight of her slit throat. "I mean, what other reason would the clones have to kill her, unless they retrieved whatever she had. Right?"

"You've just read my mind," I agreed.

The horn sounded once more, making me quiver because I couldn't tell where it was coming from. It echoed across The Shade, startling the birds from the redwood treetops. They flew away in an erratic pattern, and that wasn't normal, either. Nothing was normal anymore, not in this place. Stan and Ollie were busy feasting on the flesh of a couple of dead clones. Usually, I would've been put off, but in this case I didn't feel anything. Maybe these familiar-looking creatures with fake souls had succeeded in bringing out the worst in us. Or maybe they simply weren't deserving of any empathy on our part.

"Are you okay?" I asked Soul, and he gave me a soft smile in return.

"I'm as good as it gets under the circumstances," he said. "Considering they're using some pretty nifty tools against us, I'm proud to call myself a fast learner. I didn't get black-sprayed, not even once."

I chuckled. "Yeah, that's cause for celebration."

"Thayen and the others went after Claudia's clone," Soul said, recalling an earlier conclusion as he carefully analyzed our surroundings. "And I get the feeling the rest of the clones are gone."

Pointing at the bodies scattered around us, I found myself rather confused. "This isn't all of them, though. I saw many more on the way here."

"The horn called them away," Derek said as he stepped out of the woods. He wasn't alone. Sofia, Corrine, Ibrahim, Rose, Caleb, Ben, and River were with him. "The comms are back, too. Telluris, as well."

I immediately reached out to the Time Master through our telepathic connection. My message got through, and I received his response quickly. He was on his way to The Shade already, worried that neither Soul nor I had answered his previous attempts at communication. I looked at Soul. "Time is coming. I asked him to gather as many of the First Tenners as he can."

"And I have already reached out to Death, brought her into the loop," Soul added. "I'm not sure what good that'll do, but hey... I did my part."

Sofia stared at the clone corpses, many of them torn to shreds by our ghouls, who were now sniffing their way down a path that led to the Port beyond the woods. "We're currently receiving reports from all over the island. Some places were hit, others weren't. There were multiple shimmering portal sightings, too."

"They're gone now," Rose said. "As soon as the horn sounded just now, the clones just up and left."

"It means that whatever they came here for, they got it," I replied, shaking my head as I once again thought of Claudia's doppelganger. "Where are the others?"

"When the attacks started, they were in different locations around The Shade," Sofia said. "Some were verified by your team and Thayen's and sent back to the Great Dome. We tried to get as many of ours back that way, but without the comms running, there was very little we could do."

"The casualties are at a reduced number, too." Ben sighed, running a hand through his hair. Then he spotted his own clone among the others.

"Good grief, this is creepy and then some..."

I glanced his way, knowing I'd have a little bit of reaping to do. "How many of your people are dead, do you think?"

"Less than a hundred. We've got officers doing the rounds and scanning the island from one end to the other," Ben replied, still staring at his copy. "There's a lot we don't know yet. Hell, I've got at least twenty questions of my own about what happened here."

"Oh dear." Sofia gasped when she finally came across Isabelle's clone. "What happened to her? Where are Thayen and his crew?" She gave me a horrified look, and I didn't know what to tell her, exactly. I offered a full account of what I saw and heard during the melee, but without more information, I couldn't tell Sofia what had happened to her son.

"How did you all get here?" Soul asked the Shadians.

Derek pointed up at the trees. "We had scouts climb up to the top on a half-mile radius around the Great Dome. Some were tasked with watching the skies; the others had to keep an eye on the ground in case more people were headed toward us, originals or otherwise. One of them spotted movement in the sky near the Port. He gave us a troubling description of two dragons being shot down. We figured this was the place we needed to be."

"So, Thayen went that way?" Sofia asked, pointing toward the path that Stan and Ollie were investigating. I could barely see them now, their bony figures moving through the rich underbrush. Their heads poked out once in a while, their black eyes finding mine. I gave them a nod each time, encouraging them to keep tracking.

"Yes," I said, then turned to Phoenix. "Where is Viola? Something tells me Astra wasn't the only Daughter they were after. Of all the clones I've come across so far, two of them were made after you, yet none after Viola. Nor Astra, for that matter. It's the one pattern that stands out."

Phoenix exhaled sharply, and I almost felt his anguish as though it were mine. "I haven't found her yet. I suppose Astra didn't have much luck, either?"

There was a hopeful look in his eyes, and it broke me to have to shake my head in response. "I'm sorry, Viola wasn't here," I told him. "We need to head to the Port. Now."

We were all in agreement. While the rest of The Shade was pulling itself together, recovering after what had easily been the single most complex and brazen hostile infiltration it had ever faced, complete with raids and violent attacks, our confused little group still had work to do. A dull sensation persisted in the pit of my stomach as we made our way down the forest path, chasing after Stan and Ollie. I couldn't shake the feeling that despite the peaceful silence that had taken over the island, things were nowhere near better than five minutes ago.

This had only been the beginning, and it would only get worse going forward. Soul walked along with me, his hand occasionally brushing against mine. We exchanged glances, and I knew we were on the same page. Something was still very much off, and we were woefully underinformed about the enemy and their operations. Well, technically speaking, the clones were The Shade's enemy, but they'd become mine and Soul's, too. They were an affront to the living, a stain on the concept of souls. This fight was personal.

Corrine gasped as soon as her feet sank into the golden sand. "Oh... there was a portal here."

"How do you know?" I asked. "I thought you couldn't detect them."

"I can't. But I can see a number of footprints going in this direction," she replied, pointing toward the shipyard's warehouse.

We spent about twenty minutes searching this side of the beach. Soul and I used death magic tracking spells, while Derek and Sofia traced every single scent that still lingered in the salty ocean air. Corrine and Ibrahim used tricks of their own to understand what had happened here, while the footprints left behind told the same damn story.

"They stop here," Phoenix muttered. "You're right, Corrine. There was a portal here."

"I've got Claudia's scent, but it's weird," Derek said. "When I focus on it, it's subtly different."

"That's because it's her clone," I replied. "She escaped through a portal here, and I figure your kids went through in an attempt to capture her."

As soon as I said the words aloud, all eyes were on me. Big and glassy eyes, glistening with fear and horror and genuine concern. I felt bad for being the one to offer the conclusion, though they already knew it. It probably wasn't the easiest idea to accept.

But it had to be iterated clearly. "Thayen, Soph, Jericho, Dafne, and

Astra went through the shimmering portal after Claudia's clone."

The statement had troubling implications, and the more Shadians who reached the shore in search of answers, the greater the overall issue became. Caia and Blaze were the first to join us outside the shipyard warehouse, panting and desperately searching for their son. Lethe flew Elodie in all the way from the Black Heights. Phoenix was shaking like a leaf—he'd had it the worst. Astra had gone on to another realm, and Viola was missing.

"Do we have even the slightest idea of what exists beyond these portals?" Caia asked as she struggled to get her breathing back to normal. I could only imagine what she was going through. I'd had a son once, but I'd let him down. I'd lost him, and it had happened such a long time ago that I barely remembered how such emptiness felt. Looking at Caia's pained expression now, however, I realized I did have an inkling, at least. It hurt beyond belief.

"No, but considering the clones are designed to look like us and function like us, I think it's safe to assume our children won't be killed by the atmosphere there," Derek said. "I'm truly sorry we don't have more to go on."

The more we talked, the more information poured in from the rest of The Shade. Not everybody was accounted for. There were people missing— among them was not just Isabelle, but Richard, Voss, and Chantal, too. I had a feeling I'd hear plenty of other familiar names by the end of the day. The investigation was in its early stages, and there was so much ground to cover.

Zane and Fiona stormed onto the beach. Luckily for them, they'd been holed up inside the training halls with several daemon soldiers they'd brought over from Neraka. The portal leading back to their world—and all the others, for that matter—had been magically disabled. While the comms had been restored, access to and from The Shade was still restricted, courtesy of the clones' weird and otherworldly magic. The witches were going to take care of that, but it would take some time. They already had their hands full, since the hospital had been blown to smithereens, and there were plenty of Shadians in urgent need of medical care.

"Please, tell me it's not true," Fiona said, her voice trembling as she reached us. "Please, tell me our daughter didn't just walk through a shimmering portal!"

Derek had already notified Soph's parents through the comms system, and they were both understandably terrified. Zane's eyes sparkled red with rage as he stared at the spot where the footprints disappeared. He knew it was where the shimmering portal had been.

"I can still smell her," he said.

"How do we go in after them?" Lethe asked, a muscle ticking in his jaw as he held Elodie close. The human was doing everything in her power not to break down, but she was clearly hanging by a thread at this point.

"We find another shimmering portal," Phoenix replied. "But we don't yet have the magic or the technology to predict where one will appear next."

"Or if it'll appear," Blaze added. "What if the clones got what they wanted, and that's it?"

"I highly doubt it," Soul said. "There's more to this than we currently know. As far as The Shade is concerned, I recommend you stay on high alert and devise a way to scan the island for new shimmering portals. Have a team on standby and ready to go in at any moment. Hopefully, Thayen's group will find their way back here before you send anyone else through a portal."

"You don't think it's over?" Zane replied.

"Absolutely not. Call it instinct, call it whatever you wish, but I'm willing to bet you all the gold and riches in the world that there will be more of these clones coming. Nothing points to the contrary."

"Not even their complete withdrawal?" the daemon king insisted, raising a skeptical eyebrow. I tried to look away from the gold threads that covered his horns in a decorative fashion. He was about two heads taller than everybody else, yet the current situation had taken the edge off his massive presence. Much like the other Shadians, he was a parent whose child had run off into another, unknown realm.

"Nope," Soul shot back. "This was but one operation. I've seen similar patterns before, in faraway worlds that no longer exist. The spying through Isabelle's clone. The systematic infiltration and, in this case, collection of DNA material. The assassination attempts against Astra. The covert-ops-style effort to get her back. The entire operation of sowing confusion and sieging strategic points throughout The Shade. I'm telling you, it's nowhere near over. It's only just beginning."

The Time Master appeared beside him, startling us both. "Dude. Some notice would be nice!" I snapped, then rushed to hug the Reaper, for he was one hell of a sight for our sore eyes. "I'm so glad you came."

"I'm sorry I didn't think to pop over here sooner, before I even noticed you'd not been in touch recently," Time replied. "I should've been more... proactive, I suppose. It'll piss Death off that I left my post for this, but..."

"Hey, better late than never," Soul said. "And trust me when I tell you that you're of more use here than anywhere else. I suppose Kelara has brought you up to speed already."

Time nodded. "Yes. And the first thing we need to do is set up a verification operation. Every single person in The Shade must be checked. Every original must be marked in a way that the clones cannot copy. I've got a few spells in mind for that, but none are truly infallible unless we have a better understanding of what they know and what they can do in terms of magic."

"Still, it's worth a shot," Derek interjected. "We'll do it. We'll organize checkpoints across The Shade and start testing people."

"Have GASP officers ready to apprehend any identified clones. I've summoned Sidyan, Seeley, and Nethissis for this, as well. That gives you six Reapers to work with, and I suggest we bring the Daughters over from Eritopia to help supplement the spirit testing operation. With Astra and Viola temporarily gone, you need the Daughters because they're also capable of checking a soul's veracity. Besides, if all of them put their heads together, they might figure out a way to detect portals before they open, too. It's worth a shot."

"There's something else you all should know," Soul added. "Two of the clones trapped us in death magic. They wanted us out of the way, basically. I reckon they would've destroyed us if they could—"

"But they couldn't," I said. "That's encouraging. It means their knowledge of death magic is limited, along with their power to use it. So, we've sort of got that working for us."

"Did they say anything else worth noting?" Derek asked.

Soul and I shared every single detail we remembered from that encounter, but not much else stood out. In the end, each of us presented a threat towards the clones in one way or another. And each of us had come here to find a way to defeat them.

A plan was starting to take shape, but we were in the dark about many other important details, including where the missing Shadians had been taken. We agreed that they were probably in the same realm as Thayen and his crew, abducted by the clones. The worst-case scenario had them dead and stashed away somewhere in The Shade, but no one dared say it aloud. For good reason, too. Who would even want to imagine finding their child's body?

These were difficult times. The only upside was that we'd seen enough of the clones and their methods to build up a more accurate profile. Derek and Sofia stayed close to one another, both concerned for Thayen's safety. I couldn't stop myself from trying to encourage them.

"Thayen's more than capable of taking care of himself," I said, then looked at Lethe, Zane, and the other parents present. "They're all strong and resourceful. You've taught them well, and their will to live is strong. I have faith in your children, and I hope you do, too."

Phoenix sighed heavily. "It's not that we don't trust them. It's that we know almost nothing about the enemy they're dealing with."

And that was the real problem. We were facing an unknown that could kill more people than it already had. I wasn't sure if Death would grant us more authority to support the Shadians. I wasn't even sure we could get more Reaper boots on the ground here. I only knew that, for the time being, we had to make do with what we had, while hoping that Thayen's crew and the other missing Shadians would be okay. The clones were masterful at sowing chaos and snatching people.

And their work, like Soul had argued, was nowhere near over.

THAYEN

We spent a few minutes on this strange silvery beach, staring at a Shade that wasn't ours. The more we stayed here, the weirder it felt. We certainly didn't belong here, and we knew it deep in our bones. It was as if this replica island was telling us that we weren't welcome. That being said, we had no immediate way of getting out of this place, and Claudia's clone was still somewhere nearby, her strong scent teasing my nostrils.

"I think she went up that path," I said, pointing to where we'd come from in our Shade. The trail was there, identical to the original but infinitely darker. Shadows danced between the giant redwoods—maybe bushes swaying in the wind, or wild animals, or maybe other clones waiting to catch us and tear our heads off. Either way, we would have to go through there.

"Well, since we're here," Jericho replied, only half joking. Astra had healed his arm completely, and she looked a whole lot better than she had twenty minutes ago, prior to the shimmering portal opening on the other side. She'd definitely been onto something when she said she could recharge herself, so to speak, in that passageway. There had to be some kind of energy that filled her reserves to the brim. It was written on her face—in her pink cheeks and vivid, almost black eyes. I found comfort in knowing we had her at full power again, because we were about to tread through dangerous and mysterious territory.

We could use all the magic and power we could muster.

"Come on, let's go," Soph said as she walked toward the path. We stayed close together, careful of everything around us. The deeper we went into the woods, the harder it became to focus on only one thing at a time.

The startling similarity was just one of the aspects that threw us off. The unsettling feeling that came with it was the second. By the time we reached the small clearing where, in the real Shade, Dafne and Jericho had fallen when injured by metal arrows, I realized that we were in way over our heads. Every single detail in this place had been modeled off our world, and each second we spent here made me shudder.

"If we consider this to be the source of the clones, which it most likely is, then we'll need to be ready for an entire society of them, mimicking ours," Astra whispered. She gave me a sideways glance. "Is Claudia's double nearby? Do you still smell her?"

"Yeah, we're on the right track," I replied.

"I think Astra is onto something," Jericho said. "Just like they infiltrated us, we'll have to... you know, infiltrate them."

Lights flickered somewhere in the woods to our right. We stilled, holding our breaths for a second before we hid behind one of the trees. Dozens of clones were coming through a shimmering portal, and similar glimmers could be seen farther still. Multiple portals were opening, and even more clones emerged, coming back from our island. As soon as the coast was clear, we kept moving, my nose sharper than ever.

We reached the edge of the Vale. For a while, none of us could do anything. We just stared at the sight before us. It was a mirror image of the real Vale, though faded in color. Once again I had the feeling that whoever had made this place had been pretty cheap on the pigments. But every line and every shape, every single person walking the streets of the Vale, was identical to those we'd left behind in The Shade.

They seemed normal. Going to different places, talking and laughing among themselves. The shops were open. The bistro terraces were bustling with mixed groups of humans and supernaturals. I recognized Hazel and Tejus and a few others from GASP, and it took a surprising amount of effort not to raise a hand and say hello. My instincts had been briefly fooled by the exquisite similarities.

"Jeez... this takes the term 'creepy' to a whole new level," Dafne murmured.

"Claudia's clone is in here somewhere," I said. "We absolutely have to find her before she delivers what she took to whoever ordered her to take it."

"Look, over there." Soph, pointed a finger ahead. Up the main street leading toward the cloned Vale's town center, Claudia's doppelganger was casually walking, her rich, curly blonde hair flowing down her back. No one in her vicinity seemed bothered by the blood on her hands. Given that this whole dimension was just a massive dollop of freaky, it no longer surprised me.

We calmly followed her through the town center, careful not to draw any unwanted attention. I did notice some of the clones staring at us—particularly at Astra—but nobody said anything. "Got to keep our conversations to a minimum," I mumbled. "Smile when we're smiled at. Play it cool, if we're to blend in."

"I never thought the day would come when we'd be the ones acting like clones," Jericho said, his gaze darting left and right as we moved through the increasingly crowded plaza.

Claudia's clone looked over her shoulder. She saw me first, and the corner of her mouth turned upward. I froze because she was smiling. She knew we were here, following her. "Hold on," I whispered.

She stopped and turned around, her head cocked to the side. Pressing a finger against the side of her neck, lips moving, she seemed to be talking to someone. Chills burst through me as I instinctively caught Astra's wrist and stopped her from going any farther.

"Claudia's clone is one cold-blooded bitch," Dafne said.

No one else seemed to notice what was going on, but the horn sounded loudly enough to make us all cringe and gasp. It was way more powerful than what we'd heard in the real Shade, and it also had a robotic voice attached to it, howling across the fake Shade. "The pink-haired half-Daughter is here. She must be captured and killed. Immediately. This is not a drill. Find the pink-haired half-Daughter and kill her."

And just like that, the entire wrath of hell broke loose. Every single eye was trained on us, while Claudia's clone kept grinning. She fumbled through her pocket and showed us what I assumed she'd lifted off Isabelle's double. It looked like a small object, the size and shape of a single die. I'd never seen it before, and I had no idea what purpose it served. But it was gone and far out of our grasp.

Footsteps rushed across the cobblestone. Astra grunted as she pushed out a massive barrier, then bolted away from the plaza. We dashed after her, speechless and terrified. The move had thrown many of the clones back, but only for a moment. By the time we reached the Vale's border and entered the redwood forest again, there were throngs of them running after us.

"At the risk of... repeating myself... we're really screwed, aren't we?" Jericho breathed as we darted through the woods.

"You can say that again," Dafne replied, racing him down a secondary trail.

Yes, we were screwed and then some.

ASTRA

(DAUGHTER OF PHOENIX AND VIOLA)

Every atom in me quivered as I ran. Somebody wanted me dead so badly that they'd sent a horde of clones after me. Claudia's doppelganger had certainly facilitated my discovery, and the worst part was that we couldn't go after her anymore.

No, we were zooming through the redwood forest, our heels burning as the murderous masses chased after us. They weren't saying anything, and that just made this whole affair creepier. No order, not even a whisper or a mob- like cheer. They were so well trained and so focused on their mission that nothing else mattered.

"Head for the Port," Thayen advised. "I know we were going to take Isabelle's clone there for relative safety, but I think we're the ones who need it now."

"Yeah, the fake Shade's layout is likely identical to ours. There should be dungeons down there," Jericho replied.

Soph scoffed. "What really annoys me is that none of us thought to pack some invisibility magic. It sure would've come in handy right about now."

"Not really," Thayen said, his voice breaking as he jumped over a gnarly root I'd just hopped past. "They've got red lenses and stuff. They know our methods and protocols."

The robotic voice could still be heard, loud and high-pitched. "Catch the pink-haired half-Daughter. Kill her. Catch the pink-haired half-Daughter. Kill her." It was playing on repeat, and the clones were more than happy to obey. There was no time to think about anything other than safely making it back to the Port.

My grandparents' doubles threw barriers at us, but I responded in kind with twice as much. The pulses were shooting out of my hands like rippling balls of energy, bouncing back and slamming into different clusters of hostiles. Thayen, Jericho, Dafne, and Soph had already learned to duck whenever I launched one.

The sound of the clones' footsteps was so close that I could almost feel them breathing down my neck, their deadly intentions seeping through my soul and chilling me to the bone. Fireballs flew past our heads. Redwoods came down like defeated giants, aiming to crush us under their massive trunks. But we were fast. At least we had that working for us.

The darkness grew ahead, and I couldn't see much, even with the strong pink glow in my hands. New sounds emerged. Low growls that sent my senses spiraling into disarray, my fight-or-flight instinct blaring in the back of my head. Whatever these creatures were, I doubted we could engage them in combat.

"What the hell is that?" Dafne croaked, the alarm in her voice painfully obvious.

"I doubt it's anything good," I said.

We were finally putting some distance between us and the clones, but something else was running along the narrowing trail. Shadows swished past us. Branches broke. Heavy paws hit the hard ground, tumbling toward us.

The fear was so powerful, so intense, and the darkness so heavy and suffocating. I screamed just to ease some of the tension, releasing enough pink light to illuminate a fifty-yard radius around us. What it revealed made me scream even louder. Between the trees, black figures with enormous backs and claws ran toward us. Their eyes glimmered blue as they snarled and quickly fell back, overwhelmed by the light. They didn't like it.

"Holy smokes!" I heard Thayen exclaim.

"Don't stop!" I cried as the glow faded around us, and the creatures resumed their frantic race to take us down. "We have to keep moving!"

We didn't have any other choice. Jericho cast repeated series of fireballs left and right in a bid to slow down the nightmarish fiends. Behind us, albeit about a hundred yards away, the clones were still in hot pursuit, relentless and eerily quiet.

Ahead, I could see a faint light in the distance. The closer we got, the better I could discern the black figure standing in the middle of it. "What the..." My voice trailed off as it raised a hand, pointing somewhere to the left.

"Astra, what's that light?" Thayen asked. "Is that the Port?"

"I'm not sure," I replied, glancing over my shoulder just in time to see a black shadow jumping at him. "Thayen, duck!"

He lowered himself as though we were running through an obstacle course, and the creature missed him by inches. We heard it scrambling back into action, however, and it was only a matter of time before it would catch up once more. Energized by the earlier maneuver and determined to get to that light, I cried out and launched another powerful light pulse. It burst in every direction, again revealing the shadowy fiends with sparkling blue eyes. And again, it pushed them back by a few feet, just enough to give us a slightly better advantage.

The figure I'd seen ahead was gone, but the direction in which it had pointed remained at the center of my consciousness. I wasn't sure if it was an enemy, but I doubted we had any friends in this place. Still, every fiber of my being told me to follow its lead, so we raced down the path and right into a small clearing.

"Left," I said, my breath ragged.

We took a sharp left turn into the dark woods, the thundering footsteps of our pursuers never too far behind. Sudden silence fell over our group as we came to a sudden halt in front of a cave, nicely hidden between sprawling bushes and thick layers of mossy stones.

"In here," I added, then ran right inside, slipping through the nook that served as an entrance.

One by one, just like through the shimmering portal, Thayen, Jericho, Dafne, and Soph came in, and we bumbled through the darkness with only the pink of my glowing hands to guide us. We couldn't make any noise or use too much light, since the purpose was to hide from our enemies and those ghastly clawed creatures.

The silence was pressing, yet I didn't dare fool myself into hoping we'd lost them. I kept moving through the low and uneven corridors, losing track of where we'd come from. I only had this feeling that we needed to go deep, as deep as possible, for a sliver of safety. We ended up in a small round chamber with a domed ceiling.

Panting, we listened carefully for every possible sound. With the exception of water dripping somewhere nearby, there was nothing to hear. Thayen took deep breaths, analyzing the cold and thin air for any scent that might trigger danger. He shook his head as he looked at me. "I think the coast is clear. I think we lost them."

The robotic voice couldn't be heard down here, but I did wonder if the horn that had sounded in this fake Shade had echoed into the real one. The signals we'd heard back home could've been echoes of the signals from here. It was only a theory, however, and the absolute least of our concerns.

"Is everybody okay?" Thayen asked, measuring each of us from head to toe.

"For the most part, yeah," Jericho replied. "Though I prefer flying to running."

"You would've been a... well, a flying duck out there," Thayen said, holding back a chuckle. "We made do just fine. We're alive. It's cool."

"Claudia's clone is gone, along with whatever that die thing was. The so-called object, I mean," Soph muttered, settling on the stony ground with her legs crossed. Sweat dripped from her temples as she worked on her breathing.

It had been a crazy ride so far. "It's only going to get worse from here," I said. "But at least we're at the source of this trouble. The best thing we can do right now is keep investigating. We can't stay in this cave forever."

For a second, I wondered about the person who'd guided us here. I wondered who they were. It couldn't have been anyone from the enemy's ranks; otherwise, this whole place would've been crawling with clawed shadow monsters and killer clones. No, it wanted us safe... maybe I'd imagined it. No one else had seen it, after all. But that, too, was at the bottom of our list of problems. Briefly, I thought of my dad and the rest of our family. They had to be worried sick, not knowing where we'd gone. Mom was nowhere to be found, but maybe the other GASP officers had gotten to her. I only had hopes—the most dangerous thing for me right

now, considering how little I knew about this strange dimension.

"Well, Astra, you are officially the fake Shade's most wanted," Jericho said. He was trying to be humorous, but the strained smirk on his face told me he was just as troubled about this as the rest of us.

"We're going to have to find out why," I replied.

Perhaps that was our best starting point. Studying this alternative island and its clones, figuring out the administrative and military patterns. Understanding their goals and, most importantly, finding their leader. Somebody was pulling all the strings in this place. That somebody had put out a hit on me days ago. That somebody had the answer to every question.

I just had to survive long enough to get to them. Easier said than done, I realized as I looked around. We were worn out and terrified and utterly confused. Nevertheless, our war had only just begun, and we had enough anger in us to keep the engines burning.

TRISTAN

After some work, Unending found the runes that had kept the Mixer stuck in the soul fae's archives. She scratched each of the symbols off with the tip of her scythe while Loren was sound asleep upstairs in his house. We'd tricked him and his people, and it made me feel bad, but we had to get this done for a multitude of reasons.

"This is no longer just about us and our desire to start a family," Unending said as she destroyed the last of the charms. "It's about what Anunit's game is. There's something fishy going on here, and I intend to find out what the play is."

"I wholeheartedly agree. And if we complete the trials and get what we've come here for, even better," I replied, watching as she took hold of the Mixer and slipped it into her dress pocket. "I just don't understand why Anunit wrecked this for us. We were so close to getting this thing out without anybody suspecting a damn thing..."

Unending gave me a fleeting look. "I guess we'll find out soon enough."

She put her hand on my shoulder, ready to teleport us out of here, but something hit us with such force that we were thrown against the far end of the tunnel. We hit the floor, limp and breathless for about a minute as we tried to figure out what the hell had just happened. Joy's voice echoed through the entire underground, and I had my answer. "You traitorous bastards," she hissed, giant scythe in her hand as she stormed toward us. "You betrayed us. You betrayed the Reaper order! You took Spirit away from me! You're consorting with Anunit!"

"Again with this nonsense! Didn't Death tell you to butt out?" Unending replied, with no patience left for Joy's volcanic temperament.

"I don't care! She's not here! She cannot see your treachery like I can!"

Holy crap. Joy had absolutely lost a few marbles while being stuck here, playing the babysitter to the soul fae. It hadn't been immediately noticeable at first, but it was impossible to deny now. "You're not making any sense," I managed. "If Death gave you an order—"

"She'll thank me later!" Joy snapped.

"Okay. We're not getting through to each other, here. If you would just let me explain," Unending began, but the Reaper wouldn't have any of it. Her blade sparkled white as it cast a rippling pulse at us. It hit Unending in the chest, and she cried out in pain.

"Stop! Just stop!" I said, raising both hands in a defensive gesture. Joy definitely had the abilities of a First Tenner, considering she was able to hit Unending like this.

"I'll make Death understand your betrayal," Joy replied, completely ignoring me as she channeled all her rage at my wife. "I've always said you were a bad apple. She told me I was overreacting, that I'd never even met you to truly know you. Well, look at you now, huh? You put Loren to sleep. You're breaking my seals. You're stealing! Traitor!"

Joy was about to hit her again, this time from a shorter distance. Unending's scythe had ended up on the stone floor between us. "I'm not stealing! Our deal with Anunit for a body! Death greenlit all of this! It's not my fault you won't listen, dammit!" she said.

"You destroyed Spirit!"

"We had no choice!" Unending shot back.

My body reacted before I was even aware of what I was about to do. Joy was too focused on Unending to consider me anything close to a threat, so I grabbed my wife's scythe and slashed at the Reaper's stomach.

A glowing cut opened, and Joy screamed with a mixture of shock and pain. I was just as astonished, since I hadn't seen this coming. I wasn't even sure why I'd thought I could use Unending's weapon. My instincts had made that decision for me.

Liquid light poured from Joy's wound. She dropped her weapon and tried to cover the cut with trembling hands as she stared at me in disbelief. "How... how?" she managed.

Unending scrambled back up, grabbing her scythe in the process. She hooked an arm through mine, and we were gone. Darkness enveloped us both, and only Joy's wails of fury and desperation followed us away from the village and its underground tunnels.

We appeared in the middle of the woods about three miles south of the soul fae village. I wondered about Loren and Sissa, about how their lives would turn out over the years. Clearly, I was no longer welcome among them— not to mention Unending. We'd just stolen Death's artifact, and we were about to hand it over to Anunit.

And for some reason, I'd cut Joy, actually inflicting a wound. A very strange wound, like nothing I had seen before.

"Can you tell me what just happened?" I asked, giving my wife a concerned look.

She grunted softly, straightening her back. At least Joy's rippling pulses hadn't completely debilitated her. "I honestly don't know. I've never witnessed that type of injury before. But she'll be okay. I'm sure of it."

"How so?"

"She's as powerful as any of the First Tenners," Unending said. "And you're just a vampire who was somehow able to wield my weapon. There are some limitations on what a living creature can do with a scythe."

I sighed, the adrenaline finally wearing off. My legs were shaking. "Does this mean I'm going to be a Reaper after I die?"

"That wasn't the case before, but maybe things have changed. I don't know," Unending said. "First of all, I need to tell Death what happened. We just got into a whole lot of trouble with Joy and the soul fae. She'll clear it up with the Reaper and the village, but still... she needs to know everything that went down here, in clear detail. Maybe now she'll consider retiring Joy and tasking another Reaper to guard the soul fae. It's insane what happened."

The time we'd spent among the soul fae had helped Unending through some internal thoughts of her own, I realized. Not that our priorities had shifted, but the way we were going to approach the rest of our journey certainly had. "You should also double check that we are still to deliver the Mixer to Anunit, before the Reaper gets here. Won't Joy find a way to come after us?"

"No. She's not allowed to leave the village," Unending replied. "Death clarified this earlier, during our last quick chat. She used some mojo of her own to make sure Joy doesn't up and leave."

"When did Death clarify this, exactly?"

"You know, after I knocked Joy out. It's like Death knew that telling her to back off wouldn't be enough. She was trying to comfort me with this idea that... if we leave the village, Joy wouldn't come after us. Sheesh."

Good. The last thing I wanted was another confrontation with an exceptionally angry and powerful Reaper. Unending closed her eyes for a moment, reaching out to Death through their telepathic connection. I gazed around, watching as the jungle became aware of our sudden presence, the foliage veins glowing green.

The wind blew through the trees, its whispers making my ears twitch. I worried Joy might yet find a way out of the soul fae village, but that fear subsided more with every minute that passed without a violent Reaper attack.

Unending scoffed, opening her eyes again. "I swear, I don't know who's playing whom here, but I get the feeling we are both just pawns in this game."

"What happened?" I asked, carefully analyzing her expression.

"I told her everything that happened: our basement fight with Joy, you being able to cut her, and me having to put one of her precious soul fae to sleep. I didn't expect her to be so calm. She actually said, and I kid you not, to stay on track and give the Mixer to Anunit just like we agreed."

I was confused. "Huh? Well, look who's mission-oriented all of a sudden."

"Right? Just give the Mixer to Anunit, she said, and go through the rest of the trials," Unending replied, taking the artifact out to study it more. "No explanation. She just wants me to keep her in the loop, and I find that rather... odd, that she didn't have more questions, or at least a mild scolding about what I did to Loren..."

"What if it turns out Anunit is plotting something against Death?"

She raised an eyebrow, clearly skeptical. "I doubt it. I've actually

considered every possibility. Even with the Mixer, she can't do anything other than piss Death off more. Sure, Anunit can inflict some damage on our society, but nothing our maker can't handle. Nah, there's something else going on here, but if Death won't tell me what, despite me repeatedly asking, I'm not sure we have any choice other than to see this through."

We had to get to the end of our journey if we wanted a shot at the whole truth. I didn't like being in the dark like this. Neither did Unending, but considering our present circumstances, she was right. It was our only choice.

"So, we're giving this to Anunit," I concluded, nodding at the Mixer.

"Yes, you are," Anunit cut in, appearing next to us with a broad smile on her face. I worried she might've overheard us, but the satisfied look she wore said otherwise.

Unending grabbed her by the throat with lightning speed. The Reaper didn't stand a chance, suddenly caught in a chokehold. "What the hell are you playing at, Anunit?"

"Whoa... whoa!" she croaked, trying to set herself free.

My wife's grip was ironclad. There was no escaping it. I had to admit, seeing Anunit like this did give me some satisfaction, considering the harm she'd done to my relationship with the soul fae. They were such interesting creatures. It really annoyed me that I couldn't go near them without Joy's permission—and I doubted Death cared much for my anthropological aspirations.

"Why did you show up at the village?" Unending demanded, her tone clipped.

"I had to speed things along..."

"We were in the middle of getting the Mixer!" I snapped. "You nearly got us in a whole world of trouble because Joy is unstable!"

"Death will hear about this," Unending added, playing her part in this deception towards Anunit. After all, Death had already heard about this, but Anunit couldn't know we'd been the ones to tell her maker the whole truth. "She'll have me hunted down. Do you have any idea what a monumental mess you've made?"

"I'm sorry!" Anunit cried out, struggling against Unending's hold. "I just... I wanted to see how you'd react in more dire circumstances! At that point, you had the choice to turn against me, and you didn't. I couldn't

think of a better way to truly test your resolve. I knew that if you were determined to go through with this, I'd find you here now. If you'd turn against me, I'd be here on my own, knowing you've given up."

"What, the trials weren't enough?" I retorted, crossing my arms.

"Again, I'm sorry! I'm paranoid about this stuff. But you've earned my trust. I promise, I won't interfere with the upcoming trials. My word is my bond!"

Unending let go, and the Reaper coughed, taking a moment to regain her senses. My wife and I exchanged glances. "I'm not buying her excuse," I told her through telepathy.

"Me neither. Or maybe it's just part of the truth. We have two options going forward. I torture the whole story out of her, or we play along and see where it takes us," she replied.

We still had two trials to go through, and we couldn't risk losing Anunit's favor altogether. I certainly didn't want her skipping out on us. "I think we have a better shot if we keep her on our side," I suggested. "At least for now. If she does anything else that's... alarming, then we can reconsider our strategy."

Unending exhaled sharply and pushed the Mixer into Anunit's hands. "Here. And next time, stay out of our way.

Tristan and I know what we're doing, and we don't need your 'impatience' or 'distrust' to screw us over. Okay?" "Yeah... It'll go differently, from now on. I've gotten my assurances. You did well," Anunit replied, her voice shaky as she regarded the object with genuine admiration. "Oh, my... it's a work of art..."

"I'm going to have to think of ways to get Death off my back," Unending said, crossing her arms. "That stunt with Joy will be an issue. You'd better not make things harder going forward. We still have a long way to go here."

"On that, we agree," Anunit murmured, slowly raising her gaze from the Mixer. "Two more trials. Are you ready?"

We both nodded. Sure, we were. I doubted we were ready for any other bumps in the road, though. I didn't trust Anunit. She had a side plan, for sure. She'd messed with our soul fae strategy on purpose. Her excuses didn't hold any water. What troubled me more was Death's willingness to part with one of her precious artifacts. Why was she so cool with handing the Mixer over to the one Reaper she wanted most?

It didn't make sense. Once again, I found myself circling back to Unending's earlier conclusion. We would have to see this whole thing through in order to get to the truth. Our love was strong enough to overcome anything fate might throw at us. I just wasn't sure what that "anything" might entail.

Both Death and Anunit were keeping things from us. Then again, I was perfectly fine with playing dirty, too, if the situation demanded it. This whole thing had turned out to be a lot more complicated than we'd originally thought, and it only made me want to get to the bottom of it faster.

$\sim$

ASOV 89: A SANCTUARY OF FOES

Dear Shaddict,

See you soon!
Love,
Bella x